BEACH TOWN

APOCALYPSE

THOMAS MAXWELL-HARRISON

CHAPTER 1

Welcome To Beach Town

'Morning, Miss, how many today?' The clerk asked Sheila, who scoured a few coins in her red leather purse. Earlier she thought she might try stealing the cigs, you know, fuck it all and do it sort of thing. She found enough coins for two single cigs, she wanted three. Two shoppers behind were gossiping and it caught Sheila's ear. Sheila swore one of them mentioned major rioting in the city, she felt too low to ask.

'Two, thank you,' her voice soft with shame, barely enough money for cigarettes, what was the town coming to. She slid the coins across the counter, slipped the cigs into her cotton-lined jacket and stashed her purse, the purse catching the pocket lining.

It was common for people to stick to themselves in town. Beach Town was an isolated island fifty miles off the coast of England, frequented by tourists and thunderstorms. The city which lay about six or seven miles away via bridge – Sheila couldn't remember how far; she hadn't been out of town in over two months because she couldn't afford the petrol – was the closest and under UK government control.

'Damn,' she mumbled as she tried to avoid eye contact with the other shoppers. It was dim outside, dark clouds hung overhead and once she stepped onto the beach path, she smelt it, the musky scent of a storm brewing. Surfers rode the tides coming to a belly crawl and finally jumped to the sandy shore. Sheila could barely make them out, the salty sea air stung her eyes and she could taste it on her lips. Passers-by faded, and she dipped her head against the sand flicked by the wind and took a slow pace back to the car park. Maybe today, she thought, tugging at her coat for a single cig. It began raining, a saturating hailstorm getting colder against her tights. The path was uneven, cracked concrete, weeds sprouting through the gaps. Weather by thunderstorms and uncared for, a bit like her last week. Nothing had changed her mind that nothing was going to change her life. Being close to bankrupt, friendless, depressed and worn out were taking a toll. All hope seemed lost. She accepted it and smoothed a finger under her eye, brushing away a drip. Maybe it was rain, maybe not. She found it hard to distinguish between anything now.

The path snaked around the beachfront stores, and Sheila scanned the cars, trying to remember where she'd parked.

'What the hell?!' She gasped, spotting her car. 'For God's sake!' She cried.

Two young men sped by on skateboards jeering and taunting Sheila. 'Fuck you slut!' they yelled, rapidly rolling into the pissing rain. Skateboarding and surfing were popular sports amongst locals, the reason was because it was free. Sheila stood at five six and most young people towered over her. She hated them now and forever. Sheila regarded them as antisocial and this proved her right.

The wheels of her car were completely flat. She approached the car. The window was smashed, and the lighter inside had been dumped on the passenger seat. She got in the car; the rain had soaked her jacket. Sheila slid her hand down under the passenger seat and retrieved an envelope.

'Thank god for that,' She muttered, peeling it open carefully, holding it under her coat like a baby. It was her only resume, and a damn good one too. Ten years in customer services and twelve years in management positions, now the only thing left to add was she had become another victim to the shit in Beach Town.

Nearly all houses in Beach Town were suburbanised two stories and two tower blocks, the required amount of shops and the beachfront as the main attraction. Increasing crime and rising unemployment meant residents suffered break ins on a regular basis, Sheila saw the reports on tv a few weeks back. Even the hospital struggled to cope, she had to go for a check-up – suspected anaemia- months ago and nurses and doctors complained about the lack of funding which had caused staff to vacate to the city. Sheila was blonde back then, now her hair was brunette, she believed a new identity might help her stand out. It didn't.

A honk scared her out of the daze. She looked around, her hair drenched and her eyes blank with despair. It was Dean. One of the police officers who went the extra mile, Sheila admired that. Dean was honking and tilting his shaven head from the white police cruiser. Sheila felt like getting out of her car and slapping him for making her jump but restrained herself. She knew Dean lived alone and suffered depression, after visiting on weekends in the past for drinks, they had things in common. Scotch, chit chat and bettering themselves.

'You ok Sheila? Hop in I'll give you a lift,' Dean sounded a million miles away, the pounding rain now drowning out even the sounds of the engine.

Reluctantly she got out her car and entered the police cruiser, her legs shivered. Anything was better than this. 'Take me home,' she replied, the tears now rolling down her cheeks. But in the downpour Dean perhaps couldn't tell and that relieved her.

'Sure. I'll have your car towed, Sheila. You can't leave it here,' he said. The rain came down harder and her butt felt cold and damp. Sheila stared into her lap, lip trembling, and her hands together.

Dean flicked on the radio, a bit of Beach Town radio, courtesy of the college students.

'Never seen all tires flat at once.' The cruiser pulled away, wipers on fast and traffic speeding by. The song on the radio was some sad country ballad sung by an old man. She turned it off with a huff and searched her pocket for the cigs. When she pulled them out they were soaked, the last cigs she could probably afford to buy was fucking ruined.

'Fuck sake, what is wrong with this town?!' She slammed the cigs onto the dashboard, and they split open. The wet tobacco stuck to the black plastic like glue.

'Whoa, calm down, I told you - I'll have the car towed, jeez,' Dean mumbled, not looking so happy as he cut up a blue Ford. The freeway was busy for a Friday.

'I can't calm down, I've just lost my fucking job, and I just had my car vandalised and I can't even afford a packet of god damn cigarettes. What do people do round here anyway? Hey, I'm from Beach Town and my life sucks. Welcome to fucksville.'

'Holy shit, I never thought I'd hear you snap like that, goddamn it's good to let it out sometimes,' Dean said with a chuckle, enough to make Sheila force a smile. The police radio crackled, inaudible voices at first. But then Sheila heard a call about gunshots at a motel.

Luckily the journey was over, quicker than she expected. Dean pulled down 2nd street and came to a squeaky stop outside the apartments. The rain had stopped now, and a blanket of fog hung over the street. April showers galore, she thought. She checked her watch; it was just passing five in the evening. She was bored with time, it meant nothing to her after passing forty.

'Peculiar looking day too,' Dean added, sticking his right hand down his pants pocket and retrieving a ten. 'Here, It's better than nothing. Get yourself some rest and I'll see you soon. I have to deal with that motel again, take care,' she thanked him, took the money hesitantly and clenched it in her fist along with the damp resume. She stepped out, Dean waved and pulled off. His blue lights flickered in the fog followed by the siren. The building had a glow, a new paint job probably, she had seen job adverts for painter.

That was two weeks ago, since then her car was her bed as she job hunted. She wished she could have stayed at home, but her spouse who she regretted getting with, blamed her for losing her job as a manager. Sheila felt butterflies in her stomach, it was her home to. Now the mission was simple, leave the town and everything in it behind. Start a new life somewhere inland in the city, Sheila had heard passively that the city was recruiting lots of new people, a fantastic opportunity to get work. Sheila smiled. She walked to the front door and stepped in, finally, she was home.

CHAPTER 2

Death for breakfast

The kettle rumbled before steam began shooting from the tip. Dean took the black handle covered in condensation and poured the boiling water to an inch from the top of his 'officer of the day' ceramic mug.

'Day two begins,' Dean sighed, referring to the hunt for the vandals of Sheila's car, and lifted the steaming black coffee to his mouth and took a sip. He headed from his well-organised and clean kitchen to the living room and sat back on the black and brown chequered sofa. In one corner, his television screen was still on static. His way of clearing his mind, a good stare at nothingness. He put down his steaming mug on the oak coffee table as his phone buzzed in his trouser pocket.

'What now?' He grunted, seeing the number had no name. For a moment, he thought about ignoring the call, possibly packing up and heading downtown for a quick lunch at *la Carta*. The only place he knew in town that had a halfway decent breakfast menu on Saturday. A call so early was not the usual, and Dean suspected an office mishap rather than a crime, because he never dealt with

Saturday morning crimes anymore, not since his first days on the job.

He answered the old rectangular phone, tiny in rough large capable hands. 'Hello?'

'Dean, officer Ronald here, sorry to bother you so early, got a problem at the hospital, I need your help,' Ronald sounded concerned, Dean could not picture Ronald as he hadn't spoken to him in a long time. This must be serious.

'I'll be right there,' Dean replied, about to hang up.

Dean felt the coffee still in his throat as he gulped. Had something happened to Sheila, too damn proud to ask for help, she's probably topped herself.

'What's the situation?' Dean asked, and a sweat broke in his underarms. Dean took a bigger gulp.

'Two found dead outside the Rooster motel, hit and run. We have witnesses at the station. Both bodies have green pus pouring from their torso. I suspect it's drug related but you need to come and see this yourself, something is not right about the bodies.' Dean listened intently, it sounded gruesome, fascinating him. Was it too early to go corpse speculating? He downed the last of his hot coffee, flicked the TV off and made his way through the narrow passageway to the front door.

'Fine, I'm on my way. I assume a doctor is present. Best to double check Jamie is actually working.'

Dean hung up, stuck the tiny phone down his pants where his keys were poking into his thigh. Doctor Jamie gave him insights into deaths or drugs use. Jamie was the contact he had worked for in the hospital, a vital ally in the fight against crime. Dean spent months trying to convince him to assist his enquiries, once onboard Jamie soon began assisting with many problems Dean presented to him. They were close and Dean revered the friendship.

He couldn't tell whether the coffee had perked him up or whether it was the grim prospect of seeing death before breakfast. A quick glance towards the round wall clock placed perfectly in the hallway said ten to eight, but it felt like five. His jacket was freshly washed, smelling of chemicals with a dash of rosemary. He hunched it on and set out to his silver Honda Civic, gleaming under the bright morning sky.

He approached the freeway, intersecting some slow old man in a beetle. Momentarily the radio hissed, and voices yelled on it, but that quickly faded back to a bluesy beat. Dean yanked the gear stick into fifth, pushing over seventy down the empty carriageway. The carriageway intersected with a motorway which led to the bridge to the city. Dean followed it, traffic was dense, three hundred yards to the hospital turn off.

The hospital car park was packed when he pulled up to the ticket gate. Cars had parked on the sidewalks, staff moved car to car jotting down details. Dean had never seen anything like this before.

'Jeez, happy holidays, what the hell is this?' Dean muttered to himself impatiently something he found himself doing more these days, especially after a morning buzz.

'What's with the overload?' he asked the ticket booth operator, who looked pale and thinner than he remembered. When the operator answered, his voice sounded on the edge of collapse, it was flat and quiet.

'No idea sir, most of them came in at around sixish, I'm not sure what's going on.' The gatekeeper passed a tacky yellow note to Dean, waving him through with a lazy hand.

'Yeah, take it easy,' Dean said and pulled through the barrier, searching for an empty parking space. He crept the Civic through almost impossible gaps, avoiding the limp legs that hung from car doors. Some people coughed and others stumbled with the aid of nurses towards the large glass Emergency Room doors.

'This is crazy, unbelievable,' Dean said, as he stopped dead in the middle of the road, switching the engine off and jumping out. The sun was beating down. Dean saw looks of distress on people's faces and felt sorry for them. Was this related to an epidemic? He locked his car. The offshoot from the motorway was becoming clogged up, horns were beeping and voices shouting profanities. The hospital entrance was full of people as well. Dean walked cautiously; crime was opportunistic in these kind of situations.

Inside, he was met by the young officer Ronald who had called him, and a woman with blackened streaks down her cheeks, blobs of water dripping from her nose.

'Dean, follow me, the bodies of the hit and run are upstairs,' Ronald said. The waiting room ER was chaotic, almost like a pilgrimage of coughing and shivering people. Ronald gestured a wave to follow him. The woman did so as well, but Dean tried to refrain from asking the obvious. Ronald led the way, heading right from the ER waiting room through a door which led to the main hospital entrance, which was a large high ceiling white room, things were quieter, but many people lay around with bored expressions. To the left some elevators and to the right more people sprawled over cream waiting seats. Dean noticed the receptionist directly in front being overwhelmed by people throwing questions at her and he thought about calling for assistance in case a riot broke out.

The three of them trailed left across the brightly lit room to the elevators.

'Why is it so busy, Ron? What in god's name is going on?' Dean locked on to the woman again, then back to the desk clerk who was red as cherries, flinging her arms left, right and centre with papers falling everywhere. Dean considered calling for backup again, but his priority was somewhere upstairs.

'Docs think there's a superbug sweeping town, well, that's what Jamie says. Wait till you see these bodies, you'll understand what he means,' Ron swivelled his belt a little, resting his hands-on hips and standing nervously like a newbie.

'Superbug? I can't afford to get sick this time of year Ron, you can't either, they're making cuts to the station.'

'Yeah, I guess.' His reply was shallow. The gathering masses were now being seen to by hospital security as the elevator arrived.

Fifth room on the right of the third floor, the death floor as Jamie once told Dean on a booze up, was where they found Jamie leaning against the wall just outside. There was a nurse hurrying from a room further down to another, then a patient appeared at the end of the dim corridor, underweight and holding a drip stand slowly walking forward with a vacant face.

'Dean, good morning, I'm glad you could come,' Jamie greeted him with a firm shake, his skin smooth from the conditioner he always put on.

'No problem, when I heard you were here, I had to see the mess you created.' Dean laughed, and Jamie winced, not something he usually did. Dean felt the air solidify and the initial humour turn into a darker mood.

'Wait here, make sure no one comes in.' He told Ron, knowing Ronald had done enough for now. The woman had cleared her eyes up slightly, but Dean caught the random trickles of black liquid that fell still on her blouse. She was waiting with Ron for now. It was her worst day, he felt that, he could even feel her pain radiating, it was like iced water splashed against his spine.

Jamie closed the door and led Dean through the plastic strip curtains that smelt of strong disinfectant. A light flickered, and another went out with a snap. They walked down a sterile corridor to an open room tiled with white and five metal top tables lit by harsh surgical lights. Each table had a corpse on it covered with thick, green mucous. Dean felt nauseas as Jamie led them to the nearest table.

'We think this is some kind of superbug. The bug developed rapidly, maybe over a day; it seems.' Jamie lifted the left wrist of the body revealing a tatt. It was purple and green, the first thought that popped into Dean's head was that it must have been sepsis. Jamie released the lifeless arm and it slumped onto the table; the dull thud echoed in the silent room.

'Sepsis I assume,' Dean said boldly, feeling confident it was, because otherwise this was a waste of official police time, also the stench of the mucous was making him queasy.

'Yes, but like the bug it developed rapidly, over the course of an hour, just before she died. So why would being struck by a motor vehicle cause this?' Jamie walked over to the sink and picked up a metal clamp, scissors and two pairs of latex gloves. There was a cough sweet left on the side, he quickly dropped it into his white lab coat. Dean covered his nose and mouth with his hand, the stench was like stale milk and shit, and he gagged.

'Put these on and hold this.' Jamie passed him the surgical gloves and clamp and proceeded to make a long incision down the length of the girl's chest cavity, gracefully slicing the greenish flesh and parting the flaps of skin. Dean put the gloves on, and moved in for a closer look, still covering his mouth and nose. Still, the stink stung his eyes.

Inside the girls dissected chest there was a collection of gelatinous black fluid, it seemed to sac around the lungs, it wobbled, and it made Dean uneasy. He leant on the table, clenched his eyes and tried not to breath the putrid air.

'You okay?' Jamie asked.

'Yes, sorry,' Dean said. 'Carry on.' The room was too bright, and Dean felt lightheaded again. He wished Jamie would hurry up.

Jamie did so, pointing and talking but the information didn't sink in, at one point the lights in the room blurred into a massive static screen, then, Deans legs buckled, and he slumped to the floor.

'Dean, Dean wake up.' Jamie had his arms around Dean's shoulder and was rubbing and patting his cheeks, squeezing them and trying to bring him back to consciousness. Moments later light poured painfully into his eyes and the room seemed like a nightmare, surreal and disconnected, silent as the grave and full of death.

'Don't worry,' Jamie said. 'I didn't expect you to last long. Don't get up, so I'll give it to you straight.' Jamie reached for the cough sweet and chomped it, the menthol smell hit Dean waking his senses, easing the stress.

'Yes, please do, because I can't see how this contributes to a hit and run.'

'That's exactly it,' Jamie said. 'Being run over obviously doesn't cause this. Only a severe infection does, which means her cause of death was sepsis rather than being hit by the vehicle. There isn't any need to investigate, Dean, are you relieved?'

Jamie smiled and pulled Dean up until he managed to push himself to his feet. He was somewhat relieved but now needed a good reason not to give Jamie a mouthful for wasting police time. Dean had missed breakfast for this.

'Give me a reason not to be,' he said, tearing the gloves off and tossing them to the bin bag taped on the table leg. Let's go somewhere else, he thought and started to walk back through the corridor towards the plastic curtains, Jamie followed. Ron now stood with his arm wrapped around the lady at the door, comforting no doubt. Jamie put his hand on Dean's shoulder.

'It's not all good news. You need to inform the CDC, I can but I need someone of jurisdiction to back me up, politics you know?'

'Right, so serious then?' Dean asked, but Jamie returned to the room of death without replying. It must have been serious, and if everyone in the lobby was in the same condition, they could be on the brink of an epidemic.

'Ron, we're leaving, now.' Dean hurried to the elevator and Ron quickly followed behind. The woman stood next to Jamie who led her by the shoulders into the death room, her sobs now obvious, until they broke into screams, just as the elevator doors shut.

CHAPTER 3

Sheila's Proposition

'Harry, might you actually keep an eye on James for once.' Molly pointed from the sun-baked plastic chair across to the sandy beach where little James had fallen. They were sat on the path under an awning from a shop, James ten or so feet away on the beach. Behind in the small information shop a radio was playing jazz songs and news reports. Molly to the left of Harry drinking bottled fizzy water. Harry had a diet orange juice but hadn't touched it.

Kids swarmed the sand playing with kites and building sandcastles. Parents sat and drank and ate ice cream. The surfers were riding the waves. The day was hot, Harry hadn't felt this relaxed in a long time. Molly insisted they saved money, but Harry enjoyed seeing James play here, although today it was busy, and passers-by obscured the view now and again.

'Of course, I was seeing how he handled it,' replied Harry, who planted his orange on the table and made for the busy beach, cutting through the throng of anxious parents, helicoptering around their children.

'Okay little man?' he asked, helping his son to his feet. Little James Carrington had sand all over his shirt and on his face. Harry felt his pockets for a tissue and luckily found one, quite a clean one too. 'Hold still will you.'

James did as his father said and soon the tissue wiped the sand away and his crumpled-up face broke into a broad smile.

It was always unusual weather on the island, being in the current of western winds and southern heats. Saturday was always busy in town, Harry had to travel through most of it to work at the opera.

'Dad, can I have some more ice cream?' he asked, using the old puppy eyes trick to persuade, but Harry didn't need persuading, the sun beating down was making him crave one to, a mint chocolate single cone with flake and sprinkles.

'Mint choc chip then?' He didn't bother to wait for an answer. The sun was irritating his legs and if he stood any longer in the scolding sun it would start to burn. The crowds of hatted families strolled by and waiting for a gap to cross back to the table was a nightmare, even the animals seemed to get in the way or the owner and the leash. The day trippers gathered wearing Hawaii shirts, shorts and sun caps around the tourist information where Molly was sat at the table. Looking further down the shopfront revealed empty seats nearer the beach bandstand, Harry considered trying to get a seat, but he knew Molly enjoyed this spot. Finally, after reaching the table, he took a gulp of the fizzy orange. His forehead leaking sweat now, and the ground swayed. It wasn't usual to feel like this, he thought it must be because he'd drank orange rather than water all day.

'Just going to get ice cream Molly, you want any?' said Harry, keeping his eyes shaded with a hand. Molly sat cross-legged, her thighs reddening and her toned arms looking like a soft cake. She nodded in agreement, quickly returning her eyes to James, who appeared to be taunting some girls who were sunbathing. Birds flocked overhead as the passers-by dropped some crisps. Harry saw the crowds moving towards the bandstand.

Harry set off down the sidewalk, looking into the shops and restaurants, smelling crispy fries, ketchup and burgers. He was keeping right next to them under the shade and felt a few knocks and bumps of passers-by, some painful accidents, others he wasn't so sure. In front of the bandstand, the area was packed with families on benches, drunk tourists and a few bikers with black leather jackets drinking and jeering. Usually they kept the idiots under control, but it seemed there was only two of them, for now at least. On stage the band was setting up plugging guitars into amps and microphones into speakers.

The ice cream parlour overflowing with visitors. The queue extended across the path and down onto the beach. Harry thought it inconsiderate to block the path, so he made a point of pushing through to the bandstand. The teens at the front draped in black with mascara were going wild with excitement. They screamed and shouted, jumping around and smacking each other on the back in a buddy way. Cans of half-drunk beer flew outwards, some towards Harry and some towards the bikers, who responded with groans and then threw the cans back, hitting the teens but not damping their excitement. Harry tiptoed to see the action; a rapid drum beat that he could feel vibrating in his chest. It sounded like a giant bongo on steroids. Then a guitar squealed, drowning out the screaming teens. A man dressed in a white rob stepped up to the mike. Harry tried to see but the crowd kept pushing him and the noise of screaming and rock was all to invigorating, so he yelled, 'Wahoo!' accompanied by an air punch and subsequent head bang. The men around, whoever they were, gave an approving shove to which Harry pushed back. It was all going well, the music pounded, and the guitar was off the rails with tons of hammer ons. The white gowned singer held up a hand and the band went silent, the crowd also, and then he whispered into the mike,

'Pleased to be in Beach Town.' Followed by a scream. 'Deeeaaaddd tooowwwnnn!'

The speakers shook the ground and the entire thing was overwhelming. Then Harry felt his phone buzz, it was probably Molly checking he was okay. He quickly shut the revelry out and the surrounding head bangers gave an *aww* as he walked away. The screen on his phone said Sheila, and straight away the car incident sprung to mind. Still he pushed back through the now smaller ice cream queue and stood next to the building having to shield his remaining ear from the music just to answer.

'Sheila how are you?' he answered cheerily, still feeling cocked and ten years younger again. The line was quiet for a second, and then Sheila crackled into audibility.

'I'm good, Harry. I'm sorry to bother you but how do you fancy heading to a job interview with me?' She sounded hesitant about asking. It was never easy for anyone round here to ask such favours, people kept to themselves.

'I'm down at the beach right now,' it was his turn to sound hesitant. 'If you want…you could err, come down here with us, you know, Molly and James are here,' he said, eager for her to say yes. He just hoped she wasn't with Wendy if she did. The uncaring partner he had once called her.

'No, I'm afraid not, I have to prepare for this, it's today and I kind of really need a lift there.'

Harry smelt something funky in the air and left the side of the store, probably drugs he thought. As he paced back thinking of a response, it seemed difficult doing it today, the city was about three hours away after all.

'Why didn't you ask me before today, Sheila? I would love to help but this is the only day I have free.' As he approached Molly, she went from a smile to a frown, noting the time on her watch with a tut. James was still out in the sand, building a sandcastle with his hands. The teen girls were helping him, they looked as excited as James. The sand was crumbling but James kept trying to build it.

'Queue is too big, better wait until later,' he told Molly as he held the phone to his chest, then returned to the call, sensing a night of guilt if he said no.

'Are you there, hello?' Sheila asked anxiously.

'Yes Sheila, I'm sorry but it's not possible, we could meet up tomorrow though?'

'No, Harry! Listen I haven't got any money and you are the only person I have in the whole fucking world at the moment.' Her voice sounded shaky, like it was breaking into a tearful one. The tone and timing of the call was one thing, but the bad language, something like this from Sheila meant serious stuff. The last time she blew the local drunk got a beating.

'Okay, what time should I pick you up?'

'Umm, I have to be there for five, so two is fine.'

'Two? Okay, that shouldn't be a problem, just bear in mind I don't fancy getting cancer from passive smoking.' He gurgled a laugh to lighten the mood but was met with silence.

'No, I don't expect you to,' she retorted and hung up. Harry stuffed his phone back in his pocket.

The day was still scorching. In the cloudless blue-sky flocks of seagulls were circling overhead and the golden sand was looking mystical. The sound of the waves rushing against the beach and the background noise of hundreds of conversations was calming Harry.

'Sorry Molly, I need to go help a friend out. I'll catch up with you and James later, okay?' The water bottle he had previously bought still sat on the table, he opened it and downed it, feeling the cold liquid soothe his throat.

'I'll miss you, Harry. Hurry back please,' Molly said. Harry felt relieved that he could get of town for some time, but he wanted to go with his family, not Sheila. Behind on the radio in the shop, Harry overheard a report about a riot in the city. He ignored it.

CHAPTER 4

Lost in Transition

The two-door silver hatchback came to a stop on the third lane of Beach Town's only motorway, which led over a sea bridge to the city. The traffic was at a standstill. The turn off to the hospital was busy, but the cars were moving at least. Harry and Sheila sat in dull silence, pondering their own thoughts, each in their own world. Somehow the windowpane seemed more interesting than the rumbling engines and miles of car roofs outside. Some kid, maybe a toddler was crying in the distance, a car clanked into a hurricane of smoke and an ambulance tried to pull right down the siding. Beach Town drivers used the right side of the road. It was hectic beyond reason.

'Anytime soon we'll be skeletons,' sighed Harry, who wound the window halfway down, to be met with the smell of a cool breeze.

'It's not that bad, it'll improve, just wait and see,' Sheila said trying to ease her own doubt. But the cars edged forward an inch or two, and then stopped again. A man three cars down got out, shielding his eyes from the hazing sunlight. Then a woman smartly dressed in a grey suit, climbed out her sparkling two door Mercedes sport and the two-stood gazing into the distance. Less people honked and more engines went quiet.

'Might as well save fuel,' Harry said, keying the ignition off. Sheila looked in the rear-view mirror and saw some young men getting topless and jumping onto their wagon roof. Harry knew she was attracted when she looked at them, he didn't blame her for looking because her girlfriend Wendy was dismissive and argumentative since she lost her job.

'So, this job then, what is it?' Harry asked. Sheila swung her head from looking at the men to Harry, who frowned stupidly. She cracked a knuckle and felt her pants pocket just to be sure she had her resume with her.

'Yes, it's what I've always done, assistant managing, you know?'

Naturally her confidence shone through even though Harry knew she wasn't going to make it today, not a chance. Harry knew she was at the end of her career as a manager, companies just didn't have the work on the island anymore for them and Sheila's financial and criminal background now made her the less than ideal candidate. On the other hand, Harry supposed someone would give her the second chance she needed, the break everyone needs when they do something wrong because they might feel sorry for her. They hadn't even left Beach Town, and even if they had they'd need to get up to at least eighty on the outskirts to get there on time. Harry checked his watch, ten to twelve, just brilliant he thought. He was rather looking forward to exploring the city and Sheila's potential office space that was probably littered with sticky notes and the desk probably had chewing gum to the bottom, yuck. More the city, Harry had read about some of the lavish shops along the city street, particularly mens clothing.

He pushed back into his cushioned seat, the sagging fabric pressing against his back. 'Damn, need to get this thing sorted.'

Sheila held a cute kitten type look of disappointment that he seemed more interested in the seat than the job he just asked about. Harry knew he had a short attention span and that Sheila knew it to. The car was fast becoming a hot box, Harry fanned his face with his hand.

'Why don't we go to the cinema instead?' Harry said. 'You can call them and let them know you can't make it today.' He pushed his back into the seat and then rolled the window fully down, where a Smokey charcoal smell drafted in. Most people were on the bonnets now, some did handstands and others smoked and chatted. One woman was doing yoga in tight pants. She was sat on her roof, her ass crack slightly showing, but she soon pinched it back up.

'You're probably right,' Sheila said. 'What was I thinking taking an interview two hours out?' Her sarcasm was followed with her rustling through her bag.

'No chance, get out if you want to smoke,' Harry said. But Sheila ignored him and pulled out her chap stick, opened and applied it with pouting pop.

'Umm, cherry,' she said, smiling to Harry. Harry saw Sheila glance to the rear view again, the lads had their shirts on and drinking beer. By the looks of it, the driver was too. Harry felt like joining them, even with the windows open it wasn't enough to cool the car.

'Screw it, I'll be back soon,' she said, stashing her chappy in her bag and dunking it to the back seat. Her succulently sexy black suit would have to win these young men, and their inability to see the age difference.

'Be careful, I'll take a walk,' Harry replied before grabbing the keys and they both exited the baking vehicle.

It felt like a heat wave was passing over, but it was bearable with the salty breeze of the sea. Harry walked slowly past each car. At first people seemed to be having fun and chatting and smoking, but as he moved further up the motorway, the people began to look more miserable and more of them were sat head in hands with water bottles. Harry paused next to a red Jeep, he noticed the man inside was asleep, or so he appeared to be. He considered the heat and knocked on the window, the man was still. Harry peered in, using his hands to see past the glare. The man wasn't moving at all. The other folks around unaware. Harry tried the door, but it was locked.

He knocked on the window. Nothing. He pulled the handle without success. By now the obese man behind had notices and ambled over, much to Harrys dissatisfaction. He probably suspected Harry of trying to rob something from the car.

'Oi, what are you doing?' The fat man panted, his stubble greasy and his shirt soaked with sweat.

'He's stuck in there,' Harry replied, avoiding eye contact with the fat man's waist, which only just slid between the cars. The fat man wore oversized brown laced trainers and his trousers were like girders.

'Yeah?' the fat man said. Harry felt uncomfortable, like the man was creating a scene.

'Yeah, see.' Harry pointed to the unconscious man in the car. The fat man peered in the window, lifting his sacking arms to cover the reflecting sunlight and gasping for breath.

Suddenly the overweight giant clenched his dripping shirt with both hands and gasped like he just swallowed a bug.

'Not now!' Harry grunted. The giant fell to the sizzling motorway tarmac, clenching his chest. Other people sat on the cars spotted the man fall and rushed over, Harry knelt at his side. Harry could not comprehend the unfolding situation; it was all happening to fast.

'Help! Someone call an ambulance!' Harry pleaded to the bystanders who wore sunhats and shirts with gormless expressions. A middle-aged lady, in a pink flower blouse pulled her phone out, then a smaller bearded man.

Harry felt helpless he could not help the man; the motorway was rammed and the ambulance on the turnoff behind had gone. The people gathered in a circle, none of them helping.

They were a turnoff to the hospital, if he wasn't so fat, they could carry him. The fat nameless man's neck split into several folds as he seized, lashing his arms and shaking his head uncontrollably, foaming at the mouth and clenching his teeth. Harry stepped back, wary of the bystanders. The crowd began to step back. A man and woman went to the aid of the fallen man, attempting to hold his head still. His seizure hadn't knocked him out cold, Harry felt relief the man was still alive but the thought somebody might blame him for this was frightening. He had been blamed for incidents before, a neighbour once accused him of having an affair and his boss once had him monitored on suspicion of fraud.

Harry panicked at the thought, stood up and tried to catch Sheila's attention a few cars back. Harry remembered Sheila took a first aid course, but it seemed improbably the man could be saved now. The fat man's body was becoming limper with each gasp. Sheila was drinking, laughing and getting touchy with the lads. Harry felt happy for her. Sheila couldn't see his waves, so he rushed to the man's side. The heat pounding down, the tarmac rippling like a desert and the fumes foul.

Do something!' a woman cried from behind Harry, startling him. An Asian man beside Harry joined the chant and soon the mob pleaded, shouting for Harry to help. Harry could not escape now, he had to defend himself.

'I can't help I am not a doctor!' Harry said. 'How long is the ambulance going to take?!'

The woman beside the fat man answered, the fat man was as still as a rock now. 'They said they are busy responding to incidents in the city, they can't give an arrival time,' her face chalk white as her lip trembled. Harry could see the fear in the woman's eyes as she held the fat man's unconscious head. Then the fat man in the beating sun opened his eyes for a few seconds, vomit squirted out onto the ground, missing Harry but decorating the Asian man's khaki shorts. The crowd were becoming more distant, a couple walked away mumbling.

'That's no heart attack, that's something else!' said the Asian man next to Harry. It was as if a bomb had exploded, everyone watching reacted with panic. Smiles of the bystanders turned to worry and fear, a few of the onlookers frantically jogged back to their cars, locking their doors.

'It's a virus, the terrorists are back!' another man yelled, sending the remaining bystanders into a primal panic. The people screamed, shouting 'Get back to your cars! There's a virus outbreak!' and 'It's the black death!' One teen behind Harry tripped over in the confusion and was trampled by a woman. The woman supporting the fat man's head stood and walked away further down the motorway, vanishing between the sea of clogged cars.

'Michael, Michael Hanson,' said the now shaking Asian man kneeling next to Harry, outstretching his hand. Harry hesitated, scanning the road, realising the ridiculous sentiment of shaking someone's hand while a man lay dying or dead in front of them. Harry was grateful the car was shading them. Inside the other unconscious man whom Harry found before, Harry had forgot about him. Harry found the situation surreal. Him and Michael were exchanging pleasantries. Harry shook Michael's hand; it had a rubbery texture.

'No time for chatting, any ideas, Michael?' Harry shrugged unsure of what to do, mindful of Sheila and the still unmoving traffic. Both men beaded sweat from their foreheads.

'No idea, I fancy a drink, do you?' Michael's withdrawal worried Harry. The behaviour of the other motorists was diabolical, everyone ran off unwilling to help because of fear. The ambulance was nowhere in sight either.

'Hold in there.' Harry reassured the unconscious fat man. He wondered if the unconscious man could hear him. Unconscious but alive, Harry saw his neck veins turn bluish green and his neck muscles stiffen. Just as they did, the fat man ceased breathing. The fat man's face turned blue as his mouth gushed with foam. The arms flopped to the road surface.

'Shit! He's dead!' Michael cried. Harry felt his heart skip a beat, a nagging fear rose from his spine, his hairs were razors and he felt he had to leave the area.

'We need to get away from here,' Harry said.

Other motorists and passengers returned to see the fat man who was now blue skinned and lifeless.

'Jesus! It's a fucking virus of some kind!' Some woman huddle in the crowd shouted, her voice shrieking, to Harrys amazement he wondered why she came back if she wasn't helping.

'No shit!' A buffed-up camo pants man yelled, huffing at the shrieking woman. The crowd bickered and the voices a razor pain in Harry's ears. Michael was looking uncomfortable.

'Fuck off or help, stop causing a stir!' Harry shouted. Some of them walked away in silence. Harry felt ashamed, the fat man in front of him was cold dead and not one person helped. Did they even phone an ambulance? Was the ambulance coming?

Harry struggled to keep cool, birds were flocking overhead as the sun passed into a cloud. The car's metal buzzed with heat; the air conditioning of the surrounding cars hummed tediously.

'There's someone in the car.' Harry jumped up from the road and one punched the car window in rage, people scorned at him in surprise. His fist stung and trickled blood down his forearm.

'Jeez,' quipped Michael. 'You're gonna have to pay for that sunshine!' Harry smirked sadistically at him, the pain surged through his arm, pulsating with every heartbeat. Harry put a finger to the man's neck and couldn't find a pulse. He lifted the unconscious driver's arm; it was colder than the neck. Harry assumed the shade had cooled the body. There was no pulse.

'Him too?' Michael stepped over the broken glass peaking in the car window, pointing to the bottle of water that had turned yellow in the cupholder.

'I'm afraid so, no pulse.' Harry released the corpses arm which slumped to the bodies lap. This was making Harry faint. Michael breathing down his neck didn't help matters.

'It's the water,' Michael whispered. Harry saw the bottle shaking his head in disagreement. Seeing the demise of the fat man had eased this passing.

The air seemed to become like fog, like Harry was smelling the scent of death. A look back through the crowds revealed that Sheila had now sat cross legged on the roof with her knees to her shoulders. Harry could not see her expression.

'What can we do?' Harry asked. 'I have no idea how to deal with this, do you?' Michael put his arm around him, Harry was uncomfortable with a stranger touching him but resisted the desire to shove Michael, hoping he didn't want to whisper to him again. This short Asian Michael was creepy but friendly, and Harry had yet to determine whether he liked him or hated him.

'I suggest we return to our cars, there's nothing we can do,' Michael said. Michael turned and walked away towards Harry's car.

Harry observed the scene, the fat man on the floor, the broken window, which he would happily pay for, the body, touching it might not have been wise. His fist was sore but had clotted, the blood had stained his arm. The clouds were providing a well needed shade from the heat. The bystanders no longer watched, the people on the surrounding vehicle now resumed gossiping.

No ambulance in sight, not even a medical chopper.

Harry stepped back, speechless. Two dead bodies left on the motorway in the cars. Harry maneuverer over the fat man's body. He contemplated covering him but changed his mind. The gunk and green veins told Harry something terrible could happen if he touched the body. If it was viral Harry could have it already.

A few people approached crying and yelling, the hysterical woman was amongst them, no longer hysterical but pulling on Harry's heartstrings. They gathered around the fat man no longer laughing or crying. One woman went pale and vomited next to the body. Harry felt nauseas again, he had to get back to Sheila. Whatever had killed that fat man was not normal. Harry knew a heart attack didn't cause green pus to pour from the victim's mouth.

Harry reached his car after trying to avoid chit chat with nosy drivers who attempted to talk to him on the short walk back. He felt stupid for leaving the car window open, somebody could have taken the keys or Sheila's handbag. Sheila must be roasting in her interview attire.

Sheila was on the roof behind, drunk and unable to see if another motorist stole her bag. It was there along with Harrys phone. Harry got in the door handle burning his hand. The phone signal was one bar and the battery in the red. Worryingly Harry had a text from Molly twenty minutes ago. He unlocked the phone and read the message.

It read: "Harry, I've had to take James to the hospital, he is not very well at all!!! Please phone me as soon as you get this!!!"

Harry pushed call button to contact Molly. Harry was impatient as it rang. It buzzed some more before beeping three times and cutting out. Harry looked at the phone screen again, the battery icon was flashing. The silence was deafening.

'Bloody phone, never reliable!' he shouted, seeing Sheila in the rear-view mirror who heard him. Harry watched as Sheila slid down the bonnet and paced towards the car waving goodbye to the sunbathing lads on the car. She put her head in the window.

'What's wrong harry?' she asked. Harry was relieved she was sober, he couldn't handle a drunk Sheila as well, not after all of today's carnage. He had dealt with her drunkenness before and it always ended in arguing.

'It's James, he's sick apparently, I can't get through to Molly!' Harry gasped. Sheila ran to the other side of the car and got in. She checked the passenger door for her phone.

'Full battery,' Sheila said, and Harry perked up. 'But no signal.'

She gave Harry the phone and he snatched it from her hand. She frowned at him. He stashed his back in his trouser pocket.

'Tell me what is wrong,' she said. Sheila seemed genuinely frightened at Harry's behaviour. Before dialling, he paused, shook his head and explained quietly.

'There's a man up ahead who's just died of a possible heart attack, and another dead in his car, probably from heat stroke.'

'Oh, my god, Harry! Why hasn't anyone phoned an ambulance?!' she cried.

'Shh, keep it down we don't want to panic the entire motorway! Check what the news says about this traffic as well!' Harry became impatient and didn't want a crowd to gather around his car.

She did as he said turning the radio knob and it crackled to life. There was a snap in the radio audio, then a pop and hiss. The radio hissed silent.

'Wait, this can't be right,' Sheila said, growing concerned. 'There's nothing coming through.' As she turned the tuning knob, each frequency sounded like bacon sizzling.

Harry tried to ring Molly from Sheila's phone now he had a signal. The phone rang, with each ring sweat poured from his underarms, the anticipation and impatience were grinding him down.

'Nothing, no answer! This is not normal,' Harry blurted. 'No radio, no phone.' Harry passed the phone back to Sheila, the signal bar at zero.

The motorway was a frying pan, the human's eggs and bacon cooking until they passed out. People were sprawled on the road now, hiding under cars, spraying each other with sun block and water. They could not stay any longer, the heat would become fatal.

'We have to get somewhere sheltered. We'll walk if we have to,' Harry said. Sheila wasn't happy and removed her black jacket, her underarms drenched too.

Harry saw people jumping on cars in front, some fell over as they tried to run down the narrow gap between cars. Something had triggered mass panic. Harry felt his heart skip a beat. People were screaming. Sheila was trying to see what was happening. People scrambled running over other people as they sprinted down the motorway. Children were being carried by shocked parents and car horns sounded.

The screams scraped Harry's ears, making him angry that they wouldn't shut up. Harry covered his ears with his hands, but he could still hear the crying. It was hysteria.

'What the fucks going on up there?' Sheila snapped.

'I hope it's not another heart attack,' Harry replied. He got the impression things were about to change to dangerous.

Harry got out the car and Sheila did so as well. The masses of panicked people pushed one another to get away from the fat man, their faces pale with fear. Sheila leant on the car; strangers piled past her. The fat man had become violent attacking bystanders. People attacked one another. Harry could see them punching the faces of one another. It was violence Harry had never seen before. Something pulled Harry closer to the action.

'I'm checking it out.' Harry loosened his belt.

'No, I'm coming with you,' Sheila asserted. Walking round and standing at Harry's side.

'No!' Harry snapped. 'Wait here.' His face tingled red and his feet began to drag as he walked towards the shouting.

He got a few cars back from the disturbance. People in cars were stricken with fear. There was a moulding scent that carried in the wind. Harry gagged into his hand before spitting a thick lump onto the road.

Birds squealed overhead and the surrounding cars were now being abandoned. Harry wanted to drive on the other side of the bollards, where no traffic had travelled for the last hour at least.

The fat man's neck was puffing, oozing green hard sludge resembling lard. The smell was intoxicating Harry, he had to cover his mouth with his hand. He gagged at the sight up ahead. He was a good few cars away and whatever was unfolding hadn't notice him.

He took a few deep breaths scanning the deserted cars. Harry turned to walk back to the car, Sheila next to him.

Michael the touchy Asian had vanished a while ago. Harry was annoyed. The guy was friendly enough and may have been a counterweight to Sheila. Harry had one thought now, his son and home. They continued past Harry's car. Sheila wound the car window up and left her handbag. Clouds were blocking the sun, but it was still hot. The shouting and the crowd that remained around the fat man's car were acting weirder, shambling and groaning. Harry was nervous. He hadn't felt butterflies since college exams.

Harry turned to Sheila as they made there was back down the motorway towards the turnoff, the cars empty abandoned. 'We're walking.'

CHAPTER 5

No Way Out

Harry and Sheila reached the turn off after walking through the traffic of occupied cars, the drivers and passengers to far away from the attacks to see what was happening. Some cars smoked from the overused clutch, bored occupants smoke and sleep.

Behind, a few bored motorists had tagged along, carrying purses and bottles of water. It felt sickening to be leading them to the hospital, knowing Harry couldn't provide an answer to the traffic or to the lack of emergency services. The only motorway out of Beach Town was clogged full of cars. Harry was sure they had blocked the bridge from the city, that would explain there being no cars on the other side of the road. Harry figured the people were just as concerned as he was.

Sheila needn't squeeze through the gaps, her slim waist slipped elegantly passed them. Harry found himself the victim of an ignorant red Ford driver who opened his door to ask, 'What's going on up there?' Harry replied quickly, he didn't want Sheila and him wasting time in a danger zone, 'Collision.'

The hospital was secluded after the curved turn off which ramped down directly into the carpark. The large hospital doors were open, the car park was full of cars but no occupants.

The heat was burning a hole in Harry's back and Sheila kept readjusting her white blouse. The other motorists had stopped following once Sheila and Harry headed towards the hospital waddling back to the packed motorway with coughs and sighs.

'Hold on,' Sheila said, pausing to rub her eyes.

'What the hell,' Harry muffled.

They were nearing the car park entrance and free of the unbearably thick smog.

'What now?'

'I need to find James,' Harry said, gathering the little energy he had and marching on. Sheila pulled her phone from her trousers but then she stashed the phone to her pocket again. Her shirt was now wet, and she unbuttoned the top two buttons, catching Harry's ear.

'You feel okay?' he asked, stopping and admiring the bright white bra.

'Yes, I'm fine,' she said. 'Just a little hot.' Sheila led the way to the car park entrance, the ramp coming to an end. Harry removed his arms from his jacket and chucked it over his shoulder.

They approached the car park gate; it was open but blocked a large jeep. The guard box empty. The car park as empty as a ghost town too. Harry looked in the guard's boxes open window; it stank of hot plastic.

'Anything?' Sheila asked.

Before Harry had time to react, someone had smacked a heavy metal object over his back, sending splinters of agony through his spine. His head lashed backwards as he fell to the concrete. Sheila screamed, Harry turned and saw her take a whack to the legs, from another figure.

Two men, dressed in leather jackets towered them, snarling at their faces. They held large silver wrenches; the wrenches must have weighed five kilos easy. A dull pain coursed through Harry's back; he lay clenching his teeth. Sheila appeared to be ok.

'Alive?' One of the men scorned at Sheila. The man's brow thick and his goatee unclean. Harry could see the jacket clearly now, it had an unflinching logo of a skull with a dagger through it - the hells angels of Beach Town, as they would say - Harry couldn't recall much, his spine was in agony.

'What the fuck are you doing?' she yelled. The man got closer, the sun revealing thick and black hair. His hands wrapped in leather; his boots glistened.

'Holy ghost, they're alive,' he said to the other wrench wielder who immediately helped Harry to his feet

'Sheila, you okay?' Harry asked. After being helped up he rushed to Sheila's aid. She had a red lump forming on her shin which she avoided looking at.

'No, I'm clearly not okay Harry,' she exclaimed.

The two bikers stood swinging their wrenches like shopping bags. The day was getting more confusing, Harry didn't know why the road was packed or the men attacked them, it wasn't a normal day.

'Just who the hell are you? We came to the hospital and this happens!' Harry realised he'd lost his jacket in the ticket box, it was unimportant now. Harry approached the black-haired man, not too close, as he towered over him at six feet easily.

'I'm sorry okay,' he said to Harry. 'We thought you were one of dangerous ones, the names Charlie, Kale.' The man outstretched his hairy arm to Harry, which gave off a sickly scent of smoke, his skin tinged yellow. He was bearish, which couldn't be held against him, after he said sorry.

'Next time try saying something first,' Harry replied, shaking the hand firmly, he had to wipe the sweat on his pants after.

'In this situation, I doubt anyone will have time to speak,' his partner replied. 'Peter. I'm a close friend of Charlies, as you can tell.' He went to give Harry a handshake, but Sheila grabbed his hand and dug her nails into his skin, grinning like a school kid.

'Pleased to meet you, jackass,' she tore her hand away.

'Shit, take it easy, I'm sorry alright,' Peter cried, his hand red.

'Accepted,' she replied.

Harry saw the biker's rides near the main entrance doors.

'My sons in there, I need to go find him,' Harry explained. Charlie had a look disapproving concern.

'No chance,' Charlie replied. 'Wait until the police get here, then go in.'

'I've been waiting on the highway for an ambulance, it didn't show, then I was told my son was brought to hospital, seriously ill, I'm not waiting.' Harry walked off across the car park with Sheila limping behind. There were a few cars parked on curbs, everything appeared normal, Harry could not understand why they hadn't sent an ambulance.

'Wait,' Charlie called out, jogging his gladiator body over to them.

'You aren't going in alone, I'll come with you. Peter, wait here for the police, if anything happens just do what we said and run.' Charlie led the way to the entrance, Peter hopped on an old station wagon, holding the wrench behind his head like a pillow.

'So, what happened?' Sheila's voice trembled with pain as she walked. Charlie shook his head frowning. Harry at his side worrying for James.

'Can't explain it. We came in, one of our friends fell off his bike, ran down a girl. He came to the hospital, but when we came to visit him, he seemed…well, he seemed to have some sort of goo pouring out of his mouth.' Charlie shivered a sigh.

They reached the open entrance doors; the lobby was empty with nothing but the sound of the white wall clock ticking and the lights and check in computers humming. A dreadful wave flooded over Harry. The receptionist desk ahead was deserted.

'Was it green?' he asked. Charlie whipped around eyeballing Harry, it unnerved him.

'What? Have you seen this before?' Charlie alleged.

'Unfortunately, I have. Back there on the motorway, there were two dead guys, they both had green goo,' Harry explained. Charlie went silent. They entered the hospital lobby area. Harry was nervous that it was empty, something was seriously wrong.

Sheila was pale and sat on the red leather lobby sofas.

'What is it?' Harry followed up, holding his hands-on hips like a manager interrogating his late employee. Charlie was swinging the wrench again. It must have been his thinking tic, because it looked to Harry like a kid swinging a doll or their parents' arm.

'I don't know,' Charlie said. 'It might be an epidemic, you know?'

The lobby was unsettling because of the lack of people and the buzzing lights. Sheila's bag rattled and echoed through the room as she searched it. Something was not right, and Harry sat next to Sheila.

'I have no idea where James was taken, where do we start to look?' Harry asked Sheila, who pulled out a small red lip gloss, twisting the top and applying it to her lips.

'Third floor is the children's admissions,' she said, stashing her lip gloss back into her handbag. Harry admired her blouse that was drying, it entertained him to think she sweated as much as him. Harry got up and waved Charlie over.

'Let's go,' Harry said.

The two men walked to the elevator left of the entrance doors. Harry thumbed the fading button and it beeped. They stepped into the elevator. Charlie went to push the first floor, but Harry pushed third floor before Charlie could and he grunted.

'Gotta find your son, I get it.'

The elevator reached the third floor. It was quiet as they stepped into the eerie hallway. The elevator doors closed, and Harry felt left in the abyss.

'Disturbing.' Harry observed the shiny corridor that seemed a mile. Doors lined the corridor and piercing lights lit the ward. The administration or nurses' desk in front of them was empty.

Charlie walked to it and peered at the workstation before walking around the side of it where he began routing through the loose paperwork. Harry joined him.

'Look for last name Carrington.' Harry sat at the computer, but it was locked. He tried the obvious password, *password* and then *hospital children's ward*. The computer flashed an error box with wrong password in red. Harry began routing through the paperwork.

Gradually the paper began to have meaning. Charlie had ventured to the front of the desk, leaning on it and shaking his head. Harry read through endless medication lists and tons of names but couldn't see James's name.

Harry stopped routing, a second of waiting might help him refocus. It helped to find his keys and his phone, so why not his son. Harry opened a draw; they were packed with office equipment and some chewing gum. Looking through the nurse's station files was distressing him, nobody showed up yet.

'Dammit, we totally missed this sucker,' Charlie chuckled like a gorilla. Charlie pointed his wrench at a white board on the wall next to the elevator door. It listed patient names and bed numbers. Bed five it listed Carrington.

'How the heck did we miss that, come on let's go.' Harry got up from the swivel chair before beginning to walk off down the corridor. Charlie yanked his collar before he could get to the first room. They were going left from the elevator doors down.

'Woah, what?' Harry moaned. The yank made his back ache.

'Be cautious, the hospital is empty, does this seem normal?' Charlie set off in front. None of the patient room doors were open. There was a beeping pulsating from doors one, two and three. It sounded like the monitors had gone on overdrive.

Harry walked up to door number four. There had to be patients and staff. Maybe the staff were on another ward. Harry investigated the window of room four, but the room was empty.

'Jeez,' he said. On the floor was the green goo, it was encompassed in a red slimy border resembling a giant cell.

'Look at this!' Harry said to Charlie who looked in horror.
'What?' Charlie replied.

'This shits everywhere, don't go in,' Harry said. 'We don't know what is it.' Charlie walked off down to room five.

Harry looked in number five. Seeing the monitors flashing. There was no goo, so Harry gripped the cold door handle and stepped in. 'Where is he, where is James?' he asked himself. 'Nothing.' Harry slapped the white wall with his palm.

Charlie waited at the door but entered when Harry slapped the wall. Harry was angered and ashamed that he didn't know where his son was or what the hell was going on. Hope drained from Harry. Replaced with the magnetic shudder of fear. The feeling you get when on a high ledge.

'We have to move out, this place isn't gonna tell you anything, come on,' Charlie said, opening the door for Harry.

They stepped into the breezy desolate hallway. The cries of children sent chills down Harry's arms. It was harmonic, there was a group of children somewhere nearby.

'Shit, they are here,' Charlie cried. Like wild dogs hunting prey, they both began to search for the cries.

They paced slowly down the empty corridor following the cries. The further from the elevators they were made Harry nervous, they didn't know what they were against.

The crying overwhelmed Harry's senses as they passed room eight. Charlie gasped pointing into the window of room twelve where Harry jogged over to. Charlie was white.

'Damn, never been so nervous to find children,' Charlie murmured.

Harry felt relief and without thinking opened the door.

The crying children stopped. The room had a stagnant

odour of chemicals and rusty copper. Harry had to cover his mouth with his hand, Charlie did the same.

'Why are they on the floor?' Charlie asked.

The children turned, they were not children, they were adults. Hunched over in a circle looking like dolls. Blood and chunks of flesh dripped from their noses to their chins. On the floor in front of them lay a deceased boy. Mauled with his face torn off and tendons and ligaments pulled out like spaghetti.

'What the fuck, let's go!' Charlie yanked Harry by his fear frozen neck and dragged him from the room. The adults screamed. The monsters drenched in flesh had stood and began a sluggish chase after them. Harry picked up pace, Charlie was ahead. They raced back to the elevator.

Harry hit the elevator button.

'Shit, come on!' Harry hammered the elevator button. The monsters coming closer. Charlie stood in a defensive stance. The group of blood drenched adults waddled along the corridor, blood dripped onto the floor and left a streak of red.

'I told you this wasn't a clever idea.' Charlie leant down on one knee, as if in prayer.

'What the hell are they?' Harry whimpered. His thumb sore from hammering the elevator button. The beasts kept shambling closer. The elevator door opened.

Harry dived in. 'Get in.'

One flesh chewing monster grabbed and hooked onto Charlie's shoulder. Charlie jumped skywards crashing the wrench down on the creature's arm and snapping it. Its cries were hawkish. The bones shattered like glass and the man stumbled at Charlie again.

'Fuck!' Charlie lunged the wrench round. The blow knocked them back which gave Charlie enough time to dive into the elevator before Harry pushed the lobby button and Charlie fell to his knees.

Harry's neck flamed a sweat rash and his arms felt a ton heavier. What the hell had just happened? Harry felt panic.

'They were eating that child god dammit,' Harry whispered to himself. 'The children!' Charlie wiped the wrench with a grey rag he pulled from his jacket pocket.

'Whatever I just saw, or you just saw, is for the police.'

'What? You saw them eating that child,' Harry said feeling lost.

'You don't get it; you saw me attack them.' Charlie sounded anxious. Harry was an abiding witness.

'You think I care about that?' Harry pronounced.

Charlie pocketed the rag, got up and heaved Harry against metallic backing of the elevator and pushed the wrench to Harry's neck.

'Get off.' Harry tried to push Charlie and his toy away, but Charlie overpowered him.

'Good, cos if I hear about you mentioning it, I'll fucking break your neck.' Charlie gritted his teeth a millimetre from Harry's nose. His breath salty like sea water.

'Yes,' Harry murmured as he felt his face lose blood.

'Good.' Charlie released Harry.

The elevator shuddered as it arrived at ground floor. Immediately Sheila greeted them with a smile.

Harry hugged Sheila, a wet trickle rolled down his cheeks, a heavy weight was lifted.

'Are you okay?' he asked her. Afraid of the fate of his family. Afraid the beasts upstairs had gotten to them. Over Sheila's shoulder, he saw Charlie storm outside and flick his head around. Charlie began smacking the wrench against the concrete.

'There's someone stuck upstairs,' Sheila said, pointing to the front desk. Harry let go of her, the hug felt good. He couldn't remember the last time Molly hugged him.

'Where?' he enquired. His energy peaked.

'On the screens, you know, the cctv. I think he's a doctor, but he looks injured.'

They both walked to the front desk scurrying round to see the computer monitors. A set of keys with a plastic picture of a baby girl with bushy hair. That was someone's child too. Then Harry observed the screens as Sheila clicked the mouse trying to bring up the 'right' monitor.

'There.' She showed Harry, who's mouth dropped. He could see a doctor on the monitor, his leg wounded, and the floor pooled in blood.

'We have to help him,' Harry said. Charlie startled them as he popped up behind them.

'Where's Peter?' Charlie demanded of Sheila. Harry knew he couldn't defend her, but he knew she could withstand the violence. Ten years with violent partners toughened her, she told Harry on their drinking nights. Sheila never complained about it.

'He said he wanted to let the boys know what's happening.' Sheila's sarcastic tone lit Charlie's face like a bonfire.

'Bitch,' he commented. Charlie then noticed the camera computer monitor. 'Who's that?' Charlie's voice softened.

'Obviously a doctor,' Sheila said.

'Yes. An injured doctor,' Harry added. 'We should help him.'

Harry opened the draws which were filled with staples, tape and blue tac. Harry hoped to find a torch, something was better than nothing if more of those things turned up.

'What happened up there?' Sheila asked. Charlie sat on

the desk, it creaked under the weight of his buttocks. He tilted his wrench, so the light shone in her eyes.

'Watch it!' she complained. Charlie rested the wrench on his lap.

'I'll tell you,' Harry said taking Sheila's hand. Their eyes met; Harry felt a fire that had been suffocated.

'A child was dead, and staff were attacking him.' Harry waited for the response; Sheila held eye contact. Harry felt sick to his stomach.

'What the hell is going on here? Where are the police?' she spluttered like a weeping angel.

'They aren't coming,' Harry sighed.

'Everyone knows that. When things go downhill, they are the first to leave town,' Charlie remarked.

'Nonsense,' Sheila responded.

The computer monitors flickered. Harry grabbed the announcement mike.

'We can help you,' Harry spoke into the mike. His voice resonated throughout the hospital and the doctor became distressed at the sound. Charlie snatched the mike from Harry.

'You idiot,' Charlie snarled at Harry. 'What if there are more of them monsters here and they here that?' Harry felt frustration, James could still be here somewhere. Harry watched the screen and saw the doctor search his lab coat. The doctor retrieved a pen and paper.

'He's gonna write something,' Charlie said. The doctor wrote on the paper and then stuffed them back in his pocket.

'Can't see,' Sheila said. Harry redeemed himself by holding the computer mouse and zooming in.

'What the...' Charlie murmured. Harry was stunned. It read like coal on Christmas and a slap in the face;

GET OUT, NO WAY OUT

CHAPTER 6

Fish Out of Water

The hospital was opaque in the sunlight. A polluted undercurrent of car fumes enveloped the neglected stone pavement of the ghostly car park. No sirens sounded yet nor had any other motorist from the motorway decided to venture away from their snacks as they sat and waited.

Crows circled the hospital diving into the thick surrounding brush for worms. There was an iridescent heat pounding off the metallic coatings of the remaining ambulances.

Charlie was leaning on the door of a jeep toking a roll up cig. The smoke snaked around his ears and dissipated into the indistinguishable fume cloud accumulating overhead.

The abandoned cars had a dead silence.

Charlie lifted his head back while holding the smoke in, before exhaling rings. He became distracted by a metallic rustle. Charlie scanned the car park with wide eyes. He choked spluttering on his hand and dropping and stomping the cig into the concrete.

Inside the entrance behind the desk Sheila and Harry

were observing the wounded doctor still, the only other human they had seen in the hospital.

Charlie walked to investigate the sound, moving slowly towards the car park barrier, keeping an eye on the motorway turn off. He headed past the ticket box towards the motorway ramp. A metallic scraping scared Charlie and he jumped back.

'Come out,' he demanded. The wind picked up. There was a shuffling that made the crows overhead depart from the area.

Then a thousand footsteps pattered together, a herd of shambling green pus riddled motorists shuffled from the motorway turnoff like a pack of wolves. They horded together groaning and stumbling themselves.

'Shit,' Charlie said. Hastily Charlie began slogging it back through the barriers and across the car park. He panted and sweat flicked from his brow. He looked behind. The crowd was massive. Their bodies swaying as they continued to the bottom of the turnoff. Charlie's gasped, slowing his pace.

The motorists had the same lifeless stricken face as the nurses eating the child. Charlie stumbled through the hospital entrance.

'Get in the elevator,' Charlie shouted.

Harry spotted the beasts in the car park and grabbed Sheila's hand, yanking her from the desk and across the room to the elevator. Sheila tripped as Harry pulled her. Charlie pushed the elevator call button.

'Hurry,' Harry screamed. The hoard of pus and blood riddled monsters shambled through the hospital doors smashing the glass. The elevator was taking forever, Harry saw the stairs to the left of them, beginning his run towards them.

Charlie pushed Harry to mount the staircase first and his ribs ached from the wrench attack. The heat made him nauseas. Sheila let go of Harry's hand as they ran up the stairs.

Harry saw a sign on the staircase reading first floor to palliative care.

Soon they reached the first floor and skidded across the gleaming speckled hallway. Charlie ran to the nearest door and booted it open. The lifeless crowd still pursued, Harry could hear the determined groans, like the staff upstairs. Nobody was around, the ward was empty and cold from the breeze coming through an open window further down.

'Quick get in!' Charlie held the door handle as Sheila and Harry darted in. Charlie's face pale and beading with sweat.

Charlie pulled the wood door shut. The pursuing crowd were not stupid, they shambled onto the first floor until reaching the room and scratched at the door.

The nail scraping was deadly unnerving, claws and shuffles with no breath from the monsters.

'Where is that idiot Peter?' Charlie grabbed Sheila by the shoulders. She slapped his pale soaked face and he shunted her to the stone wall.

Harry investigated the dim storage room; one long light lit the room. It was clinical, clean and smelt of plastic as expected for a hospital. Dust accumulated around the corners of the room. Brown boxes with white labels stating ward names were stacked against the right wall.

Harry opened the top box. He shivered as he looked inside. It was red sacs of blood. If the monsters outside were like the staff upstairs they would want blood, just as the staff wanted the child's flesh.

'I didn't want to get locked in a storage room.' Sheila got in Charlies face and he stumbled onto the boxes near the door. Charlie gasped and clenched his chest. Harry saw and felt a wave of dread. A repeat of the fat man's fate.

'I can't breathe!' Charlie gasped making his face sag. Harry returned to looking in the box of blood donations. Sheila concerned knelt at Charlie's side.

'Breathe,' she said. 'It will pass, it's just exhaustion.' Sheila thumbed his neck. Harry felt no emotions other than fear for his son and wife's whereabouts. He remembered at work having to check someone's pulse after they downed a few cappuccinos in one hour. He was confident Charlie was just unfit. Charlie was probably coming close to forty or fifty.

'I…I can't…breathe.' Charlie managed to gasp. Sheila looked around, there was a water fountain at the rear of the room. The room was small, perhaps ten feet long at most.

'Harry,' she called. Harry had pulled out two sacks of blood, feeling the weight in his hands.

'Yes,' he said. Harry's zoned-out face zombified.

'Water quickly, Sheila said. Harry dropped the bags into the box.

The plastic cups towered above the fountain, Harry grabbed a cup and thumbed the blue lever and out came some cloudy water, aging and unchanged. The cup filled and he returned across to Charlie. Charlie's eyes were sunken and his mouth gaping like a fish out of water.

'On his face, he can't drink it,' Sheila commanded Harry. Harry threw the cup of water at Charlie's face. Charlie jumped to his feet. Harry tossed the cup on the floor and returned to the stack of boxes on the left, a big red cross over the stickers which read: surgery.

'Feeling better?' Sheila asked. Charlie began breathing normally again.

'Okay,' Charlie said. 'Get me more.' Charlie leant against the wall next to the door, the scratches continued.

Sheila went to get some more water.

The groans and clawing were annoying, becoming more prominent. It seemed the crowd were enraged because they couldn't perform a simple task like opening a door.

The blood bags had significance not for patients, but Harry. A potential distraction if they indeed craved blood. Harry squeezed the blood bags and placed them onto a brown box. Rummaging through more boxes, Harry pulled out two more blood bags that were coagulated like ice cream. Harry was pale and gagged.

The lights shimmered, Harry's head piercing. He held a blood bag to his forehead. The cool bags soothed his brow. Another problem in a terrible day. This must have been Harry's punishment for choosing Sheila over his family or choosing the city over the town.

'I wanted to move,' Harry said, his thoughts coming aloud. Sheila couldn't hear him, she would say something if she did, sometimes she was overbearing. He shook his negativity to positivity hoping the moral of being stuck in the dimly lit room would improve. 'Right.'

Harry threw the blood bags to the floor and the bags jiggled, sliding across to the door. Harry pulled out the normal uncoagulated blood bags from the stack of boxes behind him, gripping the bags with the hope that they would distract the beasts. He walked to Sheila.

'These will help,' Harry said. 'I'm sure of it.'

Charlie looked confused. 'Hold on,' Charlie said. 'I'm not bleeding out.' Sheila giggled to Harry's dismay, the laugh was painful and made his headache worse.

'No, this isn't for you,' Harry explained. 'These bags will distract those people, monsters, from attacking us.'

'Genius.' Harry ignored Sheila's snarky remark. The plan energised Charlie and he crushed the plastic Sippy cup and tossed it to the floor.

'What makes you think they want blood?' Charlie questioned Harry. Harry didn't have the motivation to answer questions. He just knew that somehow, this would work. It was like being born recognising your parents. Harry instinctually recognised the answer was the blood bags. Albeit it had laid dormant through his life. Harry felt confident in his plan.

'Think about it, those k... people upstairs, they were soaked with it.' Harry avoided describing the victim as a child, the staff eating the child continued to weigh heavily upon his mind.

'Yeah well fuck it if it doesn't work. I can't stay in this room any longer with the buzzing lights, I'd rather stick my head in a beehive.' Charlie hit the nail on the head. None of them wanted to be cramped up in a storage room. Harry just needed to find James and Molly. Surviving was essential.

'Damn right and we need to find that injured doctor to, he needs our help.' Sheila trying to sound concerned came out condescending.

'Honestly, he's a doctor and he has the skills to save himself,' Harry said, realising the doctor wasn't the priority anymore but their lives were. 'It can't be about other people now, not when we are stuck in a room that smells like copper.' Harry flicked his eyes, not to woo Sheila but to convince the determined broad to side with him. Sheila was a force to be reckoned with when she made a decision.

'What happened to being human?' Sheila said. 'That man can't call for help, he's locked in a room just like us. How can you expect him to help himself?' The room was too silent. The awkwardness faded. The shuffling corpses outside the door had stopped amidst the heated discussion. As if the hoard of corpses had listened to the drama.

'I don't know,' Charlie said. 'He might have answers.' Sheila's looked to Charlie with surprise. Harry supposed Charlie was rattled from nearly having a heart attack. Death had rattled his unfit cage.

'Fine,' Harry grunted. 'But we can't be running around. It's obvious that the hospital has been evacuated. I say we get the doctor then make for the roof.' Harry wanted to leave the building, but he also wanted answers. 'There might be a window cleaning lift we can escape to ground level with.' Harry glared around the musky storage room. It felt supernatural, unreal.

'So, what's the plan?' Charlie asked. Charlie used Sheila's shoulders as a crutch. She wobbled as Charlie latched his capable hands onto her white office shirt. Charlie appeared intimidating as he did in the car park. His wrench was on the floor next to the door. Harry wanted to grab the wrench and hit Charlie over the back for payback. Harry clenched the blood bags facing the door. The deranged creatures clawed at the wooden door.

CHAPTER 7

Blood Letting

The room lacked adequate ventilation, there was no window. The stench of the horde was vomit inducing and the smell wafted ungraciously under the gap at the bottom of the door.

Sheila put a hand to her mouth gagging. Charlie took small breaths.

'Ready?' Harry prompted both Sheila and Charlie. He couldn't cover his nose while holding the blood bags. Harry stood at the silent door. Sounds of rustling clothes could be heard. Harry dared not listen to closely. God forbid they get in the room. They would tear them to shreds and then what? His wife and son would be doomed to endless struggles.

'No Harry,' Sheila said, standing behind Harry. 'We can't do anything until they go, can we?' Charlie stood next to Harry at the door. The overhead lights revealed Charlie's ghost face.

'Sarcasm won't help you now,' Harry said. Sheila prodded his back.

Sheila had walked further into the storage room and retrieved a plastic Sippy cup and filled it with the lukewarm water rather than cold. She downed it and discarded the cup to the stack of boxes.

Too much was going on.

'Calm down, Harry,' Charlie laughed. 'You might give yourself a headache.'

Before Harry could reply, Sheila made a wall between them.

'Quit it. The room stinks and I can't think,' Sheila moaned. 'You two make this more depressing than winter.' Sheila got on her hands and knees. Placing her head on the concrete floor and looking through the gap under the door. Uncoordinated feet shambling around told Harry they were brain dead.

Harry and Charlie admired the view of Sheila's behind. Her body tight in her black suit pants. Harry felt aroused and unsteady. Sheila turned and saw Harry looking.

'Give it a fucking rest!' Sheila jumped to her feet and slapped Harry's chest. Charlie chuckled which angered Harry more. Charlie was just the third wheel in this trip, why couldn't he just throw Charlie out the door?

'How many?' Harry enquired. He dreaded Sheila would say too many. They could be trapped in this room some time.

'Too many for us. Unless we run for it,' she replied.

'I wouldn't risk it. They are mean killing machines. Who knows what or where this comes from or how it affects people?' Charlie said, sliding down the wall to the floor.

A small stack of boxes to Harry's right fell, they were labelled emergency use only.

'Are you an expert?' Sheila mocked Charlie. She crossed her arms and leant her back to the wall next to the door.

Harry walked to the door and put his ear against it. It was depressing having to listen their way out of that stinking box. Charlie ran his palm over his cheek and sighed.

'Sheila give it a rest. We're all tired.' Charlie sounded sleepy.

Harry glared at Charlie. He knew such comments resulted in poor outcomes when Sheila was pissed off. Luckily for Harry she refrained from arguing.

A fly buzzed past Harry. It was quick and too aggressive for Harry's liking.

The plan was going to work he was certain.

Harry stepped to the door. Charlie had his eyes closed and Sheila stood behind looking unnerved.

'This will work,' Harry said. 'You are going to have to trust me.' Harry gestured towards the door. He knew Sheila liked dominance from him.

'I'm,' Sheila hesitated. 'I'm with you.' Sheila confirmed. She brushed her hair back and stepped to the door.

'Err, give me a minute I'll be right with you.' Charlie groaned rubbing his eyes. Simultaneously the groaning monsters outside started banging on the door again.

Each bang brought Harry close to insanity. The bluebottle buzzed past Harry enraging him.

'Whatever, Charlie.'

Harry tore a small opening in the blood bag, blood seeped out onto his hand. Disgusting.

'Open that door when I say. Then slam it shut,' Harry said. 'Slam it shut immediately after I throw this Sheila, don't hesitate, no matter what you see.'

'Right, Harry. I hope this works.'

'Me too. Okay, get ready.' Harry was determined, adrenaline coursed his body. Sheila gripped the door handle.

'On three, okay?' Harry's forehead was sticky from sweat. The fly buzzed past and his temples throbbed.

'One…two…three!'

Sheila pulled the door open. Harry threw the blood bags out into the air. There was a horde of bloodied faces trying to munch their way in. Blood trickled from their green mottled skin and their eyes bloodshot with blackened veins. Sheila squealed. The blood bag seeped out over the grotesque faces.

Sheila rammed the door shut. Harry dived to the door to help. The beasts clawed at them. Scratching into the room, they had a dead foothold. Harry felt his feet slipping as they tried to keep them from breaking in the room.

A painful scream shattered their ears. The bloodied faces and hands moved away, and they shut the door. A man was screaming. Then Harry heard a snap and the man sounded like he was chocking and coughing.

'Someone's out there, now's our chance!' Harry yelled. Harry was pumped and didn't want to waste the opportunity. He pulled the door open.

The beasts had swarmed around a bleeding man who lay covered in blood and whose eyes were sockets. The man's torso looked like a salami filled bread roll, with ketchup. The blood bag had splattered on him. He must have tried to sneak past.

'Shit that was an accident,' Harry said. 'I didn't know he was there.' Harry ran into the corridor past the feasting crowd. Sheila ran behind.

The hallway was covered in a trail of intestines and organs. Harry stood on the intestine and it squished under his shoes. Sheila wobbled and vomited onto the guts and flesh.

'To the doctor,' she cried. She pointed to the staircase further down the corridor. The horde was fixated on the body just as Harry suspected, they craved flesh and blood. Harry slowed as they reached the end of the corridor and reached the bottom of the stairs. Harry's legs burned and he was hungry. Other rooms appeared empty.

Harry investigated the window of the room next to the stairs. People inside gnawed with bloodshot eyes. Harry was sick to his stomach and became lightheaded. His heart pounded and everything was tinged grey.

'Sheila,' Harry called. Sheila grabbed Harrys' arms and pulled him up the staircase. She gasped for breath, holding the staircase railing with her free hand. The staircase lights went out plunging them into darkness. Harry was dizzy from going in circles.

Sheila let go as they reached the fifth floor. Harry fell to the floor exhausted. Fresh air was coming in from a window further down the corridor. It rejuvenated his senses, but the stench of chlorine overwhelmed him. The floor seemed normal.

'The monitor said floor five,' Sheila said. 'Come on.' They crouched from the staircase into the sparkling hallway taking a right.

The howling breeze from the open window echoed along the hallway. This floor had less rooms. Harry soon tired from crouching, his calves cramping. They were near the end of the corridor, at the end a small unoccupied desk. Harry looked at the door on his right.

'There's a good chance he's in there,' Harry whispered. His eyes darted from door to door, wiping the sweat from his face. They had to be quiet. Sheila looked at the door.

It read;

J. McCormack MST, PHD, BIONEURO

'Big title, I hope he can help shed some light on this.' Harry crouched towards the door. He hesitated, fearing the doctor was dead. Harry looked at Sheila.

'That was an accident back there,' he said. Sheila placed a finger to his lips.

'I get it, survival,' she replied. 'It was a shot in the dark.' Sheila gazed into his eyes. The hospital hallway transformed. The howling wind drowned out by moans.

'Shit they must have followed us,' Harry said. 'Let's get inside. I've had enough of bloodletting for today.'

Sheila giggled and it irritated Harry. Harry opened the doctor's office door, they both slipped in and he closed it behind.

They stood up. A weak grumble halted Harry. A hysterical laugh unnerved him, like a maniacal clown. Harry walked further into the well-lit room. A face emerged from behind the grey filing cabinet to the left of the desk. A shaking man appeared with a scalpel in hand. He was thin and dressed in a hospital gown with five hospital admission bracelets. The man's face was dirty. His thick brown hair knotted. Harry pulled Sheila close to him. Harry saw the injured doctor in the left corner of the room behind the desk. He was shaking. Gripping his bleeding right leg.

The gowned man stepped forward, slicing a small wound into his forehead, blood trickled down his eyes and cheeks. He was hunching over like a gargoyle. His bony shoulders protruding disturbingly.

'Welcome to my house,' the disturbed man said. 'We're gonna have a party now.'

'Oh no,' Harry muttered. Sheila's palm slipping from Harry's. Harry was angry he let Sheila talk him into this.

'We can run for it,' she whispered from the corner of her mouth. It dawned on Harry how messed up this situation was becoming. Harry also realised something else that might come back to haunt him.

'We left Charlie behind.'

CHAPTER 8

Revenge is sweet

Charlie awoke. Smelling the air. His chest was burning. His legs shook to life, blood rushing back to the feet. The storage room was empty. Harry and Sheila were gone.

Silence filled the room. The moans had stopped. The room door was open. His right boot had thick coagulated red gunk over it. Charlie sat writhing his back. He grabbed the wrench at his side. His eyes adjusted to the light. He had an overwhelming urge to slap the wall. He cracked his neck.

'Shit,' Charlie mumbled. He pushed himself up against the wall. His feet aching. He leant against the wall. The wrench was blood-stained.

'Harry,' he whispered.' 'Are you there? Sheila are you there?' He licked his lips.

He recalled the plan to help the doctor, maybe they had gone to find him. He was overdue a check-up. He remembered that chicken bastard Peter, Peter skidded off. Either to main street or worse, the motel. If Peter had sense, he would vanish out of town.

Charlie feared going back to the motel, and what the others would think of him. Trying to clean the mess to cover his mistake. The mess here would distract them. Knocking up a hooker was seriously frowned upon in the club.

The door creaked. Charlie was still, beads of sweat trickled down his neck. He looked around the door and saw the dismembered corpse. Trails of guts plateaued across the floor. Charlie saw the trainers, there was no other way to tell it was a man.

The hallway was clear and breezy. Further down the hallway echoed groans of nonhuman origin. The elevator was opposite, the disembowelled corpse blocking the floor.

Charlie walked into the corridor scanning the area, holding the wrench to his chest.

Something glistened as he stepped over the body.

He bent down, covering his mouth from the throat grinding smell. Green pus emanated from the exposed black lungs. There was an identification card poking out from the guts. Charlie pinched it with his finger and thumb. Sliding the badge from the green goo and wiping it on his jeans before putting it in his jean pocket. It read: janitor. It may help him get through a locked door when the time called for it.

Moans rumbled louder and Charlie stood and thumbed the elevator, it opened immediately, and Charlie stepped in and wiped his forehead. He pushed the fifth floor, where he had seen the injured doctor on the computer monitor. Charlie held the wrench up across his chest ready to defend himself when the elevator doors opened.

He crossed his chest, praying it was clear.

The elevator door opened. Charlie felt the icy cool Antarctic air blow across his face. It was empty. Charlie stepped into the corridor and shuffled along the wall.

Further down, two doors caught his eye. There were people talking somewhere.

The door on his left read *J. McCormack*, the door on his right read doctor's office.

McCormack could be one of the dead now. Charlie walked to the doctor's office door.

Screams pierced through the wind. Charlie turned to the left, at the end of the corridor was a smashed window. A bed had been wheeled next to it. The bed was covered in blood. An IV drip on the floor on its side. Charlie turned his attention back to the door.

He pushed the door to a quiet dark office. He jumped as the door slammed behind him. Light came through a small open window at the back. Charlie still could not see.

From the darkness an elderly man darted, lunging a pocketknife at Charlie. Charlie dived out the way. The man wore spectacles and a woolly jumper, the name tag was still attached to the collar. The old man tried to hook the knife in Charlie. The knife skimmed over Charlie's jacket. Charlie lifted the wrench and hit him on the head and then jabbed the wrench into his stomach.

Charlie heard a crack. The old man fell backwards into the doctor's desk knocking the laptop off and the screen smashed. He dropped the knife and it clinked on the floor. Charlie bent down to pick the knife up and pocketed it in his leather jacket.

'Stop,' the old man pleaded with a dry throat. His glasses had fallen off when Charlie hit him over the head. Charlie turned and bent down to pick the glasses up. The old man pushed Charlie.

'Stop,' Charlie shouted. 'I'm leaving,' Charlie muttered and began to walk to the door.

'Wait,' the old man cried. Charlie stopped and turned around; he could not see the old man's face in the dark office. 'What do you want from me?' Charlie asked. 'I'm waiting for the doctor,' the man said. 'Where is he?' He was confused or unaware of the situation. Charlie was wide eyed. Blood trickled from the old man's hairless crown down to his ear.

Maybe the wrench disorientated the old man. He could be bleeding internally. A slow death meaning eventual prison for Charlie.

Charlie needed to take him to the injured doctor. Whatever was happening in the hospital was unexplainable, but would the authorities see this as justified, Charlie doubted it. Charlie did not want to go to prison over this. The police knew him and his band of merry bikers very well.

'I am the doctor, follow me and keep quiet,' Charlie said. 'Other patients are sleeping.' The old man stared at Charlie blankly. It was uncomfortable not knowing names. 'What's your name?' Charlie asked. The man gazed at the floor before looking at Charlie. The wrinkles heavily formed under his eyes.

'Jack Stenton,' the old man Jack replied. 'I want to speak to a nurse or doctor. I have been waiting for over two hours.' Jack coughed harshly.

'I am the doctor, follow me.'

'I'm not stupid,' Jack said. 'You're trying to send me back to the motorhomes, aren't you? Where is the doctor? You are trying to take me somewhere I don't want to go.'

Charlie huffed and lifted the wrench above a petrified Jack. Charlie lobbed Jack over the head again and Jack fell unconscious. Charlie turned and opened the door back into the empty corridor.

He turned left to enter the other doctor office.

Dark shapes danced off the walls at the far end of the corridor. Then the corpses shambled from a room into the corridor, unaware of Charlie's presence. Charlie pushed his way into the McCormack office. The refreshing breeze began to waft the stench of the corpses into the hallway.

Charlie shut the door carefully behind him, not to alert the beasts. He was met with a smack in the face and collapsed.

'Charlie,' Harry said aiding Charlie back to his feet. Charlie responded and punched Harry's in the stomach. Harry grabbed his stomach wheezing. Sheila stepped to Charlie, ending the altercation by slapping Charlie in the face. Charlie felt blood ooze from his nose and wiped it on his jacket.

'Bitch,' Charlie grunted. Charlie was unaware of the situation and raised his hand to slap Sheila but dropped his hand. 'Lucky this time,' Charlie added.

The man in the hospital gown crept forward. Jamie pushed himself back against the wall, his leg leaving a trail of blood as he slid across the floor. The unstable man walked to Charlie who looked unimpressed. Instinctually Charlie threw a fist at the gowned man, but he dodged the fist.

'Trying to attack Shane?' Shane, the deranged patient shouted.

Shane walked backwards towards the desk. Charlie watched in awe. Shane pulled open a draw and pulled out a blue stapler and then pressed it against his left cheek.

'Don't do it Shane,' Jamie pleaded, trying to push himself to his feet using the wall but sliding down in pain.

Charlie held the bloodied wrench up hoping to deter Shane. Shane ignored him letting out a shriek as he stapled his cheek. The stapler clicked a few times and blood dripped down onto Shane's mouth and gown.

Shane gritted his teeth and tossed the stapler to the floor and it broke. Shane screamed out like a wailing woman.

Harry stumbled forward as the door pushed against his back. The corridor was filled with shuffling and hands began to reach around the wooden door.

'Shit,' Harry said. 'There here!' Sheila and Harry jumped to the door, pushing against it as bloody fingers wrapped around the frame.

'Dammit lock it,' Charlie yelled. Charlie turned, Harry was weak and couldn't do this. He pushed the door like you would push a lawnmower.

Shane walked to the injured doctor and put the knife to his throat. Shane's veins rippled and bulged as he grasped Jamie around the neck.

'Don't Shane,' Harry yelled. 'Don't do it.' Harry was ignorant and moved from the door.

Harry walked towards Shane holding his hands up like an idiot.

'Put it down, we're all dead now,' Harry said. Shane grinned and waved the knife around in front of the Jamie's face.

'We're all dead because of you,' Shane screeched. The creatures outside groaned and clawed to get in. Charlie saw the tiny fingers of a child reach round. It was disturbing.

'Harry fucking get back here,' Sheila shouted.

Charlie left Sheila alone to hold the door. She pressed her back pressed against the door.

Charlie shunted Harry to the left out of the way and walked to the desk and picked up the desk phone. Shane jumped up and lunged at Charlie and they both went for each other.

Shane held the knife up and Charlie held his wrench to his side and the desk phone in the air. Charlie swung the plastic phone and Shane went to grab it before Charlie surprised Shane by walloping his testicles with the wrench. Shane sliced through the air with the knife simultaneously, successfully slashing Charlie at the throat. Charlie rag dolled to the floor, dropping the wrench which made a metallic ding, the phone went flying across the back of the room.

Charlie clasped desperately at his spurting neck veins, if it was an artery, he didn't have long.

'Shit, Charlie,' Harry said. Jumping to Charlie's side.

'Pressure to the wound,' Jamie shouted. 'Do it now.' Shane paced to Jamie and punched him in the face.

'Keep it quiet, your next,' Shane snarled.

Charlie panted and tried to talk. Blood spluttered on his leather jacket. Harry couldn't comprehend it.

Everything was blurred and Charlie struggled to grip his throat.

***

Charlie's neck spurted through his unconscious fingers onto Harry's shirt, squirting onto his face.

Sheila continued to struggle to keep the door shut, she managed to hold them off. Sheila had her back to the door and her eyes were closed as she panted through her nose, and out through her mouth.

'I can't stop the bleeding,' Harry said, feeling too responsible for Charlie after he offered to help look for James.

Harry's fingers slipped as blood pooled over his hands.

'Doc,' Harry called. 'Pass me something.' The doctor tried to move but Shane booted his back. The doctor curled up into a foetal ball, shielding himself. Shane walked to Harry and held the knife to his throat.

'Let go,' Shane said. Harry's pulse quickened. Shane pressed the bloody blade to Harry's throat. Any moment Shane could cut through and he would never see his family again. Harry had to let go of Charlie's neck, the blood was coagulating but not quick enough to stop the bleeding. Charlie would have to understand, even if Harry had to make it up to him in the next life.

'Fine,' he replied, and a tear ran down his cheek. Shane kept the blade to Harry's neck as he stood up. Behind, Harry saw the doctor crawling through his own blood towards them.

'I have to find my son, please let me go.' Harry wept now; the tears streamed down his face.

Blood had encapsulated the floor around Charlie's body. The beasts would want it, Sheila had almost closed the door.

Harry peered down at his blood-soaked trousers. Shane's blade digging into his throat.

Shane lowered the knife to his side. Jamie's face appeared behind Shane, he held the broken laptop in his hands and lifted it above Shane's unaware head. Harry stepped back and Jamie smashed the laptop over Shane's head and Shane dropped unconscious. Jamie booted Shane in the back a few times before commenting in an unfamiliar language, maybe Latin.

'Damn,' Sheila said. Harry turned to look. Her eyes now black from fatigue.

What had just happened to Harry was surreal and even more the reason to figure out what the fuck was happening.

Charlie appeared lifeless. Harry assisted Jamie to Charlie's body.

Jamie checked the pulse and began applying pressure to Charlie's neck and pointed to the desk. Harry quickly walked over to the desk and opened the drawers. The bottom draw had a packet of cigarettes and a cloth. Harry pulled out the cloth.

'Here.' Harry tossed it to Jamie who pushed it to Charlie's wound. Harry reached back in the draw and picked up the packet of cigs and pocketed them. Smoking was the least of his worries now. When things didn't work out, he used to have the occasional cigar. Sheila knew his little secret and would probably kill him for this packet.

Sheila wreathed against the door and was struggling to hold it.

Harry ran around the desk and round Jamie and Charlie and jumped at the door. Harry pushed as hard as he could.

'What's his name again?' Jamie enquired as he held his ear to Charlie's nose.

'It's Charlie. Doc we have bigger problems. Those things out there are dangerous. Can you be quicker?' said Harry. Sheila and he had just about shut the door and Sheila clicked the lock on.

'The bleeding is stable, but he might have lost to much blood to make it, if we had access to an IV drip and some blood, I could save him, otherwise he will go into coma and die if he hasn't already.'

They had just escaped from bloody blood storage room too, what a fucking nightmare. Harry tensed.

'We just came from the blood room, I'm not going back,' Sheila said. Jamie shook his head.

'This man will die otherwise, I need to get my leg sorted, otherwise I'd go' It became a bitter decision, Harry decided regrettably. Sheila would have to be patient.

'Sheila, we have to help. You wanted to help the doctor, so we need to help Charlie, the truth is, without him I could be staring at the roof of a coffin,' Harry said.

Sheila better be onboard because otherwise he wouldn't give her a lift anywhere again. Choosing to take her to the city had landed him here. At least if he stayed with Molly and James, he wouldn't be looking for them.

'I've made up my mind Harry,' Sheila said. 'Be thankful I haven't left you here, I could be at my interview if it wasn't for this shit.' Harry now noticed the smell of sweat from Sheila's underarms. That ever so special friendship had hit another speed bump. It hurt Harry, it was if Sheila had forgotten he left his family to help her and that his family weren't where they said they were.

'Sheila come on. We need to work together.'

'Yes, I'll wait here,' Sheila huffed. 'You go and save the day and come fucking back.' Harry hated Sheila when she was like this.

'Go Harry. This man doesn't have long. I think at a guess less than ten minutes before he either bleeds out or goes into a coma,' Jamie said. Sheila shook her head.

'How do we know his blood type? This is not worth the effort, if he lives that is fate. If he dies that is fate. Let fate take its fucking course for once,' Sheila shouted.

'She's right what blood type?' Harry said scratching his head.

Shane groaned and they all froze, then Shane went silent again.

'It won't be long until Shane wakes up either. I'm too pressed to be cautious, get O type blood, it's the only one that doesn't contain the A and B antigens.' Jamie crawled back to his desk. Retrieving a small click torch from the bottom draw and another cloth. 'Damn, the only time I need a cigarette and they've gone.' Jamie crawled back to Charlie.

Harry felt the pack of cigs in his pocket. The felt squashed but hopefully smokable. Harry walked and picked up Charlie's wrench. It was heavy and rough to the touch like sandpaper.

'I'll push through, they'll follow me, then try and push that desk against the door.' A lump rose in Harry's throat. His grip on the bloodied wrench loosened as he held it in his sweaty hands.

'Good luck,' Sheila said. Harry held the door handle and hesitated. Perhaps Sheila was right, let fate take its course. Her voice made him weak at the knees. It was never intentional.

Harry turned the handle. 'I'll be back, don't worry.'

CHAPTER 9

The Return To The Blood Room

Harry grasped wrench in his sweaty palms like a baseball player.

Outside the corpses had splashed blood over the office door while trying to get in. They reached out for Harry's neck and he swung the cold steel wrench into the gormless crowd of nurses and patients and visitors. Harry shunted them backwards further into the hallway, giving him enough space to run. The creatures were vicious. Children clawed viciously at his tired legs. Harry lunged forward knocking the children to the floor.

Harry kicked the door shut. Green veined arms grabbed at him. He was overwhelmed and underprepared. This was a bad idea. Harry choked at the stench of the green pus pouring from the patients' mouths. It stunk as if he had walked into a gas cloud of sewage and gas.

Harry swung the wrench knocking two nurses over, their aprons coveted in pus. The kids had begun to pull on his torso. They were heavy, a deadweight. He was being pulled to the floor and had to escape. The beasts tried to bite him on his thighs, his trousers shielding him.

Harry panicked; his brain zapped into overdrive as he was pulled to the floor struggling for breath. Harry shunted the little kids – regrettably, he had no choice - in their blood smudged faces. A skull cracked; the others gargled. His forearms burnt as they ran out of juice.

Behind in the office he could hear the desk scraping along the floor, banging against the door. Harry slid on his stomach to escape.

He crawled through the crowd, far enough that he could jump up. Harry glanced to the elevator, only a fool would wait. He ran for the staircase, but instinct said look back.

An elderly man stood confused with a cut on his head. He stood holding the doctor office door open, the room he hadn't checked. Harry's instinct changed; he should run for it. The dead were coming for him. The man whispered inaudibly; his free hand tremored. Harry's heart telling him to help.

'Shit,' Harry shouted. Harry darted past the creatures, they reached for his shirt. Harry reached the office door unscathed and pushed the man back inside the room. Harry speedily shut the door and locked it.

Harry fell against the wooden door. His back burning from swinging the wrench around. His slid to his ass, the concrete floor was uncomfortable. He slid the wrench across the floor, the metal wrench screeching as it moved.

The old man walked to Harry and leant near Harry's face in admiration. The blood on the old man's forehead was dry. Harry prayed to be out of the hospital soon, he didn't like the fact he might meet new people, that would slow him from reaching James and surviving this mess.

'Are you the doctor?' the man asked. Harry felt seduced into fatigue. For the first time in ten years his thighs ached from stress. Just as they did when he used to get overworked at the beach when he tried to save bad swimmers from drowning. Harry wished he had remained a lifeguard, he would still be fit if he was.

The office was darker than Jamie's. Jamie was a real doctor who depended on him, just like Charlie.

'I'm Harry. We have to go.'

'Go?' the man retreated further into the black room and rustled onto a dimly lit office chair. Behind, the door bangs began and the scratching of nails on the wooden door.

'Jack Stenton and I want to make a complaint. Do you know who I am? I am Jack…Stenton.' Jack spoke down to Harry, it was condescending as if he thought Harry was stupid. The wound on Jack's head could explain the confusion. Maybe this is how the creature thing starts. Harry was losing his patience.

'Jack, pleased to meet you,' Harry said. 'Would you like to follow me to the doctor?'

'Doctor?'

Harry walked to and sat on the desk. Harry was concerned and tried to look at the wound. As Harry leans in Jack kicks his shin.

'Shit,' Harry yelled.

The creatures at the door persevered. One ward of people fallen victim to the illness. God knows how many people have been affected by the disease in the hospital. The diseased people prevented his escape, prevented the night he had planned and prevented a lovely stress-free life.

'Don't touch me then, I have rights,' Jack responded. He tugged at his sagging neck. Harry routed through the desk draws for some identification that would convince the senile man. There was no ID, but there was a little brown bottle with a white cap. Harry checked the label: codeine.

'Thank god for that.' Harry opened it, it was a push and screw bottle, there were a handful of pills left. Harry took two pills out and put the bottle in his pants pocket. Jack wasn't paying attention. Harry sat in the doctor's chair behind the desk. Time was running out for Charlie.

'So, Mr Stenton is it? Should I call you Jack?' Harry rubbed his chin and cracked his knuckles. Jack stood up using significant effort and walked behind the desk to Harry. Harry pulled a sheet from the top desk draw and slid it shut.

'Doctor I've been waiting for hours, what kind of service is this?'

Harry eyed the sheet which was a checklist for some disease that he couldn't pronounce. He placed the paper writing down on the desk.

'So sorry Jack, we have been rather busy. How are you and what can I help you with?' Harry falsified his grin. Jack started reaching into his pocket. Harry was nervous because the wrench was at the door. Jack might knife him like Shane, he had to squelch his paranoia.

'I was told to come here before my surgery, I'm due an operation on my prostate you know?'

What had Harry got himself into. Honestly ten minutes must have passed since leaving the other room. Charlie was probably knocking at hells door and being refused no doubt.

'Interesting Jack,' Harry said, trying to keep things flowing smoothly. 'We should look at doing the operation another day. Now you need to take these for any pain.' Harry passed two codeine pills. Harry wanted them for his back pain. He did have the entire bottle. Letting two go to sedate the man wasn't going to matter.

'Good,' Jack said. He snatched the pills from Harry's hand and swallowed them dry. 'I am not happy doctor,' Jack groaned. 'I want a refund.'

Harry was certain this was a free healthcare facility. Jack's confusion was apparent. Harry had doubts about the codeine, it wasn't a promising idea. Harry had to decide to either leave Jack wounded and confused or escort him to the other room and risk being killed. Harry jumped as a thump rattled the office door.

'Are you coming with me?'

'Are you taking me to the complaints department?' Jack replied. Jack's memory of complaining wasn't failing, so he might not forget to follow Harry. If Jack lost his way, then it would be sayonara amigo. Harry couldn't save everyone. There was a glimmer of hope in trying to save people, but how many people could be saved? How far did this disease go? The motorway, the hospital, the town? Where were the police? Harry was battered with stress and tension in his shoulders. He had a deceptive idea.

'Carry the wrench Jack.' Harry was suspicious that Jack's confusion meant he would easily attack people. He had tried to go assault Harry earlier. Jack could beat the shambling beasts, fighting them back whilst Harry collected the blood. It wasn't perfect, it was a substantial risk.

Jack walked over to the door and picked up the wrench. Harry walked next to Jack. It was a bizarre situation. Harry felt shameful, torn between good and evil. Jack could die trying to get there, Harry accepted the possibility.

'Ready?' Harry asked. They stood at the door.

'Yes,' Jack replied. Harry unlocked the door, taking deep breaths. He pictured a variety of situations occurring. He saw James' face as he closed his eyes and James turned into a scrounging attacker. Harry jumped. Then Molly's face appeared, she was alive and trapped. Harry's mind cut to James and Molly being chased along the roof of the hospital, forced to jump to their deaths. Harry shuddered.

Harry turned the handle. The gnawing bloody mouths began to rush for him. Harry thumped them as hard as he could. He punched the unrecognisable faces whilst avoiding touching the mouths. Harry kicked out and walloped a few back. He shoved and kicked. Harry tried to grab and throw a nurse, but the nurses top ripped off and revealed green veined breasts. Harry zoned out staring at the breasts, the left one had a nipple piercing.

Jack began to swing and yell as the beasts grabbed his shoulders. Harry continued to fight.

'Doctor these bastards have gone crazy.' Jack smacked the corpses on the heads and fought valiantly.

Harry kicked them and a small circle had formed with a gap to the staircase. The child patients continued to crawl and eat Harry's feet. The topless nurse swayed in the crowd.

Jack jogged out of the circle, turned and faced the crowd whilst Harry pushed the male patients back. They were stiff, their necks cocked. A man wearing a blue golf shirt shuffled forward and his golf hat fell to the floor. Harry launched a boxing jab at the golfer. The black-eyed golfer grabbed Harry's arm. Jack was being encircled by the pus ridden corpses. Jack hit them hard with a scowl, he smashed a nurse to the floor and brought the wrench down on her head. Her head split in two and green blood spilled onto the corridor floor along with chunks brain matter.

'Help Jack,' Harry cried. Harry felt helpless, the golfer was strong. Harry fought to keep the golfer's mouth from his shoulder. Jack pushed through the shamblers and swung the wrench at the golfer. Jack's face was covered with blood.

Harry rolled onto the floor. The concrete made his back hurt from Charlie's inconsiderate attack. Harry crawled to his feet and ran to Jamie's office. The crowd had thinned, a mess of bodied lay on the corridor floor coveted in green pus and blood. Jack slaughtered the remaining two.

'Sheila it's Harry,' he shouted. 'Open the door.' Harry was nervous and didn't expect the bodies to pile up so quickly. Jack was breaking their skulls with the wrench like an executioner. Jack attacked the last corpse. A man in his thirties wearing a t-shirt and shorts. Jack punched the wrench into the man's face and the creature sagged to the floor. It was a blood bath of disintegrated brains.

The corridor was not sparkling anymore. It was vomit inducing and dull. The floor painted in red, blood was splattered on the elevator doors and the walls. The open window at the end of the corridor, the one with the bed and IV stand blew the stench further down the ward.

'Harry hold on,' Sheila replied. Jack walked to Harry and handed the dripping wrench to him. Harry was in awe; Jack was a ferocious warrior and had saved his life. Jack was a hero. Charlie was still dying; Harry was running out of time and patience. He didn't know anyone except Sheila. In life and death situations people only cared about themselves, but not Harry and it annoyed him that he couldn't leave people in harm's way.

'This is going on the complaint,' Jack said. 'That nurse had no top on.' Harry chuckled. Sheila opened the office door;

Harry pulled Jack inside and closed the door behind him. Sheila was pale.

'Is he still breathing?' Harry asked Sheila.

Jamie was at his desk, waiting for Harry. Shane was still unconscious, now propped up against the left wall. Charlie wasn't moving yet.

'Faintly, have you got it?' Sheila asked.

'I need more time,' Harry said. He turned and opened the office door, exiting to the carnage in the corridor. He felt no fear, only motivation. There was no time to be afraid, because he had wasted too much time with strangers instead of looking for his son. He jogged to the staircase, heading down the steps one floor to the storage room. All was quiet. He held the rails for momentum.

Harry jogged to the deserted ward. The blood room door was open. The body was lying in the corridor. Harry froze, his mind flashbacked to the screams of the man as he had been ripped apart. A horrific reminder of his mistake. Harry held the wall, lightheaded. He gathered the strength to carry on. He walked around the body to the blood storage room. Coagulated blood fell off his shoes in chunks as he walked.

Harry pushed the door to the wall, it was empty. The storage room reeked of body odour.

'Which blood type?' Harry asked himself. The brown boxes had tumbled to the floor. Harry walked to them, the white labels read A, then B, then AB and finally O. 'That's it.'

It was distinctive, a man's life hung in the balance, he couldn't afford to make a mistake. He felt obliged to save Charlie. Charlie was a rough man but had helped him into the hospital in the first place.

Harry pulled out two blood bags labelled O type. Having no spare pockets, he tucked one bag down his pants and carried the other bag. He had the wrench in his left hand.

Harry paced back up the stairs and to the doctor's office. Sheila stood waiting.

'Harry, get that IV.' It was extremely lucky that the IV was at the end of the corridor.

Harry handed the blood bags to Sheila who darted back inside. Harry ran over the wrangled bodies down the corridor to the IV. He wrapped the tube and needle up carefully. Harry looked out of the window. Beach town, the motel visible about a mile away. The dirt road was a quiet unused path from main street reserved for emergency use when carriageway was busy. Harry spotted movement along the dirt road. He squinted. Perhaps he was cracking up or stressed to madness. Two police cars were speeding down the dirt road, kicking up a dust hurricane around the vehicles. They were followed by a black van.

Harry watched, relieved, some hope had arrived. The police cars rolled into the car park below. Harry saw officer's hop out the cars and a four-man swat team jump from the rear of the black van. Harry couldn't hear what was being said as the police huddled into a circle. Harry saw they were armed, the police had pistols and the swat had assault rifles. One officer wearing a cap made hand gestures, Harry could tell he was in charge.

Harry yelled out of joy. The police couldn't hear him If they were as useful as everyone says they are, they can clear this mess up and restore the hospital and save them. Harry turned and carried the IV drip back to the office. Sheila shut the door behind him.

Harry looked at the people before him. Survivors. They would need counselling to recover from what they had seen. Except Jack who needed more substantial psychomotor help. Shane needed a fucking lobotomy. Charlie needed a rehabilitation order.

'Get it done.' Sheila took the IV from Harry. Jamie was waiting on the floor next to Charlie. Harry felt his pocket for the codeine pills. They were still there. Jamie could use some. Harry looked at Jack sitting against the wall on the right. Harry changed his mind; the pills were sparse and unprescribed.

The police had arrived, and Harry didn't know if theft of prescription medication was a priority for them.

'Well done Harry,' Jamie complimented Harry and he felt good. Jamie started to insert the needle into Charlie's left arm. Attaching the blood bag to the other end of the tube.

'Sheila,' Jamie said. 'Hold the bag in the air it needs gravity.' Sheila came to Jamie and knelt beside Charlie. She took the blood bag and held it in the air. Sheila stroked Charlie's cheek with her free hand. Harry noticed and a flare ignited and niggled at his stomach, why was she stroking that criminal? Harry walked past Charlie's body with clenched fists and sat on the desk.

'Doctor when can I make a complaint,' Jack said. Jamie had crawled back to the desk and pulled himself onto his desk chair. He looked at Harry with concern and the silence gave Harry knots in his belly.

'He's confused Jamie,' Harry said. 'I had to help.' Harry wasn't sure why he was trying to win the moral approval of a doctor. To Harry's pleasure Jamie cracked a smile.

'Harry, saving that man is a good thing,' Jamie said. 'You may have saved two people today.'

'It was life or death,' Harry explained. 'Jack could have died. I defeated them monsters out there to get him to safety.' Jack walked over to the desk.

'I saved myself,' Jack said. 'You were cowering.'

'A liar? How nice,' Jamie sniggered. Harry couldn't tell whether he was being serious or sarcastic. Harry didn't care. Jamie would forget about him soon and they would be evacuated by the police. If the police made it here alive.

'Okay Jack, you were the fighter,' Harry replied.

'You bet,' Jack said. 'Twelve, no, thirteen years in the military, shooting those goddamn communist bastards.' Jack saluted with an enthusiastic approach to storytelling which Harry couldn't help but smile at.

'By the way,' Harry said. 'The police are here, they have guns, rifles. I believe they will get us out.' Sheila looked to Harry; he could see desperation in her eyes.

'Police? Is Dean with them?' Sheila's nagging annoyed Harry, he didn't know everything.

'Calm down. I couldn't see who it was. They couldn't hear me, I tried to call for help if you were wondering.' The wrench was heavy, so Harry placed it on the desk. The metal had cut into his hands, they were superficial wounds. The cuts were minor, the backache however felt like a lifelong problem and it only happened earlier.

'We'll have to wait and hope for the best. I don't know what created these creatures or how to deal with them, they are clearly dangerous.' Jamie said. He swivelled around in his leather desk chair. When it spun the mechanism broke and Jamie was left facing the rear wall. He rotated back to face the room. Jack slid down the wall next to Shane. Sheila switched to holding the blood bag with the other arm. The bag was emptying quickly.

'Yeah this is more than dangerous, this is pandemonium,' Harry said. 'I can't understand how this started, what would cause people to eat each other? People who look dead?' Harry crossed his arms.

'I was investigating a new bacterium before this occurred. But I can't see how that would lead to people eating each other.' Jamie rested his elbows on the desk and closed his eyes. Harry prayed the police would escort them back to safety, that they would help find James and Molly.

Sheila waved Harry over. Like a lonely puppy Harry walked over to her and knelt beside her. They both had bad body odour. They needed fresh new clothes and coffee. Harry wanted a pizza with donuts for dessert. Harry remembered he hadn't bought an ice cream for James. The queue had been too long. It was minty chocolate chip and strawberry with a chocolate flake and rainbow sprinkles.

'Harry,' Sheila said gazing into Harry's tired eyes. 'When we get out, I don't want things to change.' The blood bag was three quarters empty.

'Jack come and help,' Harry said, Jack waddled over.

Jack stood over Harry. 'What?'

'Hold this up please.' Harry took the bag from Sheila and passed it to Jack. Jack held it high, pinching the hole where it hangs on the stand. Harry returned to Sheila's eyes.

'How so?' Harry asked. Sheila twiddle her thumbs. They sat on the floor like teenagers. Harry smelt Sheila's breath and could taste the alcohol she drank on the motorway. They both sat in dried blood.

'I wanted you to come to the interview with me. Then this happened and we ended up here. I got you to come with me when your family needed you most, that's why.'

Sheila wiped tears from her cheeks. Harry wrapped his arm around her.

'Not at all, friends are friends, it's not like we knew this would happen is it? I wouldn't worry if I was you, if anything, coming along helped, it's brought me closer to you.' Harry smiled and rubbed her shoulder. He was felt as if he were lying. But it was true that their friendship was far reaching. This merely built new bridges.

'Thanks Harry that means a lot.' Sheila pecked his cheek. Sheila was vulnerable and if he continued to gaze into her deep emerald eyes, he might end up initiating something.

Charlie began to move his arms. Jamie scrambled from the desk chair and crawled over to Charlie. Jack dropped the bag and walked off to the wall and sat down. Jamie placed his index finger over Charlie's carotid artery and waved a fist in celebration.

'Yes,' Jamie exclaimed. 'We did it he's alive. Harry, you are a lifesaver.'

'I'll add it to my resume,' Harry replied. Sheila giggled.

The lifted spirits were dashed as the sound of boots marched around the corridor. Orders were being shouted. They all looked to the door. Harry heard someone give the order to breach the room.

The door smashed open and police stormed the room and aimed their pistols at them. The police held flashlights that blinded Harry. Behind the police were the black uniform swat officers all geared up. The swat team were aiming into the corridor.

'What in the hell happened in this place?' an officer said. Harry couldn't see his face through the flashlight. 'There's an emergency and I'm afraid I can't explain everything. The hospital is now a quarantine zone and we've been ordered to extract any remaining survivors.' The officer lowered his flashlight and pistol, the two officer's behind him did the same.

'Dean,' Sheila cried. She jumped to her feet and ran at him and hugged him.

'Sheila, what are you doing here? Thank goodness you're alive. I thought you had to head out of town to that interview, I assumed the worst.' Dean squeezed Sheila and the let go and bent down to examine Charlie and Shane.

'Is that Charlie?' Dean said. 'My god he is in a state.'

'Thank goodness you are here. This man has had major blood loss and needs immediate help. I've injured my leg but it's minor,' Jamie said.

'That's Jack, he's senile and this gowned fellow is Shane, a dangerous man. He slit Charlie's throat,' Harry explained. Harry just wanted rest.

'I'm not senile, I came in for a prostate surgery, then that man hit me on the head.' Jack pointed to Charlie.

'We'll deal with the law you just be thankful to be alive Jack,' Dean said. 'Listen carefully. The CDC have faxed over emergency quarantine instructions along with government procedures that are to be enforced immediately. Because the hospital is no longer safe, we have had to set up a field medic behind the station. We'll take you all there,' Dean said. The two officer's behind Dean holstered their pistols, walked to Charlie and lifted him out of the room.

'They got my observations?' Jamie asked.

'No, Jamie. The CDC claim they never received a report,' Dean replied.

'Right, well when I go down there they'll listen,' Jamie snapped.

'Slow down, you lot are not going anywhere, your all going to the station, the CDC procedures state we, and the doctors, have examinations to conduct.' Dean chuckled a belly laugh. Sheila was distraught with tears running down onto her white office shirt. Harry felt shitty hearing Dean say that. Harry stood and stepped next to Dean.

'Where are my wife and son, Dean?'

'Probably at home, that isn't my problem, you lot are. You are the living normal people we have found so far.' Dean turned and walked out of the room. Dean began to give inaudible instructions to the swat officers.

Two of the swat officer stepped in and one aided Jamie to his feet and escorted him out the room, Jack followed them. Harry lifted Sheila to her feet and the pair were escorted out by the other swat officer. Harry waited with Sheila at the elevator. The swat officer's black bullet proof vest had blood on it.

Harry turned and saw Dean re-enter the doctor's office. Again. Another police office followed him and shut the door. The elevator arrived. A gunshot went off. Shane had just been executed. Harry was sure of it.

CHAPTER 10

The Police Station

Beach town police department is situated in the centre of main street. Worn untended brown brick exterior, four stories. A UK flag was housed into a suspended pole overlooking the centre of the building. The police station windows sparkling clean.

The entrance to the police station, two solid wood doors up six steps. Two armed police officers with belted pistols stood silent at the front doors. It wasn't regularly guarded but new rules were in play.

Cars drove slowly down main street, the occupants going about their day, unaware of the horror that had taken place at the motorway and hospital.

Opposite the police station, the street was lined with two clothing shops at the left end of the road. Next to the clothes shops an Italian restaurant, a western style pub, a post office, an independent bank –Independent Finances Co. Beach Town Daily newspaper sat directly opposite the police station and housed the town radio on the first floor. Next to the paper radio shop was a fish and chip shop, a cafe and Harry's workplace the opera house which sat next to a large supermarket at the right end of the road. The pavements were lined with strips of grass that separated the road from the path.

The street was bustling with shop goers and parents and children. They dressed in dresses and shorts and hats. Heat waves rippled from the road surface. Shop goers chatted to one another and laughed. Kids ate ice creams with rainbow sprinkles as they waited for their gossiping parents. Beach Town's postmen were striking outside the post office, eight people held and waved signs reading "more pay". A yellow vested traffic warden was writing a ticket for a poorly parked Ford outside the bank. Residents were going about their lives, there was no sign of a pandemic.

Behind the police station in the car park, police cars were parked against the bushes and a white tent was erected in the centre of the parking lot. People dressed in hazard suits tend to people inside the tent. They take blood samples from the visitors. Five officers patrolled the police car park whilst drinking coffee and smoking. Police radios were irregularly quiet. A call came in for a social disturbance at the beach front, they ignored it.

Inside the police station, things were different. Officers wore casual clothes and paced through the offices; tension was high as if they all had a strict deadline. The officers didn't talk to one another. If they did it was to ask for paperwork or spare pens.

The police station entrance opened to a large rectangular marble floored reception area. A bearded whistling janitor mopped the entrance. The receptionist's desk was directly in front of the entrance, twenty paces. The desk was occupied by an officer filling out paperwork. Other plain clothed officers loitered in the main entrance frustratingly trying to use their phones. They could not call because there was no signal.

A two-in-one coffee water machine was to the right of the check in desk. To the right was a railed stone staircase which led to the first floor. Staff could only gain access to the first floor through the staircase. Contractors had failed to install an elevator stop because of "structural limitations". The first floor housed the evidence room and three offices. The evidence room full of confiscated marijuana and knives. Beach Town was low on crime. Major crimes were rare with an occasional murder and criminals appeared to prefer drowning their victims. Dean was forced to discover more than six people along the island coast during his employment. There was an elevator to the right of the reception desk and left of a canteen. Four officers sat at the metal tables eating handmade butties. The microwave had broken.

In the cellar of the police station were the cells, stone slabs and cold. Three people awaited sentencing or release. Two interview rooms were on the second floor and the third floor was weapons storage. The third floor had offices each with a coffee machine and an in house first aid room. Officers preferred working on the third floor. The heating worked on the third floor. There was also a radio player screwed onto a desk in the hallway. Officers weren't allowed to move it.

Sat in interview room number one on the second floor was Harry. An officer had asked him a set of questions about the situation and left with his notes. Silence surrounded him. The room was dim and dirty. It was unpleasantly spacious. Harry sat on a silver steel chair and leant against the wall. A steel table in front of him. On the table was a black recorder box and its red light hummed like a bee. Harry looked behind him out the window. Seagulls circled overhead amidst the clear skies. The interview room door opened, and a casual clothed officer entered followed by Dean. Harry had known Dean through Sheila and met him years ago, but they never spoke until now.

'Officer P. Smith has just entered the room along with detective Dean Harrison.' Officer Smith waited at the door after announcing their arrival. Dean sat opposite Harry and his chair screeched on the stone.

Harry's was next to a hot radiator and still felt cold. Officer Smith looked laid back as did Dean. Harry assumed they were both detectives as they never wore uniform in tv shows. Only a bullet proof vest and badge at most.

Harry was relaxed yet the perplexing situation was difficult to comprehend. Dean handled a brown file, Harry failed to notice the file as Dean entered. Dean ran his index finger along the file and opened it. Dean then pulled a black ballpoint from his trousers and began to write in the file. Harry could see his name inside the file and suspected he would be sworn to silence.

'Harry, Harry Carrington?' Dean said, straightening his name tag. Dean held the file up to Harry. Harry's back ached against the metal chair and he bit his tongue in frustration. Finding his family were the priority, not sitting in a police station. If his family had been hurt at the hospital, Harry could never live with himself. 'Confirm your name and your address and date of birth for the recording, please.' Harry crossed his arms.

'Harry Carrington, Leaf Drive,' Harry said. 'Born nineteenth of the sixth, nineteen eighty-four. Thirty-four years old. Staff manager for the opera house. Enough?' Harry grinned obnoxiously and Dean was un-humoured.

'This isn't the time for jokes. We have a serious epidemic on our hands and have been given government guidelines to follow. You are aware you need your medical examination.'

Dean glared into Harry's eyes; frowning. Harry thought Dean talked too much and never enjoyed his company. Sheila liked Dean but Harry never understood why.

Harry felt his trouser pocket. The cig packet was still crumpled. Harry wanted to get rid of them, he wasn't in the mood for tobacco. Harry wanted to give them to Sheila, but she was taken for her medical examination. Harry didn't want a medical examination but if he was at risk of contracting the disease, getting checked would reassure him. Sheila was distraught at the hospital and hadn't mentioned Wendy her partner. Harry disliked Wendy's attitude towards him but Sheila should have notified Wendy. Harry's neck muscles tensed, his scalp was prickling, and pain resonated over his head.

'Epidemic?' Harry yelped. Dean ticked something on the file. Harry couldn't see what. Officer Smith held his hand over his pistol, a threat. Harry was fearful. 'What is this? I'm not dangerous.' Harry worried the law had gone rogue, somebody had shot that crazy bastard Shane and they might do the same to him.

'We're following government procedures to establish whether you are in fact a threat,' Dean said and ticked something on the sheet. Harry lifted his head to see.

'Why?' Harry quickly responded.

'Because that is how this procedural checklist goes,' Dean said. 'If you are so concerned, it's the checklist for Z C dash one eight, eight, nine, dash zero. See.' Dean briefly showed Harry the checklist. The file had an official address and logo of the dispensing CDC centre. Harry saw a section labelled informal observations with tick boxes. Dean continued to ask questions.

***

An hour after bickering and two interruptions, the checklist was complete. Dean escorted Harry out the interview room. Harry saw a water machine but there was no time to stop. They took the stairs as the elevator was out of service.

Outside the police station main entrance, it was dusk. Main street was quiet, and shopkeepers were closing for the night. They walked around the side of the police station to the rear car park. Dean led Harry to the white medical tent and returned to the station through a rear entrance.

'Harry,' Sheila cried. Sheila jumped up from a plastic chair and hugged him. She looked ragged.

'Jeez,' Harry said. 'Have you been here the whole time?' Two doctors in white hazard suits were busy with vials of blood and microscopes.

'Yes, I have,' Sheila said. 'I've given blood and I've had to give oral swabs; they swabbed my woo-hoo too.' Sheila blushed. The doctors tended to a table in the centre of the tent with files. One doctor approached Harry. The doctor breathed as if through a gas mask.

'Lay down sir, we need a blood test, we won't be long.' Harry complied and walked to the bed on the left. Sheila held his hand as he lay down. Harry assumed they would immunise him.

'Done,' the doctor said. Harry felt a pinch he assumed was from Sheila joking. Harry felt woozy. Time was precious. The sun was low, and an icy breeze whistled through the tent. Harry shuddered.

'Can we go?' Harry asked. He let go of Sheila's hand and watched the doctor examine the blood sample. The doc placed the blood in a glass machine that spun and then used a small glass tube to place a drop on a slide of glass before placing it under the microscope.

'Sixty seconds sir.'

'What's happened to the hospital, what about those people, what happened to them?' Harry asked. The other doctor was attending to a man with an oxygen mask.

'The police have orders to quarantine the hospital,' the doc said. The other man was attached to a heart monitor machine. It skipped a beep. Harry thought nothing of it.

'My family were there, what will happen if they are still there?' Harry was afraid his family were shambling through the hospital as one of the creatures. He got off the bed.

'Sir, step back,' the doctor said. His raised voice attracted the attention of the two officers outside the tent. The officers stepped in and drew their pistols.

'Step back,' one officer said pointing his pistol at Harry's chest. 'Back away from the doctor.' The officer was unshaven and bag eyed. Harry stepped back. The doctor turned to face Harry. Harry could not see his face through the plastic window.

'Clear,' the doc said. 'You're free to go. A curfews in place now, I suggest you adhere to it.' The doctor walked to his colleague next to the man on the other bed. Harry saw the frail man's eyes had gone black. The officer lowered his gun and led Harry and Sheila out of the tent into the darkness while the other remained inside.

'Curfew?' Sheila asked. They headed back down the side of the police station.

'First I've heard of it. I need to go home,' Harry said. 'My family might be there, and they are the only thing I care about now.' They stood at the foot of the police station steps. The pub opposite was closed. This was serious and getting worse. The opera house was closed, and Harry didn't know when anything would be open again, if ever. Harry hugged Sheila and departed. The night air soothed his pulsing temples. Would the town survive the night or would the disease sweep through town and kill everyone? Harry knew one thing; he was alive and not infected.

CHAPTER 11

Not Contained

Harry was awoken by the plastic blue alarm clock ringing on the bedside cabinet. He thumbed it quiet. He had survived the night.

It was seven. On a normal day, James, Molly and he would prepare to go to church. Harry was depressed that he was unable to contact his wife. The signals died yesterday long with Harry's spring spirit.

His head still hurt. The dark room was lifeless. Today would be worse, the search for his family would continue. Tiredness last night ran him into the ground otherwise he would have scoured every square inch of the town.

The red bedsheet thick with soft feathers. The texture calmed Harry. He felt as if he were on a cloud, content to peruse the days plan.

Harry could not smell syrup pancakes or black tea and he couldn't hear James playing Lego at the end of the bed. Something he enjoyed. Everything was strange and unfamiliar. Harry had checked the landline last night. The phone was reading out a pre-recorded message: "Due to a recent curfew you are not permitted to use a mobile phone or landline. We hope to have the problem fixed soon."

The curfew was a ghost rule, rules Harry considered useless. Harry thought they may be announcing it on the radio or tv.

Harry gathered the strength to push the quilt off and slide his legs out of bed. He was fully clothed after returning home too stressed to undress. The shoes had left mud under the sheet. He pulled his shirt off and patches of dried sweat decorated the underarms. He kicked his shoes off and took his trousers and socks off. Harry turned and walked into his en-suite bathroom. The cabinet neatly arranged, and the shower head glistened under the automatic lights. He grabbed his razor from the sink and had a shave before brushing his teeth.

The house was modern. A one story detached with a large rear garden. The interior was featureless in Harry's eyes. The walls cream with a red flowered feature wall in the living room. Two bathrooms and two bedroom.

Harry paced back into the bedroom and retrieved some clothes from the built-in sliding door wardrobe. Harry looked at Molly's clothes neatly stacked next to his, her shoes lined up on the floor. Harry noticed the watch he bought her just months ago. He slid the wardrobe door shut.

Harry walked down the cream carpeted stairs and took a left down the laminate floor hallway to an open plan kitchen. He opened the fridge. Checking the curfew seemed more important than food. Harry walked into a large sitting area and sat on the sofa. He found the remote under the cushion and changed his mind again. He got up and walked back to the kitchen where a radio sat on the white marble countertop.

Harry clicked the radio on, the button was sticky and reminded Harry of cake icing. The radio crackled and after some silence an announcement came through.

"It's just turned half seven, we have plenty of fine tunes coming your way right after a brief news report," the reporter sounded cheery. 'Beach town police department have issued an official curfew, the first in over thirty years."

Harry turned the volume knob.

"All residents are ordered to stay inside their homes between the hours of eight pm and nine am until further notice. Residents are also advised that communication via mobile, landline and post will remain unavailable until further notice and the towns WIFI has been disabled. Anyone attempting to leave town will be arrested. What is this Mike?"

Harry had felt the same as the reporter when he saw the nurses devouring the child.

"And if that isn't enough it seems the government have issued emergency vaccines to doctor's surgery's, with flu jabs being given near Haker Street Medical. Suspicious behaviour should be reported to the police immediately and all residents are warned against going to the hospital. Avoid travelling alone. Okay folks, I think that does it, oh wait, hold on, there's something else. Well the police are going to need to explain this to us, they are setting up regular foot patrols around the town, all officers will be armed and are instructed to shoot anyone posing a threat to others and to the town hall or surrounding buildings. Whew that was a lot to take in folks, so I guess we'll be together till nine am, so stick around for more banging tunes." The presenter put a song on, Harry didn't recognise the tune. He leant on the counter staring at the radio, stunned.

'Fucking hell,' Harry said. Harry turned back to the fridge and opened it. He scanned the shelves and pulled a carton of orange and some bacon and brown sauce.

Harry ate some fried bacon with sliced bread and drank a few glasses of the orange juice.

Harry walked back into the living room and slumped onto the sofa. Harry dreaded what news reporters would say. Harry didn't like the news but, in a crisis, it might come in handy. Harry's ass was aching, and his spine sore with bruises after the wrench attack. The firm sofa cushions did little to help. Harry clicked the forty-inch plasma on, and channel hopped until he found the international news channel. He bit his lips with impatience.

The road outside was quiet. There were no cars or dog walkers, joggers or postmen. Nothing. The news repeated the weather for several minutes before cutting to a suited lady, a government representative. She sounded bleak giving vague details about people killing other people in mass groups and eating them. Harry's ears perked up. She said the attackers had come back to life from the dead.

Harry's mouth dribbled and he wiped it on his arm. Unbelievable. Unbelievable. Harry was not prepared for such news. The people who he had narrowly escaped from at the hospital were in fact, dead. The crisis became real now. The woman was shaking as she held the microphone. Swat officers appeared into view behind her. Police joined the tv swat.

The camera didn't show the soldiers, but Harry heard military orders. It was getting stranger. Then the tanks rolled by in the background. Soldiers escorted the tanks carrying assault rifles. Irrelevant details passed over Harry.

Harry snapped out of his gaze. A woman cried outside. Harry leapt to his feet, his heart pounding. Was it his imagination running away? Harry stepped to the windows and looked at the street. Someone was crying loudly, then another cry. Harry darted to the hallway and grabbed his black waterproof jacket.

The curfew made Harry stop with his hand on the front door handle. He waited for another scream. He pulled the handle expecting the beasts to be swarming the street. It was clear. Harry walked down the garden path and scanned the road. To his shock a neighbour was screaming for help further down the street. She was surrounded by the creatures. Her house was mobbed by at least five of the dead. She was trying to run out of her front porch, but they attacked.

Harry panicked. Should he go back inside and phone for the police? Of course not, because the government had cut all communication. Yet the police demanded we call them when exactly this happened, idiots Harry thought.

Harry watched in awe as a patrolling officer ran to aid the woman with his pistol drawn. Harry leant on the picket fence. The officer gasped and let off two rounds.

'Get inside sir,' he yelled. The woman could not get back inside, she was trapped. The officer kept aim at the monsters. The dead wore patient gowns and had nurses' uniforms on, some wore shorts and t-shirts. Harry suspected the police were able to properly quarantine the hospital, but the dead had escaped before their arrival.

'Call for backup,' Harry shouted through his hands. Teamwork was critical, Harry watched as the officer took out another with a headshot. Harry wanted a gun, wanted to run and take a few out himself.

The officer fired round after round to no avail. The woman was being eaten alive by the mob. Harry saw a man leaning out from a window upstairs, he tossed some glass bottles, but they did nothing. The dead swarmed the officer as he tried to reload. Harry saw him using his chest radio. The officer slipped a clip in and Harry could not see him as the dead had surrounded him. Five gunshots echoed through the street, two more popped and the dead dropped around the office as he reloaded again. Harry squeezed the fence, the officer was brave, he was doing well, and Harry hoped backup would arrive to help him. Otherwise the disease would-be all-over town in a short while.

A black swat van zoomed past Harry startling him. The van drove into the crowd of dead people. Their heads were mashed under the tires. Four swat officers pushed open the rear door and jumped out. Automatic rifles went off. The swat team fired relentlessly into the dead. The valiant patrol officer was crouching at the rear of the van. He glanced at Harry. Harry saw the fear in his face.

Instinctively Harry crouched back to the safety of his house. Locking the front door behind him. He ran back into the sitting area to get an unobstructed view of the danger. The radio in the kitchen was announcing the incident and Harry figured the radio station had access police frequencies to keep people informed. The announcer said to stay inside and lock doors.

'Shit,' Harry said. 'This is not contained.' Harry could see other neighbours peeking from windows and hanging out of upstairs windows.

The patrol officer had begun to walk down the street, seemingly unscathed. The gunfire had ceased. The woman had been killed. The swat officers swiftly piled the bodies into a pile. One of them retrieved a large gasoline canister from the van. Then he poured the fuel onto the bodies. Another officer stepped forward, lit and tossed a match to the deceased.

The smoke was black. Harry could not believe how diabolical the situation was. The police burning the diseased bodies in the street rather than taking them away was stupid. Harry saw the incident unfold and it wasn't a mild problem, it was potentially lethal to the entire town. If more of the dead wander into the streets people will be killed.

In the house on the opposite side of the street, in the living room window Harry could see a man vomiting. Harry was blocked up and couldn't smell anything. The couple there had been caring to Harry and his family. Harry wondered if he should go and ask about James and Molly. They should be in town somewhere; Harry knew in his heart they could not be at the hospital. It was deserted and the ward with James's name had given him hope he had been discharged or Molly took him to her parents.

The reality sunk in; the radio continued to play tunes as he sat there watching the news for another hour. Harry turned the tv and radio off at nine. At least news channels were reporting something. But the details didn't say anything specific such as how it started or where, or even what caused it.

Harry stepped onto the pavement and the street had come alive. Neighbours packed luggage into their cars whilst crying. They hurried their children into the backseats. To the right of Harry, a young woman was loading a baby into an Alfa Romeo, she was sobbing. Harry knew the bridge was clogged up and the families could not leave. Survival instinct told Harry that trying to escape to the city was a bad idea. Judging by the traffic jam, Harry presumed the bridge toll booths had been shut, that would explain no traffic coming the other way. At this point, it was safer to stay inside.

CHAPTER 12

Deterioration of Beach Town

Main street shops opened as usual on Sunday. Until the local radio started announcing the curfew forcing residents to stay at home and businesses to close early.

Harry walked down main street toward the police station. He looked down the side of the police station to the rear carpark. A queue of people lined up waiting to enter the tent and be tested.

Main street was unfunctional. The café remained open, police would need to buy refreshments and lunch from somewhere. Harry saw people wander in and out of the café. The blissfully hopeful people who think it won't get worse and the police can handle it.

Harry was lucky to be alive. There were a handful of others who knew the reality that you can't contain something so ghastly. He walked up the police station steps past the guarding officers and pushed his way into the entrance hall. The reception desk was empty.

Harry waited for the desk clerk to arrive. He wondered where Doctor Jamie was. Was Jamie one of the hazmat guys or had he gone home. Harry was confident there were enough doctors living in town to treat everyone. Even if they set up more tents. The lack of officers walking around the station told Harry that at least a third would be keeping the hospital in lockdown.

After some five minutes a woman in her thirties with an athletic build and blonde locks stepped forward from a door behind the desk. A fruity overpowering fragrance hit Harry and he accidentally ingested the scent.

'I'm here to report two missing people,' Harry said. 'They were at the hospital last…' Harry realised his keys were at home and the house was unlocked. His wallet was on the bedroom cabinet. He'd forgotten his wallet when he took Sheila to the interview. With the current situation people would be tempted to steal from others. Harry shook at the thought.

'Okay,' the clerk said. 'Can you fill out this form with their names and dates of birth.' She picked a yellow tinted sheet up from the desk along with a black ballpoint chained to the desk and passed them to Harry. Harry filled the details as quickly as he could. One question that stumped him was the last known location. Harry saw his family at the beachfront. Molly said they went to hospital, the ward sign confirmed it.

'Hospital,' he muttered. The clerk opened a drawer and flicked through some papers. 'Here.' Harry passed the form back and the clerk scanned over the document.

'Okay we'll investigate sir,' she said. 'As you know there is a government curfew in place, and we are extremely overworked. I don't want to give sad news…' Harry interrupted her.

'It's okay I was there, I've seen them.' The clerk's mouth dropped. Harry started to walk towards the entrance doors. He may have said something he shouldn't.

Outside the station, the occasional car drove past and some folks were bickering outside the café.

Harry's looked at the opera house, it looked open. He should have been at work but continuing life after losing contact with his family was overwhelming and the incident at the hospital had frightened him. Residents went about their lives and two or three businesses were open. Harry had to return to normalcy. Too much alienation and he would lose motivation altogether. If people saw the monsters roaming the hospital, they would change their mind about keeping calm. As the residents on his street had panicked, so would the town.

Harry stepped down the police station steps to the pavement. The pub had a few drunk punters outside. Harry wanted some alcohol, but he didn't have his wallet or the patience. A drink would calm the anxiety rising in him.

Losing his family was too much and it was destroying him. Harry couldn't keep it together. His thoughts were astray. A gunshot abruptly boomed through the street, people screamed, and the café goers ducked. Harry ran around to the side of the police station. Officers had shot a man who lay bleeding out. It wasn't clear why. Harry assumed it was another infected who had escaped the hospital. Harry realised the motorway was not being watched and the queue had gone on for miles. If the disease had spread the entire length of the bridge then the batch that had wandered in from the motorway turn-off was the least of the towns worries. The entire fucking city could be overrun. Harry left the scene and walked down main street to the opera house.

The opera was locked. Harry looked inside the glass doors, the entrance was polished, and a red rope hung from two golden posts, blocking entry to the venue.

A mob of drunk pub goers began shout, taunting the police outside the station.

'What's this curfew about then? I'll go out and go anywhere I want to,' one man shouted. Another lugged a stone narrowly missing the police. The police were unmoved. A mother shielded her son outside the café and rushed him inside. A couple walking past the bank turned around and headed the opposite way. Anyone who walked onto main street hid around building corners. Harry saw a man spying from behind the pub.

The drunken men continued to yell insults. Harry decided it was time to visit Sheila. Molly may have taken James there; it was a long shot. Harry needed to see Sheila regardless.

Four officers exited the police station and stood in the street in a stand-off against the punters. The drunks shouted racial insults at a black officer and threw stones at him. A woman came from the pub and taunted the police with the birdie. The officers were holding their ground. Harry recalled the radio, if anyone posed a threat to the police station or town hall then lethal force would be used.

Harry was about to walk away, but an officer equipped his pistol and aimed at a man who stumbled and vomited. The crowd of drunks turned to him. Harry ducked down behind the black bin outside the opera house. The vomiting drunk was hacking all over the road on his hands and knees. The crowd had taken a step back from the vomiting man. An officer stepped forward aiming at the man on the floor. The drunks went in to help the sick man, but the police yelled to stay away and pointed their guns at the crowd. 'Move back.'

Harry looked at the police station. Dean was looking out of a top floor window. Dean was pointing and explaining something to another officer next to him.

The sick man dropped to his stomach and black goop poured from his mouth and nose. The crowd were aghast. The sick man began to groan. The gargling took Harry's mind back to the hospital. Being trapped in that blood storage room surrounded by the dead. Harry wondered who the man was whom he accidentally threw the blood over. It didn't matter now.

'Get back,' Harry shouted from behind the bin. 'Listen to them.' The crowd ignored Harry. The corpse rose to its feet, as the news had said, and the drunk was now dribbling green and black pus, his eyes streaking in tar gunk. Harry saw Dean open the station window.

'Fire,' Dean shouted. The officers began to fire round after round. A barrage of lead struck the diseased man in the head and torso. Blood sprayed amongst the tarmac road. The drunks dispersed, running frantically back to the pub. Harry looked to Dean who spotted him. He waved to Dean, but Dean ignored him and shut the window.

'Fuck you,' Harry grumbled. His leg's stiff from crouching and his spine solidifying from the lack of movement. Harry watched as the officers returned to the station carrying the body to the rear. It was surreal the drama had come and gone all in the space of five minutes. The drunks were probably in the pub shaking and getting afraid. It was time they did, it was time the town did. Harry knew Beach Town was not prepared for this.

Harry stood and began to walk down main street. To Sheila's to try and formulate a plan. An evacuation from Beach Town was needed. But not without his family.

CHAPTER 13

Riots And Rations

The walk from main street to Sheila's was ten minutes. Harry took a right at the end of main street down and headed down a residential road towards Firtree park. Sheila flat was in a tower block at the end of the park.

Firtree park was full of gossiping parents. Harry walked slowly to try and catch a conversation about the situation. They chatted about their lives, seemingly oblivious to the outbreak. Dog walkers jogged around along the path past Harry. Kids played on the swings and roundabout. School must have been shut as precaution.

Harry saw two officers patrolling the perimeter of the park. The thick brush and various trees were beginning to flower an assortment of colours. Harry lost sight of them. Harry hadn't seen any ticket wardens today. He hadn't seen postmen or milkmen. The unusual was the new normal.

Harry approached Green Life elementary school. James was a pupil there. Harry investigated the deserted classrooms as he walked towards Sheila's. At the front of the building the front door was covered in police notices. Harry stopped to read one. "The education of pupils is important. Due to a government notice we have been closed down until further notice." Harry wasn't surprised anymore. He continued towards the block of flats. Its exterior clean white. The doors shone in the midday sun.

Harry reached the door and pushed the intercom to Sheila's flat; number one, one five, tenth floor.

'Who is it?' Sheila answered quickly. The dirtied speaker hissed as usual.

'Harry.' Sheila buzzed him in instantly.

The tower guard sat at the elevator looking sombrous. Hunched over reading last week's newspaper. Harry was annoyed the local paper had been cancelled due to financial reasons. Beach Town Daily had ceased trading about five days ago. Harry thought it might be connected to the outbreak but that was too farfetched.

Harry stepped into the gloomy hallway of the tenth floor. Neighbours radios and tv's were blurting the news out. Harry knew people would be too interested not to find out the truth. Harry knocked on Sheila's door. He heard some furniture being moved and then the door opened.

'Finally,' Harry said and stepped inside. He walked over to her sofa and planted his backside down. Sheila was still limping, but she moved about ok. 'It that necessary?' Harry added. Sheila struggled to push the bookshelf back against the door. The kettle was boiling in the kitchen. Harry's legs melted into the purple fur blanket covering the sofa.

'Yes, after the hospital do you really think anywhere is safe. I tried calling, nothing.' Sheila struggled with the bookshelf, so Harry go up and pushed it the rest of the way.

Sheila walked into the open plan kitchen and brewed two cups of coffee bringing them back into the living room.

The smell of black coffee and her flowery perfume was a little sickening. Harry took his cup from Sheila. This was what he would do if he fell out with Molly. Molly and he wouldn't talk for a day or two, but things always got better. At Sheila's he'd have to endure Wendy. Wendy governed the Town Hall planning department, according to some people she did a decent job. All Wendy would do is bicker about Harry's lack of moral compass and lack of work variety. She always urged him to consider applying to have the theatre seating area extended to bring in more cash, but what did she know about money and business, nothing.

'I still can't find Molly or James,' Harry said. 'I went to the police station. I even considered going to my parents, but it's unlikely they went there it's too far. It just gets worse Sheila, seriously.' Harry sipped his coffee and picked a few sugar cubes up from the table and waited for the sugar to dissolve before gulping. Sheila reached for the tv remote on the table and turned the tv volume down. It was showing a program on nature and animals.

'Is Wendy here?' Sheila sat back and crossed her legs, her skirt lifted revealing her knickers. Harry ignored it.

'I don't know where they can be other than the hospital, you said they were going there didn't you?' Sheila huffed. 'Wendy, don't mention her to me yet.' Harry tensed his shoulders and sank further into the sofa. He was thinking of all the locations they could be. This was all a wasted journey. He would have been better driving around, but he couldn't because his car was lodged on the motorway.

'What's happened?' he asked. Sheila shuffled next to him. They both watched the television whilst drinking coffee and talking. Something they were accustomed to.

'She's a little annoyed about the car, that's all, I can't seem to convince her to buy a bike instead, she always runs.'

'She'll get over it,' Harry replied. 'Trust me.' Harry took the remote from Sheila and flicked through the channels until the news came on. Harry placed the cup on the glass.

Images of Buckingham Palace flashed onto the screen before cutting to Westminster, London. A man in a black raincoat stood with police behind him reporting the armies' deployment to protect her majesty. The news cut back to Buckingham Palace gates. A young female presenter wearing a bullet proof vest over a yellow blouse stood outside the gates. Tanks resided inside Buckingham Palace's perimeter. Soldiers patrolled the area and a helicopter sat directly behind the reporter. Harry was in awe. This was frightening, everything was changing fast and Harry didn't like it. The reporter described a very serious threat to national security that was beginning to overwhelm the countries defences.

'This is why I'm glad I don't live on the mainland, or the city for that matter,' Harry commented. His body sank further into the sofa, his palms sweaty. Sheila wept.

'How bad does this need to get?' Sheila was crying. 'They can't contain the hospital, can they? What happens if they come from overseas?' Sheila struggled to get her words out.

'Hold on…' Harry turned the tv volume up. The camera cut back to Westminster. The man was pale. Behind him the soldiers stood in rows with their rifles to their chests. The camera cut back to Buckingham palace. Red palace guards stood on the roof and marched the grounds. Harry wanted information and fast. If London was falling, the whole country might fall.

"Westminster has issued an international cry for help to the United States and Russian governments for military assistance.

It is believed the crisis has originated somewhere in western Europe and prime minister Carl Longwood states the crisis may have completely overwhelmed Europe. The United Kingdom is still fighting, and the prime minister has issued emergency warnings to all citizens, stay away and inside from the threat."

'What the fuck,' Sheila said. Harry could not believe it.

'It's more than a threat. It's a plague of psycho's and monsters is what it is, if the governments can't contain it, nobody can,' he replied. 'I've got to find my family. Please tell Molly and James to come home if you see them.'

'Harry, look at the front door I'm not going out,' Sheila said. 'When this thing gets worse, I'll be safe inside.' Harry could see the fear on Sheila's face.

'Please, if you see them out of the window in the park or anywhere, try to shout them in at least.'

'Okay, but I'm not risking going out,' Sheila replied. 'I don't fancy getting attacked again.'

Harry smiled and stood and walked to the blocked front door. He struggled to slide the bookshelves out of the way. Sheila continued to sip her coffee and watch the news. She didn't offer Harry a biscuit this time. They had to ration now, with Britain falling the commodities wouldn't be imported to Beach Town. Harry wondered if people would forget about them.

***

Harry had to walk back past main street to get home. The post office strikers had gone.

Harry walked slowly past the supermarket; a large crowd had gathered outside. The talking was like a seashore wave.

Men and women complained to each other. Scared kids held each other's hands whilst their parents chanted for food. Three officers stood at the supermarket entrance attempting to calm people. Harry walked towards the police station. Three officers now stood at the station entrance. At the town hall building to the right of the police station, two swat officers stood guard. Thing had changed. The security was increased. Harry feared it was too late. The disease would spread. The diseased would travel and kill everybody unless they could escape, he was sure.

Harry turned back to the crowd outside the supermarket. One man caught Harry's eye. He recognised the short black hair. Harry jogged back over, keen to dig deeper.

'Jamie?' Harry asked the man, patting his shoulder. The man turned; it was Jamie.

'Harry, nice to see you again,' Jamie said. 'This is the hospital that's triggered all this, guarantee it.' Jamie put Harry at ease, it was nice to speak to another survivor. The hospital had formed an invisible bond between them. But Jamie seemed to be unaware of the bigger picture, London was falling, it wasn't just the hospital that was responsible. Harry had an unobstructed view of the supermarket doors.

'What's this for?' he asked Jamie. Jamie cupped his ear with his hand. 'What happened? Is it open?' Harry shouted. Jamie nodded folding his arms. Jamie leant closer to Harry.

'Yeah, we're waiting for our rations,' Jamie shouted. 'New curfew rules by the town hall. Apparently, there are enough food boxes for everyone, although I can't see those arriving tomorrow getting the same things.' Jamie grinned. The bickering got quieter.

'I haven't heard about this, when did it happen?' Harry asked. Jamie shook his head.

'Just half hour ago, the radio announced it.' Jamie lifted his sleeve and checked his watch.

'How long until they let them in?' Harry asked.

'Not sure, they said we could get our stuff ten minutes ago,' Jamie replied. Harry patted Jamie's shoulder and walked back towards the police station. The crowd were pale, worn out and fearful.

He had to go to the town hall to find out about evacuations. Harry stopped his stroll as chorused shouts rattled his ears. He turned to look at the crowd. Men had grappled the officers and were attacking them. The crowd shunted the supermarket doors and booted the glass. The glass cracked scaring a flock of birds from the supermarket roof. Harry watched as five officers came running from behind the police station.

'Stop now, we have orders to shoot, one officer shouted. They equipped their pistols. Harry ran to the alley at the side of the town hall. The men continued to smash through the doors, and they swung open in pieces. The mob of ranting people stormed through.

'Stop, take your children to safety if you want them to live,' another officer shouted and fired a gunshot in the air. People trampled over each other. The angry town goers forced themselves through the doors, trampling over broken window glass.

Women picked up their children, holding them to their chests and moving to safety. A bloody faced man got up from the stampede and limped towards the bar, where pub goers were watching from the Victorian windows. The officer fired another two shots in the air. Another officer shot a man running out of the supermarket with a bag of unpaid goods. The bullet impacted his chest sending to him to the concrete.

He dropped the bag, fruit and tins rolled onto the pavement. The police moved into the supermarket where the crowd were looting. A few people lay in the doorway crying in pain from being stood on.

One policeman came back outside and used his radio. Then the other police joined him. Harry ducked down, afraid of the consequences of the death of the man. The police stood in a row aiming their pistols into the supermarket. One officer fired another shot into the air. Harry watched as people began to run towards the supermarket doors. The police opened fire, spraying the crowd with bullets, it was a massacre.

CHAPTER 14

Brutus The Mutant

Charlie awoke in a strange room on a bed of thin sheets. He could see through some iron bars. An officer sat reading an outdated newspaper with a picture of the town hall on the front page.

Charlie's hands, feet, face, bones and ligature were aching. Not fatigued, but sorely exhausted. The last he remembers is talking, voices that hadn't previously made sense, but those voices had returned, it might have been his cell mates sharing the lower floor of the station with him. He wriggled but it was too difficult to get out of bed. All he could do was flick his eyes. He tried speaking but only mumbled sounds came out.

Beating down was a brilliant white light. Needles migrated through his pupils. The cell walls blurred and clouded. Charlie held a hand over his eyes. All fathomable energy was spent, he believed he was dead. The officer placed his newspaper on the floor and approached the cell bars. Charlie heard the radio bleep and fizzle. Time distorted. Charlie could feel a pin prick on his left arm like a bee sting. He shut his eyes. His chest tightened at the sounds of gunshots. The guard panicked and

Charlie opened his eyes. The officer entered the single elevator. Any hope of Charlie getting answers was gone.

'You awake?' a deep voiced man called, tapping a pot or can on the bars of his cell. Charlie could not tolerate the rattling; nor could he shout a reply, his lungs rippled with tension.

'Yes,' Charlie said. It felt like an iron blanket was placed on his head and face. All he wanted to do was sleep. More gunshots came from above the stone cellar. Charlie looked at the needle prickling his skin. Whatever it was pumping was making him feel woozy. He hadn't the energy to take the needle out yet, so he tried to kick his leg.

'Charlie it's Peter, what happened to you the other day?' Peter clung to the bars; Charlie could hear the rasp of his knuckles against the iron. Charlie heard the faint whispers. Charlie sensed the drug euphoria fade and elation left him. Peter's voice made him tighten his jaw; he felt betrayed.

'You been to the motel?' Charlie asked trying to lift his IV arm to rip the needle out, but his arm flopped lifelessly onto the bed. Charlie heard Peter slip away from the bars and begin to pace.

'Yeah, err no,' Peter trembled. 'I kind of let everyone else deal with it, you know?' Charlie could feel a fire rising in his stomach. Peter had deserted him.

'Anyone coming for us?' Charlie said. Anger fuelled his mouth. An invisible scorpion stung his muscles into action. Charlie reached for the needle and tore it out. He was lightheaded and thumbed over the injection site. The stone walls swayed and the ground shook as he pulled himself onto the edge of the bed. Silver specks dotted his sight and shimmied out of sight. His body rocked as if on a carousel.

'Yeah, I told them anything happens to us, come get us, that was when I got my free call. The police aren't too happy with you though, I heard them talking and they said you have to submit to blood tests once you wake up, they been sedating you since you got here, after the blood transfusion that is.' Charlie heard Peter jump on his squeaking bed.

'No chance, we're getting out,' Charlie said. 'And we're gonna clean the mess at the motel.' Charlie stood up.

The floor was stained in dust. The walls decaying and cracked. A mirror sat above a sink that was rancid with blood.

Charlie stumbled towards the cell bars and grasped them. He looked at his arm. It was a mess. Plasters were half pulled off the left arm. He tore the plasters off, they stung as it ripped hairs out. He tossed the plaster to the guard's drink next to the chair. 'Enjoy that.'

'What we gonna do?' Peter asked. Charlie didn't have a plan yet. The grooves of Charlie's brain were lacerated with endorphins. His hands shook in sweat.

'I'm not staying. You should have stayed at the hospital. That place is gonna be the end of this town, full of monsters.'

'Yeah. I saw them on the news the night I got brought in, something about the fall of Britain. You can't take it too seriously, can you?'

'Peter, if you had had the guts to stay at the hospital, you would see this isn't worth shaking off.' The elevator beeped and the doors opened. Charlie's eyes darted at the officer who stepped out. He carried a steaming cup in one hand and a piece of paper in the other. The officer glared at Charlie.

'You need that medicine, why did you take it off? If you're that keen, we'll take you to quarantine now.' The officer stood out of reach. Charlie's ribs hurting on the bars.

'I can't hear you,' Charlie replied. The officer stepped towards the bars.

'I said…' The officer didn't have time to finish, Charlie reached his right hook through the bars and wrapped it around the officer's neck, he dropped the coffee on himself, Charlie muffled the scream with his other hand. The panicked officer reached for his gun, but Charlie gripped tighter then cracked the officer's neck sideways. His neck snapped instantly, and the officer rag dolled to the coffee covered floor. He had his hand on his pistol with his head cocked to the left.

Charlie bent down and pulled the officer's body closer. He grabbed the keys out the policeman's trouser pocket.

Charlie keyed the cell bars open and stepped out. Stepping over the officer and walking right, passing an empty cell before reaching Peter's. Peter was alone just as Charlie wanted him.

'We'll bring a whole lot of shit to this precinct after, I'm right with you,' Peter said clutching the holding cell bars. Charlie turned from Peter and walked back towards the elevator.

'Fuck you Peter, you are a backstabbing chicken.' Charlie thumbed the elevator and the doors opened. Peter mumbled.

'Fuck you for leaving me here, I'll fucking tell them about the motel, you knock up whores,' Peter shouted.

The words pierced Charlie. Charlie walked back to Peter's cell. It was time to cut Peter loose.

'Nobody is saying anything about the motel.' Charlie reached through the cell bars and grabbed Peter's hands and pulled him towards him. Charlie was in a daze from the sedative. Charlie pulled Peter's arms harder and held the officer's keys above Peter's head.

Charlie keyed Peter in the right eye and it popped. Blood poured onto Peter's jacket and he screamed and thrashed as if he was a fish. Charlie twisted the key; Peter kicked his body about crying out.

Charlie yanked the key out. Holding Peter's arm, he put his foot on the bars for momentum and pulled hard. A hollow pop sounded, and Peter's arm went limp. Charlie released Peter who slumped against the bars in a pool of blood.

Charlie walked back to the elevator whistling. Charlie waved goodbye but Peter had lost consciousness. Charlie pocketed the bloody keys. More gunshots sounded overhead. Charlie stepped into the elevator.

***

Amidst the supermarket chaos Harry hadn't seen Charlie leave the police station. The officers hadn't either. The receptionist was too busy shuffling papers and the police were occupied with the supermarket.

Harry could see through the row of officers that at least twenty people were shot. People lay injured and bleeding to death. Blood spurted from a man's neck and a woman lay bleeding from her thigh. Four people were dead, and the kill count was rising to seven once the other victims bled out.

Harry crouched back into the alley. Flies and unmoved trash bags lay untended. Shoppers began to surrender. The shoppers with brains. The looting continued.

The officers moved into the store again. They reloaded their pistols. Harry heard gunshots followed by screams. A barrage of bangs and snaps filled the street. Food was being thrown around; meat tossed towards the exit.

Those who surrendered gathered around the bleeding victims. They were bleeding to death. It had been shoot to kill orders. Not shoot to wound or deter.

Harry crept further down the alleyway; the red stone walls became tighter. Sunlight was being blocked. Harry crouched to the rear of the town hall carpark. Harry saw the white tent in the police station car park. Harry stood oblivious and realised he was stood in a car park filled with body bags. It was a betraying sight.

'Oh no,' he gasped. His breath was shallow. Harry clenched his shaking fists. The carpark was devoid of cars. The black body bags were around six-foot long. Harry needn't count, there was over thirty at a glance.

The gunshots stopped. He heard officer's barking orders and looters begging for mercy.

The bags were laid in rows with tags with names written on them. Harry looked at the closest tag. It was blank.

A rustling caught him off-guard, a squeaking and shuffling. Harry froze, one of the black bags was moving. Harry walked over to the bag out of fear. As he got closer, he heard groaning. Then the other body bags began to rustle. The deceased were back. Harry watched the mass of body bags twitch and shake.

Harry knelt next to an unmoving bag; the tag was blank. It was possible his family were here, but something told him they weren't.

Police were approaching, their heavy-footed belt clinking alerted him, radio static filled the air agitating the corpses more. Harry dived behind a dumpster. The police emerged from the alleyway. Both stood in awe.

'Look at this, their moving,' one officer said. The other officer bent down next to one of the body bags and then kicked it. It didn't move like the other bags.

'What is this? Get Dean on the radio,' he said. 'Town hall to Dean, over.' They waited and paced through the walkways between the bodies. The officers neared Harry's position. Running to the rear entrance of the town hall was too risky. The officers might shoot him or mistake him for a criminal. Harry stayed put, he wasn't risking anything.

The officer's radio hissed.

'This is Dean, what's wrong.' The officer held his walkie as if eating a hotdog. The other officer mazing around the corpses, he stopped at a bag. Harry watched closely. His partner was occupied with the radio. The officer bent down to the black bag, reaching for the zip. No, idiot, Harry thought. Harry couldn't let the officer open the bag. Harry searched the floor for a stone and tossed it at the town hall. The stone made a knock on the concrete wall. The officer jumped to his feet. His partner was still on the radio.

'What was that?' The officer looked around. Harry hid further behind the dumpster. Harry heard Dean's voice; he was in the carpark somewhere.

'See.'

'This is very bad. Get rid of them immediately, whatever you do don't open them.' Harry heard the officer reload their pistols, a metallic slide and click, then a snap.

Harry peered around the dumpster; Dean was gone. Harry saw the police pistols in hand, hesitating.

'Take them out,' one said. They watched the bodies moving.

They lifted their pistols and opened fire. The bullets impacted the wriggling corpse and it went still. They let off a round in each body bag. Harry saw a chance and ran for the rear door of the town hall, opening it and slipping inside.

CHAPTER 15

Power

A crew of police had been assigned to patrol the hospital twenty-four seven. Two police cars were parked in the hospital car park. Seven officers patrolled the perimeter and watched the hospital entrance. The door had been barricaded using the waiting room chairs and biohazard tape stuck across them. Two snipers were stationed on the motorway turnoff.

The police were drinking bottled lime juice and eating peanuts and dried fruit for snacks. Taken from the station canteen. They had been accustomed to having their lunches brought to them.

Two officers stood at the main entrance chatting. Another four officers circled the hospital perimeter in pairs, complaining of the moisture air. One officer sat on a plastic white chair on the motorway turn-off chatting to the snipers. One of the snipers interrupted the mundane conversation on energy saving light bulbs so he could announce his kill shot. He believed he found a survivor, but it turned out to be another monster.

The officers had been instructed to report each kill back to the police station, so they had an official body count for military arrival. Corpses raggedly straggled across the corridors briefly in view through the windows. When they shambled into sight it was difficult to get a clear shot. Using the rifles scope didn't make it any easier. The scope lens glared in the sunlight, making any shot tedious. One sniper lay on the bonnet of the police car resting his eyes. Rifle by his side, waiting to take his position when the other rotated. They had successfully picked off the few corpses in the car park before barricading the front doors.

At the rear of the hospital the officers were under attack. The other police, and snipers lay oblivious to the threat. A breach had occurred. Two officers were tackled by the beasts as they fell from a broken first-floor window. The corpses smashed through the day previous unknown to the police. They toppled over the shards of glass poking from the window frame, guts split and fell onto the concrete. The beasts munched at the officer's necks.

One officer grabbed his pistol and let a shot off. The beasts were relentless and crazy. He accidentally shot his leg amidst the struggle. They continued to topple out. At first ten or twelve, but fifty zombies had poured out from the hospital window. The patrolling officers were shredded to pieces.

Another window further along smashed. This time the officers at the main entrance heard and radioed the patrols at the back. They were met with death like screams dissipating into static. The sniper on the motorway turn-off ordered a round up at the main entrance.

The shambling blood drenched monsters hobbled, limped and stiffly marched on with broken bones protruding from the fall.

The recently deceased officers were amongst the horde as it wandered around the hospital towards the car park. The sniper panicked and struggled to cock his rifle. Then a crowd groaned behind him and tore into his arms gnawing at the flesh, tearing his ligaments. They ripped the intestines from the sniper laying on the police car and gouged the officer on the now red chair.

The four officers at the hospital entrance were swarmed. They open fired. Firing shot after shot into the undead, but they kept coming. The dead huddled round the officers and swamped three of them. It was a thunderstorm of killing. The guts of the officer squished under their limp feet. One officer made a run for it, to the rear dirt road of the hospital. There was no time for cars, the hospital and motorway were overrun. The officer tried to radio the station. There was no answer. The officer stopped and took off his bullet proof vest and tossed it to the dirt road. He set off running, back into town, the longest route.

***

On main street the remaining civilians had fled. The supermarket doors had been pulled shut, but they were broken and wouldn't lock. The dead bodies had been removed. Those that were shot dead were now being covered by shamed officers.

Dean had decided to dump the bodies with the others in the town hall car park until they could be buried. They were dumped there without care and the officers returned to being order abiding robots.

A few pub goers shouted from the windows, taunting the police were corrupt. It was true, they were rogue.

Dean watched from the top floor of the station. He had seen people escape with hands full of things that would last two days at most. Food distribution was a big problem along with medicine. Dean's friend Jamie lay in the carpark, dead. Jamie hadn't intentionally gone into the supermarket; he was pushed by the mob. Dean had to watch as his friend had been trampled to death. Dean shed a tear and was interrupted by a radio call from the carpark.

He was back at that desk with neatly stacked paperwork and a stapler aligned with the corner of the table. His mug cold and adjacent to the papers. Dean adjusted the clock; somebody must have changed its position because it had to tilt to allow the small hand to tick.

Dean knew the mayor was asking for trouble. The mayor hadn't done anything useful other than taking people's liberty. Dean believed he could do better. He had to convince the current mayor to step down. If he resisted, something would change his mind like bribery, threats or a good old-fashioned coup. If the mayor had seen the hospital, he would be shitting his pants. Dean sighed and walked to the office door and left for the town hall.

Dean met the mayor with a flimsy handshake, a shake of the level of respect he had for him, quickly wiping it down his trousers. The mayor's cocky smirk whipped Dean like ice.

'I'll get to the point, we need to start distributing food,' Dean said. 'My men have had to kill innocent people today, people who have no idea what is going on and are trying to get basic resources, how can you possibly expect us to suppress this any longer? They aren't the threat, trust me.' Dean slammed his fist to the wood table, knocking a statue of big ben over. The mayor looked fraught, glaring at Dean. The mayor cricked his neck and fiddled with his pen. He sighed at Dean.

'Dean, Dean, Dean, why do you insist on coming here to tell me this? I have had contact with London. It's over, there's no hope, there's no scientists or cures or anything coming to save us from it, we are one of the few remaining islands to survive this thing. I think we should very much be concerned with the food supply, because once it's gone, we'll have to start growing crops. It's over, this is the end, Dean.' The mayor had jotted a few notes. The mayor had an extremely irritating rung out voice. He sounded dry. Dean spotted a half full whisky bottle on the shelf to the left.

'I don't believe it, the end of what? Your sanity?' Dean snapped and grabbed the whisky bottle from the shelf showing it to the mayor. 'Drinking on the job? What happened to you?' Dean added. Dean launched the bottle across the office at the door. It smashed and glass and whisky decorated the walls and floor.

Jimmy the mayor jumped up off his seat. Dean approached him and grappled his shirt, shunting him against the window behind the desk, hard enough to make it crack.

'Let go Dean, I'm not kidding, I'll have you scratched from the force. It's over, what more can I say, we need to pull together, not apart,' Jimmy conveyed. Dean shoved him to the floor and Jimmy stumbled back up. 'I'm in charge now, go home. If this is the end for us, then we need to start building the future today. I'm ordering police escorted food and medicine distribution of at least two weeks to every house in the town.'

Dean wrinkled his nose and walked to the office door. His feet crunched on the broken bottle glass and he left the office. Outside the office Dean gritted his teeth; it was the end. Dean marched back through the door.

Jimmy was sat down at his oak desk and held a large knife. Dean froze. Jimmy sobbed and stood up. Dean walked forward. Jimmy the mayor gave a final salute to Dean and slit his throat, ear to ear.

CHAPTER 16

Radio Apocalypse

The lone police officer gasped for breath on his run down the dirt road, he was nearing the motel. It was over a mile from the hospital already and a mile more to main street.

The officer stopped and equipped his pistol and then carried on running whilst spraying single shots into two oncoming undead. They fell in a synchronistical shamble. He unloaded bullets into the pursuing horde until his gun clicked empty.

He was out of bullets and he tossed the pistol to the dirt and continued to run. The horde stumbled over the corpses he had shot.

The officer only had one weapon now, it was a taser strapped to his leg. The officer limped and was nearing the motel and petrol station. The boulders to the right prevented him from cutting across to main street. The dirt road turned into concrete as he neared safety.

The petrol station was clogged with empty cars. The officer waved at the motel trying to catch someone's attention. The creeps gained ground, nearing the officer almost within an arm's reach of him.

The officer was reduced to a snail jog and almost tripped as he equipped his taser from his leg, it was black and yellow and loaded. There was a man stood outside the petrol station, but he soon turned and ran back inside at the sight of the horde.

The officer panted then stopped in a puddle. He turned, taser aimed. He shot the first one coming at him and it fell into the puddle where he stood. The electric taser surged through the water and through the officer. Their bodies buzzed until their skin burnt and they fried in the water. Other beasts clambered down onto the officer and ripped at his skin and face.

Charlie sat on the bed in the motel room talking to Delila, the prostitute he knocked up. She cradled a baby who was suckling on his milk bottle when the horde alerted Charlie.

Charlie walked to the bathroom and looked in the mirror, his razor was on the tiled floor. He'd pick it up another time. He lifted his chin and examined the stitches in his neck. The stiches were rough and bloodied. He couldn't remember anything after Sheila slapped him.

Charlie walked back to Delila. She had placed the baby in his chaffed pram, the corners of the pull-down hood dog eared and ripped.

'You can't keep avoiding this,' Delila pleaded. 'He is your son, accept it.' She sat with her petite pale hands between her jeans.

Charlie gazed out of the window. He saw the horde of beasts approaching. His muscles tightening in his face with sweat. The hospital was getting to him now. He must have been imagining the crowd and shut the curtains. He turned around and backhanded Delila's face. She whimpered and covered her face with her hand.

'How many people have you been with? I was with you a few times, god dammit there is no way this is happening,'

Charlie shouted. His voice startled the little baby boy who let out a cry. Charlie could unwittingly attract the munching creatures if they were real. Charlie was pacing the small room.

'He is your son, I promise. Just accept it and we can move on.' Delila carefully picked the baby up and held him to her chest. Delila took the formula bottle and hand fed him.

Charlie admired the tiny grips, one day they would be like his. He walked back to the curtained window and pulled the curtain out of the way. Charlie jumped back. A group of bloodied gnawing corpses clawed at the motel walls. The horde shambled moronically into each other. Charlie closed the curtains. He turned back to Delila, she had calmed the baby and placed him back into the pram. She sat wiping her tears with used tissues.

'No one can know,' Charlie grunted. 'No one can know how I've knocked up a whore.' He slid down against the door. He was close enough to realise the groans were real.

Hands scratched at the plaster walls. Other rooms were breached, Charlie heard windows being smashed followed by screams.

Delila looked startled and the baby began its painful cry. She couldn't calm him. The more he cried the more they tried to find him. The more they groaned, the more Charlie sweated, the room looked like a pixelated video mirage.

'Shush, it's okay, shush.' Delila calmed the baby to a snooze. Delila rocked the pram back and forth.

'They won't find out, I promise,' she replied. She smiled at Charlie. Charlie was unimpressed, giving the thousand-yard stare with a grunt.

'Look outside now.' Delila walked to the window and looked outside. She gasped and retreated to the back of the room.

'What the fuck are they Charlie,' she shouted, the baby didn't wake up.

'The same things I saw at the hospital, now do you believe me?' Charlie felt the weight of the beasts behind the door. It was thick wood and bolted and chain locked. The room was kitted out with hundreds of stolen cigarettes. They were no use unless Charlie set the place alight.

'They can't get little Samuel, they can't,' Delila cried to Charlie's dismay.

Charlie crawled under the window and watched the corpses attempt to climb the boulders that separated the motel from main street. The wall that separated the rich from the poor.

'They won't get in. If they do then I won't be waiting for you,' Charlie said.

Charlie looked out the window and the corpses had wandered off. Charlie watched as Douglas; the petrol station attendant ran across the road for the boulders. Charlie remembered him, he was a good kid and a budding candidate for the club. Douglas was scrawny and into video games as he told Charlie. He ran for the rocks and mounted them. Charlie watched through the motel window. The dead were surrounding him and reaching for the kid's arms. Douglas vanished into the sea of freaks. But he emerged from the crowd and clambered up the rocks to the top. Charlie grinned. Douglas was a survivor and someone Charlie might need in the future. Douglas looked to the motel and Charlie stood up. Douglas gave a sympathetic wave to Charlie who scorned and then Douglas disappeared behind the rock wall.

***

It was night and darkness filled main street. Harry managed to sneak up to the mayor's office, determined to find an answer.

The building was empty, Harry had to sneak past a suited woman in the main hall but that was all. He had reached the mayor's office without detection. He knocked on the mayor's door and waited for an answer. Nobody answered and he pushed the office door open. It was hard to see, the window let in enough light for Harry to see the mayor's body slumped on the desk chair.

Harry walked over the broken glass; the crunch surprised him. As he got closer to the mayor, he began to see blood dripping down the mayor's shirt. Harry saw a large knife on the floor. The mayor was wheezing, and black gunk foamed in his mouth. Harry looked around for a weapon. The mayor stood up and straggled around the desk. Harry knew what had become of the mayor.

The creature dived for Harry. He dodged and lunged to the desk. A clear oval paperweight filled with bubbles caught Harry's eye. He picked the paperweight up; it was the size of his fist.

As the dead mayor grabbed at Harry, he smacked him across the head with the paperweight. The mayor's face caved in. A few teeth fell to the floor. Harry kicked its stomach and black pus poured from its mouth. It reached out for Harry.

Harry whacked the mayor in the forehead and dented the skull. Brain fluid oozed through the cracks in the skull. The paperweight was slippery in Harry's hand from the blood.

It dived again. Harry threw the weight at its face and it impacted the head. The skull collapsed and brain matter mushed out onto to the carpet. Harry jumped back and struggled to see the beast in the darkness.

Harry booted the mayor's ribs. The mayor stumbled back towards the window. Harry pushed the dead mayor, the window smashed, and the mayor was impaled on the window frame.

Harry tried to push the legs over the frame, but its body was impaled at the waist. The stomach began to tear open. Harry heaved and threw up over the carpet. The mayor's stomach ripped open and his top half fell out the window to the car park below whilst the lower half remained impacted on the broken window.

Harry stepped back towards the office door. He daren't look out the window. An acidic bile rose in his throat and he vomited again, this time on a bookshelf to the side of the room. The disease was rancid and stung his nose with each breath.

On the way out of the mayor's office Harry overhead a radio that had been left on in another office. He waited and listened to it. Dean's voice announcing the curfew. Getting to the radio station was his next destination. He carried on out of the town hall; there was nothing else to find here.

Harry walked across main street; it was deserted. Streetlamps were working, but for how long would the power grid stay on. Harry walked into the radio station, they had left the doors unlocked, not a wise decision.

Harry paced through the hall to the stairs and made for the broadcast studio. Upstairs Dean had indeed hijacked the microphone. The radio presenter sat with him looked unamused. Harry kept low and hid behind some seats to the left of the studio. Harry could see through the plexiglass and could hear them chatting, they must be broadcasting to the whole building as well. Not wise if the disease had spread to main street.

'You'll broadcast the curfew daily, twelve till two, along with your normal schedule, until the electric goes out, okay?' Dean said. The host didn't look impressed, but he nodded in compliance.

'Residents of Beach Town,' Dean announced leaning into a microphone. 'Men, women and children and to anyone who is tuned in, this is now radio apocalypse. Spread the word because the radio offers the only way for authorities to contact you with vital information. For that reason, you need to tune in everyday from twelve noon till two past midday. Anyone not tuning in will not be able to receive information and it's very, very important to be in the know, trust me. New curfew rules are in effect, and just so there is no ambiguity in it, it has been labelled aptly, the apocalypse curfew. All residents are to stay inside their homes at all times, no exceptions. Food will be distributed by our officers to every citizen daily for two weeks or until the food runs out. All cars are hereby banned, we need to save our fuel for the generators. Oh, I forgot to mention that medicines such as paracetamol, aspirin, codeine and basic antibiotics will also be included with the food, and will be delivered weekly, provided we have the resources. Switch it to music or something.' Dean finished and the radio presenter switched a song on.

'That just about does it, we'll have to see how many people actually abide by these rules. Shit. I forgot to mention about church, there'll be police attending for an hour on Sunday for anyone who wants to attend.' Dean was getting frustrated with being unable to work the mike. The host flicked the song off.

'This is the new mayor. I forgot to mention that church will be open for an hour on Sunday. Police will be attending for your safety. Don't worry we don't want to interfere we just want to make sure it's safe. You'll be much safer now I'm in charge, don't worry.' Dean chuckled.

Harry snuck through the dark studio to the plexiglass and stood at the studio's door. Dean jumped as Harry peered through the doorway. Dean left his seat in the studio's booth.

'How did you get in?' Dean said. 'Wasn't there an officer at the door?' There was no officer at the door and Harry suspected he had gone home to be with his family. Dean was losing it, there was no need to incite panic on the airwaves.

'Found my family yet?' Harry asked. Harry tried to get into the studio, but Dean held his arm across the doorway. The studio lights were fuzzy and dim. The presenter sat with his headphones on and ignored Harry.

'This isn't time to go looking for missing people. The curfew was brought into effect to prevent exactly this from happening.'

'They went missing after this started. My wife and son were at the hospital. Now they're nowhere to be found,' Harry said.

'I remember you now, you came from that mess with Sheila. Think about it, be straight with yourself, there unlikely to have survived, they won't be coming back, I'm sorry.' Dean patted Harry's shoulder. Harry prayed to god they weren't dead. They were missing.

'They aren't dead Dean,' Harry shouted. 'They're missing.' Dean shoved Harry back and Harry wanted to punch him.

Harry took a breath. He hadn't felt this angry before, maybe it was denial. Harry heard groaning and ducked down. Dean chuckled and left the radio broadcast room. Harry stood back up and waved goodbye to the presenter. Harry walked over to the windows where he could see main street. He looked to the clock on the wall, it was eleven. He needed to go home and recuperate. Dean was trying to help but making things more complicated. Maybe he should let them do their jobs, they could keep them safe. Harry had a tough time accepting it. It was safe enough to walk around so it must be safe enough for now. The hospital was in lockdown and government would devise a plan.

He walked to the exit and began the journey home.

CHAPTER 17

Nightmare

His eyes stung and his belly rumbled. He didn't want to eat what little food they had left.

Harry had placed the radio in the en-suite before slouching into bed fully clothed.

The glow in the dark clock beside his bed said three in the morning. He rolled around the bedsheets unable to sleep; too energised from the supermarket riot.

He slipped his feet onto the floor and got out of bed. Harry walked across the dark bedroom to the bathroom. The en-suit light wasn't working. He flicked the light switch twice for good measure.

The radio was bright and clear to see in the dark. It was positioned on a table next to the bath. Harry unzipped his trousers before realising he was about to urinate in the bath. He shuffled left to the toilet.

A pot smashed and Harry jumped. He reckoned it was the neighbour's cat breaking a plant pot. There had been strange cat noises emanating from outside all night. The cats had been restless lately, Harry believed it was because of the lack of food. Harry zipped and walked back into the bedroom. The moonlight crept through the window and illuminated him.

The radio was turned low and continued to play songs throughout the night. The presenter made an occasional announcement about the curfew. Harry remembered the look on the radio hosts face; it was a look of helplessness. The presenter must have been sleeping in the broadcast studio.

Harry routed through the built-in wardrobe next to the en-suit for a new shirt. It was too dark; he couldn't see anything. He reached into the wardrobe and tried to feel for his clothes.

The noises were muffled. Harry's attention was drawn to a thump downstairs. Harry walked to the bedroom door. Something was on the staircase. It could be a burglar trying to take advantage of the crisis or it could be his family. Harry put his ear to the cold door.

He couldn't hear anything. He got on his knees, accidentally clipping his elbow on the bedside draws and knocking a bottle of perfume off. Something grunted in the stairway. Harry daren't turn the bedroom light on. He pulled the bedroom door open. His throat tightened and he jumped back petrified.

The beasts were in his house shuddering up the stairs. The corpses wheezed.

'Damn,' he muttered. He had moments to find shelter, safety. He couldn't see the bathroom anymore. He looked to the built-in wardrobe; it would have to do.

He scuffled over the carpet to the wardrobe. Groans filled the bedroom and the door creaked open. He shuffled into the tight space, clothes draped over his shoulders and shoes dug into his back. The wardrobe door was open.

Black swaying figures walked into the bedroom. Harry heard screaming and shouting from outside. Car engines fired and metallic crashes and bangs filled the air. The dead had overrun the neighbourhood.

Harry attempted to pull the wardrobe door shut. One of the dead stopped grunting and more entered. Harry counted six. He was trapped in a claustrophobic box. A prisoner to undead shadow figures. Sweat trickled down his torso, his palms shook.

He wiped the sweat from his eyes and pinched his forearm and prayed.

He closed his eyes. This was it; the end.

Harry held the wardrobe door.

The skin on his hands chafed as he clasped them on the wooden frame. His knees were in his chest. His breathing contained.

Some of the dead shambled into the bathroom and knocked the radio off the stand. It smashed on the tiles and went silent. With every bump his heart thumped faster. Any minute now and he would drop dead from fear. His forearms ached from holding the wardrobe door shut. He let go and shuffled further into the clothes.

He looked on the floor but could not see. Molly had a torch for reading that she kept stored in the wardrobe. Harry couldn't feel it.

A mental light lifted his spirits. If the light was gone then Molly could have taken it. If she was smart enough to escape the hospital. She was probably smart enough to leave town and head to a military checkpoint, wherever that was. It was speculation but better than giving up hope. James hadn't taken any Lego from his room. Harry's attention was drawn to the groans as they waddled around the room. It was if they were searching for Harry.

He rummaged around the floor. He could feel the edge of indistinguishable objects and shoe boxes. He put his hand on a soft patch before realising it was socks. Harry saw shadows cast on the walls through the cracks in the wardrobe door. The dead knocked a mirror off and then Molly's perfume from her bedside cabinet.

One of them had fallen face first on the bed and couldn't get off. It groaned into the sheet and gnawed at the fabric. Harry had little hope, he would have to wait for rescue or sunset, whichever came first, if rescue was coming.

His senses electrified. Had he dozed off or passed out? Time was missing; it was hunger. The dead shuffled to the closet and clawed at the door. He scuffled further into the closet. His back ached as he slid against a pointed object. They could smell or hear him. Something drawing them to his presence.

Harry pushed what felt like soft squishy socks and pants out of the way. Then his hand met a hard-oblong object. It could be useful. He picked it up. It was rubbery but he couldn't see it in the dark. He squeezed it. It was robust and it would suffice for now.

The wardrobe doors were beginning to open from the dead clawing at them.

Harry stood and banged his head forgetting how small the closet was. He had no time to count how many beasts there were. They were scattered, the one on the bed had struggled over to the window. Harry prepared himself for the escape; it was better than waiting in a closet all night. The dead has given up trying to get into the wardrobe and wandered around the bedroom. Now was his chance for escape.

Harry rammed the wardrobe door open. Then the vibrating began in his hand. Harry held the object up in the moonlight. The beasts made towards him. Harry hit them in the head, but the vibrating rubber wasn't strong as he hoped. He smacked a beast on the head and the rubber bounced off its heads with each hit. They were grabbing for him, four of them clawing for his blood.

He dived for the bedroom door. The undead reached out for him. He turned and booted one, he had no shoes on and his toes crunched. Harry jumped out the bedroom door and landing hallway was clear. He made for the stairs.

Harry tripped down two stairs and took a break figuring out the escape. The front door was wide open, and it was heaving with rain. He looked at the rubber thing in his hand; Molly's vibrator, disgusting. He tossed is back upstairs, it was still vibrating. Harry continued down the stairs. He turned and ran for the kitchen, more dead shambled around the countertops. Harry could outrun them…for now he darted back towards the hallway and out the front door. He saw the carnage unfolding like a scene from a cannibal's orgy.

It was raining, rain that washed away the blood of the neighbours as they yelled for help. He had no coat and would become hypothermic quickly if he didn't find safe shelter.

He didn't know what to do. The dead scrambled along the street. They raided and destroyed the house windows and doors. They attacked everyone and a group was coming for him.

The dead stumbled towards him. Harry's instincts said run but instead he turned to the left where an alley led to the rear garden. He ran to the alley, clear, and ran through to the garden. The dead pursued. Harry saw the trampoline and mounted it. It was about a foot from the house. He could make it, he had to make the jump to the roof.

The dead swarmed round the alley; Harry could see the dead in his kitchen trying to claw their way through the glass doors. He began to bounce, until gaining enough height to jump. Harry leaped mid-air onto the roof tiles, his ribs crunched as he impaled the wet roof. His feet dangled as he scrambled to climb up.

The creatures gathered around attempting to pull his legs, but Harry kicked them off. One of them tried to bite his feet, but he footed its face, cracking its jaw. He pulled himself up onto the roof. It was wet, slippery and risky. He was stranded and exhausted. He carefully manoeuvred across the wet roof to the chimney and wrapped his arm around the stone. Looking around revealed the extent of the outbreak, it had ravaged the street.

Harry waved his free hand at people trying to cram their frightened children into cars. The families were trapped by the hordes and brutally ripped inside out.

Neighbours were bitten and torn apart. Harry watched as they rose back to their feet and joined the ranks of the dead. Corpses invaded gardens and houses and they clawed at the windows of the unaware. Harry saw in the distant streets the spreading fear. The town was being overwhelmed and was in downfall. They were all doomed.

A man began to shout and run through the street. A portion of the horde scrambled after him.

The dead continued to feast on dismembered citizens in the road. Some houses were untouched, the dead waiting outside for the unsuspecting occupants.

Harry could see a car creeping forward. In the back seats two children sat crying. The car was slowed by the dead bodies in the road. It stopped and it was breached by the undead. They smashed their diseased hands through the car windows. The occupants were killed, bitten to death as the beasts piled into the car. Harry saw a man further down the street, he was stood on his porch whacking them with a bat. Harry watched helplessly; he could see a corpse sneaking round the man's garden in the bushes. The man turned as the beast dived him and he lodged a meat tenderiser into its skull.

'Hey, up here!' Harry cried. The man became distracted by Harry's shouting and had to vault across his garden fence to escape them. The courageous neighbour weaved through the crowds, soaring across the road. They were dangerous, but they were slow.

He reached Harry's back garden after batting them out of the way in the alley. The man swung and chopped at the horde in the garden. They fell to the grass but continued to outstretch their arms, clawing at the man.

Harry slid down the roof to help him climb up. The guy was breathless and was wearing his pyjamas. He jumped to the trampoline and pounced onto the roof ledge.

Harry held his weight by placing his bare feet into the damp guttering. He reached for the man who tossed his wooden tenderiser to the roof. Harry squeezed his hands, but he was too heavy. Harry looked into his eyes as he began crying out. They were biting his legs and starting to devour him. Harry saw the beasts bite into the calf muscle, and he heard the bone snap. Blood spurted onto the corpses faces; the dead were loving it. Harry let go, his hands shaking. Harry picked up the meat tenderiser. Immediately he retreated up the wet roof to the chimney. It was increasingly cold, and it heaved with rain.

He watched the beasts tear the man's thigh apart. The man began to groan as he lay bleeding on the grass. He rose to his undead feet. His eyes opaque black. The leg muscles like straw as the corpse limped to join the others.

***

Dean had managed to run down into the garage where he changed into his day clothes.

He had a spare pistol stored in the garage with old tools, hammers he'd once used for his car, and a clip of ammunition.

The dead had swamped the house when Dean was sleeping. They attacked the garage door, he was stuck, no heater.

Dean holstered his gun in his pants and searched for his spare walkie talkie radio. He had to get through to the station and call for backup. He had to warn any patrols, if they were still alive, that they need to deploy now, no exceptions.

The church was a few houses away. It should be secure enough. The church had large wooden doors that could be fortified, and stone walls made it weatherproof. It should have a radio to. There was no time to drive it, it'd be quicker running. He couldn't drive, the dead would clog the road and block him and then tear him to pieces. Dean gave up trying to find his radio, he gazed at the garage walls and his car. Life as he knew it was gone.

Dean walked to the garage doors and prepared to push the garage door button on the wall. The garage lights hummed. The dead groaned; their undead nails scraped along the metal door. Dean thumbed the button. The aluminium door jolted and slowly lifted open. Dean equipped his pistol and cocked it.

He aimed at the feet that appeared in the rain. The garage door rose higher, the dead were preventing it from opening, then it finally lifted knocking the beasts down.

He shot a round off, a headshot, the corpse fell face first into the concrete drive. Dean fired, the surrounding dead fell and tripped a few others. The rain was washing the blood down into street drains. About six dead neighbours began to close in and Dean dashed for the road. His heart thumped and his fingers pulsed on the trigger. They were slow and gormless, but Dean didn't want to wait to find out if he could take them all on. He weaved through the attackers down the road. He had run out of ammo and had to tuck the gun back in his pants. He sprinted to the church.

The dead were scattered all over the street, slow but aggressive. They were breaking into house windows and front doors. Those who hadn't bothered to lock their doors were probably dead. Dean hadn't locked his, and in hindsight it was foolish.

As he ran his lungs burned and the humidity stuck to his neck like bee nectar. Survivors were piling into the church; he could see people pushing each other out of the way to get inside. Dean slowed to a jog; the dead pursued from all sides. Dean reached the church, the hanging lights beaming through into the dark street. Faces of fear and confusion looked to him. He began to push to the doors to get inside. The crowd was fierce. Behind, the dead were approaching. The panicked neighbours slipped on the cobblestone path as they ran inside. Dean slipped in along with four others. The masses gathered on the benches and the ceiling lights illuminated a sea of pyjamas and fear. Kids cried. Dean prepared to shut the doors and stood next to them; bloody black-eyed faces shambled towards the church.

'Get inside, come on,' Dean yelled as two more survivors ran inside, their dressing gowns drenched. They fell to the floor as they entered, the woman whimpered, her husband comforted her. Dean waited for survivors, two more were running through the street naked, the dead grabbed and circled them.

A woman shouted, 'close the doors.' A wave of people rushed towards Dean to close the doors. At least ten survivors pushed the doors shut. Hands soon clawed on the thick wood.

'Lock it,' a man shouted into Dean's ear. Dean shunted the man aside. Another man picked up a wooden beam and carried it to the door. Dean placed the wooden beam over the steel holders. It was secure, for now.

Survivors sat on benches panting and crying, parents tried to comfort and calm their screaming kids. The response had been worse than Dean anticipated. Things could turn barbaric. The government had failed to respond to the threat in time. Wherever it started and whatever caused it was old news. It was a new world now and Dean felt it resonate within, an horrific apocalypse. Safety was out there, not in London, but somewhere. Throughout history countries had fought and come together to help one another, this was no exception. Dean was certain a resolution would be found.

The hall was bickering unintelligibly. Dean looked around the church, the walls and windows reached at least thirty feet and there was scaffolding up near the organs. Dean felt for his pistol and was relieved it was still in his pants. Relieved that others had the same idea to come to the church. It was safety. The scaffolding reached towards the top stained-glass windows with a stack of metal poles and planks leading up to the bell tower, which was about thirty feet above the vicar's stage.

This was how people lived before this, it was no surprise that they now returned seeking solitude and comfort, answers and salvation from a place that once brought them peace. Dean remembered that he too felt the peace a long time ago. Not as a true Christian, but as a believer in a higher authority. That changed now. The beasts outside rising after being attacked, that was not peace.

Most survivors wore pyjamas and dressing gowns. A few were fully dressed. They sought rest on the wooden benches. Dean scanned the hall for a fellow officer. Nothing, no backup. It was time to take charge and lead these scared survivors to a comfortable mindset. Evacuation to a more secure site was improbable. The dead banged faintly on the doors. The worried cries and bickering had quietened.

Dean spotted the priest or vicar, he wasn't sure what the official title was, coming from a back room to the left. The priest always lived in the church; it was a requirement of the job. The priest was dressed in a black top and jogging bottoms. He was frail, his face thin with strands of grey hair. Dean walked through the crowd of survivors, kids were sleeping on the benches and men and women huddled and prayed. Nobody noticed the priest; they were too occupied. A handful of kids played tag and had forgot what they just saw, or perhaps didn't want to remember.

'What is this?' the priest asked as Dean stepped towards him. Dean gestured to people with waterfall tears flooding their nightgowns. Some kids now sat on their mum or dad's laps, others cried, asking for food or bed.

'A nightmare is what this is,' Dean said. 'I'm afraid we'll need the church for safety until we can find refuge for these people.'

'Why, what's happened?' the priest enquired. A woman stepped out of the back room towards them. Her eyes bagged and she rubbed them. Dean saw the wedding rings on their fingers. She stood and held her husband's arm. They were easy on the eyes.

'I'm afraid there's been a dangerous epidemic. I can't explain because I don't know all the facts. These people have been forced from their homes and need shelter.' Dean scanned the room of survivors, at least twenty. He saw someone who worked at the station offices, no frontline.

The priest comforted his wife. They held each other. She kissed her husband on the cheek and walked off to the children playing on the front row of benches. Their parents tried to smile. She knelt next to them and assured them they could stay for a sleepover.

'We have sheltered the homeless in the past and we will shelter these people. This is a house of the lord and all are welcome. We have food supplies and bunk beds in the basement, in case of hurricanes and earthquakes. It's secure and warmer than this hall,' the priest said.

Dean was relieved. He thought he'd be stuck trying to calm the crowd down. At least there was food and beds, something to keep them quiet until he could figure out what to do.

'We need to keep those front doors closed at all times. The threat is high. Do not open them for any reason. I assume you have an emergency radio as well?' Dean replied, folding his arms.

'We do, it's in my study,' the priest said. 'We had to move it because we couldn't plug it in downstairs.' The priest began to walk to the back room. Dean looked around.

'Hold on,' Dean said, the priest walked back to Dean and leant on his pedestal. People rested on benches or the floor. A small group huddled in the middle walkway. Cuddling each other.

Rain pattered on the stain-glass windows. The hall lights flickered.

'Okay listen up. It seems our officers have been unable to contain the threat. So, from now on everyone stays here until I've established had bad the situation is.' Dean halted; a crack of lightning whipped through the sky; the windows flashed. Kids snuggled closer to their parents and one man fell to the bench in shock. Lightning lit the church. Dean knew it was a matter of time before the power cut out. He looked to the priest. 'Do you have a generator?'

Thunder boomed through the hall, lightning flashed, and the wind and rain lashed against the windows. The dead pounded relentlessly against the doors. Wind howled through the hall. Dean felt the floor rumble beneath his feet.

'Err, I think so…ah yes, I remember they installed one last Easter because we were having electrical shortages.' Brilliant Dean thought, a lifesaver too good to be true. The church was a sanctuary.

'Brilliant,' Dean muttered. 'Okay this place has food, beds and electric, so you are all going to be staying here until proper accommodation can be established. Try not to worry. Please understand that this situation is unlike anything we've dealt with before, it's new and it's intimidating, I get it. But please be patient.' Dean turned and began to walk to the back room.

'There eating people, what the hell is this?' Dean turned to face the woman. She stood gazing harshly, her retinas piercing Dean.

'That's why we need to stay calm and not frighten our children anymore by shouting things like that. Everyone rest and try to sleep, don't worry,' Dean replied.

Sleet hailed down on the windows like popcorn in the microwave. Thunder rumbled overhead, it drowned out the moans of the undead.

'This is stupid, is this what the curfew was supposed to be stopping. Useless town hall,' a man yelled. Dean tried to walk away but the abuse continued, and the shouting got louder. Dean felt halted.

The thunder and shouting rattled the building, the scaffolding shook. Dean heard the metal clang. Thunder and lightning were coming constantly alternating.

The priest leant on his pulpit. A figure of Jesus was hung to the back wall bearing his look upon the church.

The scaffolding swayed. Dean heard the planks crack but without notice the scaffold fractured around the bell tower. Thunder shook the building and a lightning bolt shot through the top stained-glass window striking the bell.

'Move,' Dean cried, diving out of the way. The bell jolted from its hook and came crashing through the scaffold tower, the planks splintering as the bell smashed down onto the priest. The priest was crushed. It wasn't over. Planks fell and poles clanged to the ground. Survivors scattered to the sides of the hall.

Dean saw the priest legs visible from one side of the bell. Amputated, trailing blood and shattered bone. A metal pole bounced from the stone floor and speared through the air, striking a man in the face, impaling and pinning him against the stone wall. His body slumped unable to fall flat. The pole scraped down the wall to the floor and his head slid down the pole until it hit the floor. The pole held upright by his skull.

Dean gagged. People screamed and hid under benches. The thunderstorm was in full swing. The scaffolding dropped a few more planks near the bell.

The priest's wife ran to the bell and got on her hands and knees sobbing intensely.

Dean couldn't tolerate it and he walked to the back room. The distressing cries was too intense, headache inducing. He stepped in and closed the door from which the now deceased priest came from and locked it.

CHAPTER 18

Liar

Harry spotted the little boy in the window of the house on the other side of the street. At first, he felt empathetic and then angry that he couldn't find James.

Harry saw the child alone and afraid. But he didn't feel the hero in him now.

Harry realised he might have to get to the child and save him if his parents were dead. He couldn't leave him, it wasn't human. Surviving the thunderstorm wasn't human; Harry was lucky to be alive, if the lightning had struck him, he would be dead. The rain was pounding down, but the thunderstorm had settled.

The child could barely see over the window frame. Harry had his sights on the boy.

If he dwelled on the infinite possibilities of where Molly was, he would freeze to death, zoned out in anger. He'd end up hurting Molly if he did find her. Hospital? Harry gripped the chimney harder and stone chipped off and slid down the roof. She could have found shelter in a broom closet; she could have taken James home. She had vanished and taken their son with her; it was selfish. The dead broke Harry's train of thought.

The corpses continued attempting to climb up to the roof. One corpse accidentally pulled the guttering onto itself. Harry turned his attention back to the child. The street was swarming with diseased dead.

The child had disappeared from sight. The garden was infested with the undead. The door was shut but the downstairs windows were broken, and zombies clambered through the window. That's what they were; zombies. Harry didn't want to believe it but there was no other word to describe them anymore.

Harry scanned the road and tried to plan a route through the zombies. Mr Brown wandered in the middle of the road wearing green joggers, his fat belly exposed and torn, intestines trailed behind him. Harry heard a cry; it could be the child. Harry wanted to get there and save the kid; it was a stupid shot at redemption for losing his own child.

Panic spread across his chest; his glutes tightened. He struggled to breath in the humid air. He let go of the chimney and slid down the roof to the front garden, scraping his ribs along the tiles. He landed on the concrete and jumped to his bare feet.

The zombies were hidden beneath the roof out of sight and latched onto him, Harry punched them away and his knuckles cracked. Harry went primal and twisted one's neck until it snapped. Harry felt no fear. The adrenaline kicked in and his skin tingled. He kicked three of them back and shook them off. His hands pulsed and his legs cramped.

Harry ran from the house into the road swerving past Mr Brown. More zombies tried to grab him and missed. Harry was fast approaching the neighbour's house and he lunged onto the garden path. On final leg to touchdown, Harry kicked open the front door, it smashed against the wall and a shard of glass shot into Harry's hand. He pushed the door shut and hopped up the staircase. The kid was crying.

'Help me mummy,' the kid screamed. Harry encountered the neighbour at the top of the stairs coming out from the bathroom. She was dead, her eyes black pus. Miss Penny tried to bite Harry. She had been kind towards him and his family. She must have forgot because she grappled Harry's shoulders trying to eat his face.

Her overweight boyfriend exited from a bedroom to the left. He was a zombie and clawed at Harry who stepped out of the way and the man fell down the staircase.

A bookshelf was behind Harry and he grabbed the thickest hardback and smashed Miss Penny's face until the teeth caved in and she fell dead to the bathroom floor. Harry turned, the boyfriend was laying dead at the bottom of the stairs and the kid cried from a room to Harry's left. Harry opened the door and stepped in. He had to stop his hand bleeding. It was warmer in this house and Harry was glad he came to help.

The boy stood in a puddle of urine clutching a teddy bear. He wore frog pattern pyjamas. 'I'm her to help,' Harry said, closing the bedroom door and getting closer to the child. People would judge Harry, no doubt about it because he was in a neighbour's house trying to help a kid he only briefly knew after James had him over for tea a couple of times.

It would have been nice if the neighbourhood wasn't so reclusive. The days of Beach Town barbeques and picnics were long gone.

The kid screamed. Sweet mother, Harry thought. He attempted to pat the kids shoulder but the boy was afraid and stepped back. The kid stopped crying and bit the arm of the teddy in comfort. Harry then recognised the teddy bear. It was James's, and he always had it with him. Harry checked the tag, it read James Carrington. Hallelujah. Harry smiled; this was a successful rescue mission. A teddy was better than nothing.

'Where did you get that?' he asked. The kid pointed to the wardrobe behind him. Harry's heart sank. Could it be that James was already dead in the wardrobe, or had James given him the teddy bear? Harry walked towards the wardrobe.

There was a shuffling in the closet. Harry dropped to his knees. A tear trickled down his cheek. The pain in his hand subsided. There was no noise. Harry braced himself and opened the wardrobe doors.

The wooden doors slid open and a little boy jumped out. Harry grabbed James as hard as he could and sobbed into James's shoulders. It was his son, alive in the neighbour's house. It was a miracle, a true miracle.

James held a kitten and it sniffed Harry. Harry let go and kept hold of James's hand, he wouldn't let go of him again.

The dead banged on the front door. A car screeched followed by a metallic bang and a flash of light pulsed through the window to Harry's right.

'James?' Harry asked. He hugged James again, it reminded him of the day he was born. He would never let him out of his sight again. Little James pushed his dad back and stroked the kitten's head.

'Careful you'll hurt the kitten,' James said. The kitten was cute fresh with glistening eyes and groomed brown fur. Harry wept tears of joy. James had found life and happiness in all this death. James was young and appeared unfazed by the reality of the situation.

'James, where is mummy?' Harry asked. He had forgotten about his hand bleeding and grabbed the bed sheet to clean the blood. He picked James up and placed him on the mattress.

The other boy was distant, and he fondled with the pillows. James held both palms up with his lower lips extended, he didn't know. Molly had been selfish leaving James here. Harry squeezed his hand, the stinging wound stopped bleeding. A white light of satisfaction grew inside that his genes, flesh and blood was alive.

'Where did you see her last?' Harry asked. He was interrogating his own son over his mother's incompetence. The marriage had gotten a bit worse over the last year, but to abandon James, that was petty. Unless she did him the favour of topping herself, he wanted to feel her beg for life in that moment. That WAS THE RAGE again. He took a deep breath and sat on the bed next to James. His buttocks sank into the star covered quilt.

Little James held a finger to his lips, using every bit of strength that he had to figure out where mummy was.

'She went to grandpa's,' James cheered, smiling in victory. Harry felt like everyone was against him now. His son abandoned amid an epidemic. Was she at the hospital before or after he was? When he finds out they better answer for this.

The only things that mattered now were the kid's lives and finding secure shelter. The church was a street away and the fire station adjacent.

Once he visited the fire station for fire extinguisher training for his workplace. The station housed a padlocked room containing emergency supplies for earthquakes, but so did the church. It was difficult to conclude. The other option was the police station. The three of them couldn't stay huddled in the cupboard all night. It felt strange caring for a stranger's child. The child was Harry's responsibility now and he would protect both children.

The dead had broken into the house and shambled upstairs. They clawed at the bedroom door. Harry had locked it and returned to the window. He counted thirty zombies wandering the street. To the left on a dresser, a note caught his eye.

It had Harry's name on it. Harry picked it up. The reverse side read: "Miss Penny for Harry Carrington". The note was a red flag. Harry examined the note before opening it, the paper was dog eared and stained. The town was a cake, and this note the icing. Harry opened and read the letter. His heart fluttered. Harry could see the dead invading his porchway.

He tried to let the words sink in. Obviously, the neighbours had slept in the spare room and let the boys share. Why not take James to her dads? Why not let Harry take care of James rather than fobbing him off with the neighbours? Molly's dad lived so far North he might as well live in the sea.

Miss Penny had a profound drinking habit as evidenced by the empty bottle of vodka in the trash can next to the dresser. The bloke, Harry wasn't sure of, but a stranger and probably not police vetted. The note had read a solemnly goodbye, akin to a suicide, but Harry would have preferred her death to this;

For Harry,

I have been with you now for some time, and every day I remember when we got on the road and began our journey into love. That was then, and this is now. Things change, and people change. All I can think of is James and so I've had to break our hearts as they beat as one. They used to be one and now they are nothing, you don't feel the same and I don't either. We cannot pretend forever, even for James sake.

You'll probably wonder why I didn't tell you to your face, but it isn't like that. I wanted to, and I was GOING to. When I told you, James was at the hospital, it was a minor cut that needed stiches, and that was when I wanted to do it, so that you could take James home and be angry as you should be. So that I could have some time to get over it too. I am angry as I write this, because I couldn't do it and I felt ashamed afterwards. So, I left James in the care of our neighbours, Margaret Penny and her boyfriend Henry. After I said my goodbye and wrote this, I departed town and made for my mother's house, where I will be staying until you come to terms with this. By the time you get this letter, you can forget about trying to amend anything, and to just move on.

I know about you and Sheila, and how your life would be better with her and Wendy sucking on your dick, you can have that now, so enjoy it. I won't leave this letter bitter because I have too much self-respect. I'll have to go to a solicitor about the custody of James so make the most now while you still have access.

I was always faithful, loyal and caring and loving and you threw it back at me and I've had enough.

Molly x

The letter ended with a dark kiss, the real heartbreaker of it all. Perhaps being eaten was the only redemption left in this sin ridden world.

Her mother lives near the docks on the North West part of the island. Like her father, it was at least ten miles out. There is a road that leads off from the beachfront to the Northern part of the island. It is rarely used as the dock's community is self-sufficient and receive goods from freight ships. The entirety of the Northern community could be safe.

James and the shy kid were playing with the kitten on the bed. Harry was zoned out. The dead on the landing had quietened, they didn't scratch at the door.

What he couldn't understand was why she would lie about James. That grinded him. He massaged his cheeks. If she had told him it was easily remedied, he could have avoided the hospital and avoided having his back impaled and bruised by Charlie. He could have avoided the dreary hours in that doctor's office saving lives. Oh boy, she better have a good solicitor, because there was only one way this could go, his way.

Harry walked to the bed. 'Kid, what's your name?' Moonlight shone onto Harry's face; tears streaked his cheeks. The corners of his mouth were dry. The boy looked in awe. He smelt of urine and needed some new clothes, but Harry didn't know where the clothes were. He didn't know if this was Miss Penny's son or someone else she looked after.

'Sam,' he said. Sam cried the mucous in his eyes dry. That was something they all needed, water. Harry reached for James, lifted his shirt and examined the bandage on his shoulder. The bandage was well covered, it shouldn't be a problem. The pyjamas could be a problem if the rain didn't let up. They were silk black long sleeves, a size too big. The neighbours must have given him them. Another point for the lawyers, Molly couldn't be bothered to bring fresh clothes before leaving.

'Nice to meet you Sam,' Harry smiled reluctantly. He was drained. He used tampons left on the table to wrap around his hand.

They had to evacuate off the island. There had been no news of any government safe zones or quarantine zones on the radio.

The church was the safer option with its big doors and high windows. It was a haven during earthquakes. An earthquake had struck a few months ago, it was big enough to destroy the church gates and dislodge the bricks around the bell tower. If one happened now it would be a blessing. The earthquake would knock the dead over and give them a chance to escape. *God, if you are listening, send me, James and Sam an earthquake.* Harry felt selfish for meddling with such thoughts. *Wait no, don't do that, just help us.*

His thoughts were out of focus, he was dumbfounded, why say a prayer to god? Harry didn't believe in him. Only when his family were gone did he truly want to believe. It was faith or adrenaline or a primal thing. Yes, a primal urge for survival integrated in his DNA.

Deciding where to escape to weighed on Harry's mind. It was more difficult than deciding whether to buy Coke or Diet Coke. It was more difficult than deciding whether he should watch another episode of a tv program, than tea or coffee, than bare or bareback.

He had to let the children of tomorrow, future leaders, start to choose. Because eventually they'll have to decide the fate of their own family's lives.

'Kids let's play a game. James, let the kitten go,' Harry said. James released the kitten and it skirted under the bed and peeked out. Harry knelt on the floor beside the bed. The dead in the house had returned to the bedroom door. Time was short. Both kids sat on the edge of the bed in awe. Sam urgently needed clean trousers, otherwise he'd end up with a rash from the urine.

'Church or fire station?' Harry asked. They looked at each other and giggled. Sam was becoming more open with Harry and was acting normally. Harry was unsure how to deal with a kid with learning disabilities. He had nothing against them, but he knew they could be difficult to manage. James held his hand up to Harry. Harry jumped.

One of the dead had fallen down the staircase. Waves of groans carried through the street. It was unnerving.

'James, go ahead.'

'Fire, fire struck,' James said, bearing a wide grin. One of his teeth was stained. *Sam please concur.*

'Sam.' Sam shuffled closer to James. The kitten happily bounced around Harry's legs and then pounced to the bed and clawed at the string on their pyjama bottoms. 'Your turn.' Sam shook his head. Please answer kid your life may depend on it.

He felt sorry for Sam. Why was he so shy? Were his parents abusive? Who the heck were his parents?

Harry was thinking when a stone hit the window. He quickly walked to the window and a face popped up and startled him. The kids jumped back. Little James slid onto the floor and under the bed with the kitten meowing as he followed. Sam did the same.

The lady was pale and young. She must have climbed the gutter to the window frame. Harry pushed the window open, after assessing her on his life scale, she was alive.

The young girl rolled through the window. Her clothes and backpack wet as she rustled onto the floor. Harry looked outside, a group of undead eyes gazed back, they had gathered around the front garden. He shut the window.

The weather had deteriorated to post thunderstorm rain. It wasn't unusual for the island.

The girl panted and lay on the carpet. Harry knelt next to her patted her shoulder. She didn't mind. She rubbed her ribs; it was probably bruising from the window frame because Harry couldn't see blood.

'Fire station,' Sam shouted peering from under the bed. James and the kitten shuffled out from under the bed frame, the quilt hung over them. Harry heard and nodded to Sam with a relief grin. That was a load off. No more decisions until rescue arrived.

The lady was dressed in cross country hiking gear with a small backpack. Her boots looked new. She had her eyes shut and took slow breaths.

'Where did you come from?' Harry asked. He looked into her thick hazel eyes, her skin was velvet, youthful. It was a vulnerable time for Harry. He wondered if it was safe to be around a female. Even with the dead roaming the streets, Harry wanted to lock the kids in the closet and fuck the lasses brains out. Maybe even use Molly's sex toy on her for revenge. The fantasy was becoming too real and Harry refocused.

'I live next door and I heard a kid screaming. I had to help. Have you seen what's going on outside?' she said smiling. Harry returned the smile. He had seen this from the start, the motorway and the hospital. He admired her courage and patted her again in appreciation.

She shot him down with a stern look that said don't look at me like that. He stepped back to the bed, mindful not to stand on the kids or kitten. She stood up unsteadily. She was fit and his height. Her breasts were plump and…Harry refocused.

'We're heading to the fire station,' Harry said. 'We've voted and it's the safest place for us. I saw this days ago at the hospital before the police and the town hall covered it up. They can't control this it's everywhere. Not just in Beach Town. It's London and Europe, they're falling to the undead.'

She sat on the side of the bed and unclipped the backpack and placed it down. Sam had crawled out from under the bed and retreated to the closet.

The dead weren't banging on the bedroom door anymore.

'You voted with children? The fire station isn't safe,' she said. 'The church or the police station will be. If this is an international crisis what can we do? she said. Harry didn't have a response formulated. She crossed her arms. Twenties, no wrinkles or decayed teeth yet.

'It's the plan and it's final, you can join us or stay here and wait for rescue,' Harry said, she blushed. 'How come I've never seen you if you live on this street?'

The kitten bounced around her feet, playing with strands of cotton from the bed sheet. She looked down at it pitifully. He could see her holding onto an invisible coil of sanity.

'If you think so, I'm with you.' Harry was surprised. Two was company and three a crowd. A crowd that he felt obligated to protect, a group he didn't want to get killed.

'Good, how can we get to the fire station? he asked. He hadn't a clue how they were all going to sneak through back gardens.

She slipped off the bed and walked over to the window. She pointed and Harry walked over to look. She pointed towards the silver Toyota Yaris outside.

'That's mine,' she said. 'I have the keys. We can use it.'

'We can't drive through them,' Harry said. His hand stung and he clenched the wound.

'I've got a windup car that makes noise, when I wind it up and throw it they follow it. That was at home. If I throw it away from the house, we can get to the car and escape.'

'Fool proof,' Harry said. It was ridiculously simple, Harry hoped it worked.

'You want my help? I can't sleep here with them things trying to get in and you and two kids I don't know,' she said.

'We do it and we have a chance to survive till the sun rises.' She was firm, the children watched in amazement. James probably wondered why a strange lady was telling his daddy what to do. Molly never did. Maybe that was one of the problem with the marriage, Harry had been too hard on her.

'Let's get ready,' Harry told her and returned to the bed. First things first, change Sam's clothes, there had to be something they could wear lying about.

Fear might stop Harry on his journey, 'kids, get ready for a game.'

That's what it was for them now, a game of hide and seek, of run or die For Harry, a horror game.

CHAPTER 19

The Plan

The strange woman who struggled in the window hadn't introduced herself yet. She hadn't shown caring love to the children either or taken a liking to the kitten. Every time the kitten meowed she shoved it away with her foot and it would be jumping and scratching at loose fabric or anything it could get its paws on.

Poor James looked depressed. Sam, whoever's kid he was, he didn't look like miss Penny, but he did have the crooked nose of Henry, looked down in the dumps.

Harry had no idea if taking the kitten would get them all killed. To break the news to James that he couldn't take it would break his heart. Harry hadn't seen him bond with an animal before. He should have bought a kitten for James to grow up with. Kids with pets appeared robust and mind strong, leaders by the age of ten and in government by twenty, according to the 'benefits of animals on humans', a study he read a while back. The kitten could stay if James held him close. Harry would have to find a bag to put the cat in. He was carrying James out of there himself. Sam too.

Harry had managed to find some spare clothes for the kids, and he let the girl change Sam whilst he changed James. He found them in the corner in a bag. Molly had brought spare clothes and shoes, but it didn't get her off easily.

The woman rooted through her bag and pulled out the wind-up car she mentioned. The kids waited to be picked up. Harry was ready. He had put the kitten in the bag the clothes were in. He secretly named the kitten *cinnamon,* after his favourite cake topping. What he wouldn't give for a few cinnamon biscuits dipped in hot cacao and steaming with whipped cream. Perfect weather for it too. Wrap up warm with James and Molly on the sofa and watch a movie. Complain ab…. his thought was interrupted.

'Ready, let's go,' she said standing at the bedroom door. She had her backpack on, the toy in one hand and the door handle in the other. Harry looked around the bedroom. Nothing important left. He picked James up who held the bag tight and then Sam who was a little heavier, his shoulders tensed under them. His hand wound stung.

It sounded like a lone zombie roamed the landing. He had left the note from Molly. He dumped the note into the trash after reading it. He was glad to see the crumpled words go where they belonged.

'Shut your eyes kids,' Harry said. 'James keep hold of that cat and don't let go. If you let go we can't go back for him.' James sighed in agreement and they closed their eyes. The adrenaline coursed through his body. He was a warrior, there was no danger.

'What's your name? I don't want to do this not knowing who helped me save my son,' he asked. She looked into his eyes but remained silent. She turned the door handle and opened the door. The zombie dived in for her and she booted it back. The beast stumbled backwards through the banister before crashing down the staircase. It was dark and the house eerie.

The kids cried. The kitten meowed. The danger was real.

'Keep your eyes closed,' James told the kitten. Harry waited for the girl to lead the way.

She took the lead down the landing and the staircase. There was no light and it sounded clear. Harry was close behind. If she turned around he'd be hit accidentally. She wound up the toy car and approached the front door. She looked back to Harry and nodded before opening the front door. Two large zombies waited at the porch; she tossed the toy far into the darkness. Moments passed before it rang out.

Sam cried. Harry couldn't help, his hands were tied.

She shunted the dead back and they turned and headed for the ringing toy. Harry saw the street of the undead surrounding the toy car. She led them into the night and down the garden to the pavement.

An explosion rippled through the street; flames erupted from Harry's next-door neighbour. Flames extended to the electric lines and the streetlamps went out. The house began to crumble, the roof caved in and the zombies nearest set alight.

Shambling corpses vanished into the dark. The moon was obscured by clouds.

Harry looked to the car; she was already opening the doors, but more dead wandered their way.

A man ran out from the burning building, he was on fire and screamed before running into the dead and disappearing into the black road. Harry didn't see them eat him and he didn't want to.

She kicked a zombie back and shoved her backpack in the car.

Harry walked to the car. He was grabbed from behind and he dropped the kids. James dropped the kitten.

If Harry was to die like this he had to give the kid something to love after he's gone. Harry tossed the terrorised kitten to his son. The woman ran to the kids as Harry fought off the beast. She took them to the car and locked them inside.

The dead swarmed Harry and encircled him. He couldn't fight them all off bare handed. One scratched his thigh, Harry heard a chattering mouth and watched as a crawling zombie bit into his calf. The girl appeared like superwoman and booted the zombies back.

Harry could feel the heat from the house fire. He fell to the floor.

Harry came to, his mind whirly and disorientated.

She shoved the zombies back. The toy was no longer ringing, and Harry saw shadows approaching from all directions. It was like a nightmare, she was the saviour, an angel.

The world was sharp contrast and time froze. Harry looked to James who watched from the car window. James was safe, Harry could die now.

Harry felt the wound bleeding. Inner flesh was exposed. The zombies ignored him and tried to claw at the girl. He crawled along the wet pavement towards the car. The gravel stung his hand wound.

Harry opened the car door and pulled himself into the driver's seat. The kids were distraught. He closed the door; the keys were on the passenger seat. In the side mirror Harry saw smouldering corpses falling from the windows of the burning house.

The dead hadn't followed him. They hadn't attempted to enter the car. It was harsh but the children were more important. Not a nameless woman. Harry grabbed the keys and start the car. Blood pooled around the pedals. Harry's head was fuzzy.

Harry regained consciousness again. The girl jumped in the passenger seat; blood splattered over her dark green waterproof coat.

He was losing blood too fast. Something dark and inhuman was happening in the world. Harry didn't know why he wanted to leave her; he just did.

Harry hit the accelerator and the car moved slowly down the road. The closer to the junction they got the less zombies there were. Harry turned left, the pavements crawling with the undead. They passed the first street on the left; they passed the church and zombies were attempting to get in the doors. Harry clicked the fog lights on. The fire station was in the distance on the right surrounded by fields. Lights were on inside. Harry increased speed and drove around two zombies in the road.

The mysterious young woman wasn't talkative. The kids checked on the kitten.

Harry saw the fire station on the right and pulled the car into the car park, there was one car parked up. The station entrance was clear. In the rear-view Harry watched the night carnage. Zombies were unaware of them.

He panicked; the disease could take him any minute. It wasn't safe to be around the kids.

'Let's get inside quickly,' she said. She got out and got the kids out. Harry turned the car off and pocketed the keys before limping from the driver's seat to the concrete.

They had little time to discuss anything. The pain was like bee stings. He limped to the station entrance, a big sign above the door read: Beach Town Fire Department. They were waiting in the entrance. An empty receptionist desk, waiting seats and an empty water fountain were the only things there. There were two doors, one behind the desk and one to the right. The floor was shining, the janitor must have been here as recently as last night. The stone walls were decorated with health and safety signs and pictures of Beach Town and fire chiefs. A gold-plated plaque was placed above the doorway behind the desk. It read: changing room.

Harry saw no other option; his leg was becoming heavier by the minute. The other door to the right had a glass window and Harry could see it led to the fire truck bay. There was one fire truck and it was on mounts with paint cans scattered around it along with cleaning canisters.

'To the changing room,' Harry said. He limply led the way through the door. The girl pulled James and Sam along. She was rough.

The door led to a long narrow corridor with rooms on either side. They walked down the hallway, Harry looking for the changing room. At the end of the corridor was a door to the staircase.

'Wait, here,' the girl said. Her brunette hair swayed around her shoulders. Harry saw a tattoo of a lily pad on her neck.

She opened a door to the right. Harry had missed it. James stayed close to Harry and Sam leapt forward to the girl. She took Sam's hand to Harry's surprise.

This was surreal. She looked in the room and without hesitation flicked the wall light on. She had good instincts. Harry closed the door behind them.

The room was small. Two bunkbeds were placed against the far wall. They were neatly made, and Harry could smell the detergent. There was a sink with a mirror above it in the left corner. But no toilet. It made sense to keep the latrines and showers separate. They didn't want to see or smell that while sleeping.

Harry walked to the bunkbed, he had to lay down. The itching wound was unbearable hot. The room was spinning. It had to be mild shock; the infection couldn't have taken hold that quick. He rolled onto the bottom bunk bed.

'You need to get out, or get rid of your leg,' she said. She dropped her bag on the floor. Harry's worries were just beginning. She knelt, unzipped the bag and pulled out a seven-inch carving knife. Harry gulped. James and Sam were preoccupied with the kitten.

She approached the bed and he held his arms up.

Moments or hours could have passed when he woke up. The bitten leg was no longer in pain, it was agonisingly tight as if someone had wrapped a compressor around it and sucked the air out. Harry's forearms bulged as he grabbed at his calf.

James and Sam were nowhere to be seen. Good god what had she done to them. The girl knelt looking at Harry. The bloodied blade on the floor.

'What have you done, where are the kids? Nothing made sense. Fire station was all he recalled and everything else literally shimmered. She was moving her lips. Her hands planted firmly on his shoulder now. She looked very graceful. Sound popped back into his ears.

'I saw them die and turn after being bitten,' she said, looking at the wound. Harry could feel a sheet bandaged around his calf; it was tight. 'I've had to use the spare bed sheet, there was one under the bunk. I've got painkillers, there should be more in the station somewhere. Don't worry,' she comforted his shoulder, but he shook it off and pushed her away. *Whatever she's done, she's going to get it.*

Whatever had happened at the hospital was behind him. Charlie was a no-shit-kind-of-guy. Charlie would have her by the throat. But not Harry. He wouldn't and couldn't, it wasn't in him.

He tried to move his leg, but it was stiff. 'Painkillers now,' he said. 'Right now. What did you do?' he asked but she didn't answer. She just pulled a small brown screw cap bottle from her bag along with a flask. Harry took it immediately and drank. The cool water flushed his throat. She snatched it back.

'Save that, it could be the last fresh water in town. Just take two of these,' she said. She placed two large red and white multicolour capsules into his palm which he willingly threw back in his throat. He was about to swallow dry when he realised the pills could be anything. Poison, ecstasy, painkillers so strong he would overdose. Before he could panic and protest she pushed the bottle on his lips, and he swigged them. It's too late now. He needed to trust her more and stop worrying about mundane things.

The painkillers were fast acting and kicked in moments later, placebo effect and a good one. An empty stomach and little water didn't help.

The girl walked to the door and opened it, James and Sam stepped in with the kitten. Harry was angered she left them outside, but it was for their safety. She walked back to Harry looking down at him.

'I cut away the bite wound so you won't be able to walk properly for a while. Maybe a few hours or days, I'm not sure.

I've never done this before,' she said. She grabbed her bag and sat on the bunk parallel to Harry. Harry heard her unzip the bag and gathered the mental energy to lift himself up. He leant on the back wall. He could see her writing in a notepad. Her pen had a pink feather on the end. The kids played in the corner next to the sink.

The room was dazzlingly bright. Harry had a bout of vertigo. He leaned over the bunk to check the wound. She had wrapped and knotted it extremely tight. But it covered the mess he didn't want to see. Whoever she was, she was smart. She had cut away the infection, she had saved him, but Harry had a suspicion something inhuman lurked within her. She continually kicked the kitten away and the way she dragged the kids in the building earlier was uncalled for. She could have carried them or told them to run.

There was little chance of getting to the North of the island and zero chance of escaping via the motorway bridge. The town was overrun, the city was overrun, and London was falling. The fire station would suffice for now.

'Do you think I would have become one of those creatures,' he said. She was lost in her notepad and then he added, 'do you?'

'I was up reading when they invaded the street, I tried calling the police but there was no answer,' she said. Typical crisis response. Harry knew cutting the phone signals was ridiculous, there was no way they were planning to help people after disconnecting them. The government could have at least left the WIFI on, but nothing. It could only mean one thing. The news was correct, and London and Europe were falling to the dead. Harry wasn't sure about the rest of the world, but he prayed United Nations or NATO would get involved and save them all.

Considering how quick the superpowers are at responding, the fact they hadn't was terrifying, this could be global. 'Yes, I do.'

She flicked through the pages of her notebook. It had a brown leather cover and sealed with a magnet lock that popped over the edge.

'How did you know that cutting the bite would help?' Harry asked. She shrugged. She rustled her hair with her hand. Her locks swaying. She unbuttoned the top of her jacket and it revealed a blue shirt.

After reading the letter from Molly he had no time to process his feelings. The attraction to the girl was uncanny. Was it the lack of sex? He remembered all the sleepless nights and early awakenings where nothing occurred. How long had that gone on for? Years.

'I was on the motorway a few days ago, I think that's when this thing started,' she said. 'They died and came back. The dead people came back to life and attacked the living, they bit them and then they rose and then it happened all over again and again and again…' she burst into tears and wiped the tears away with her finger.

Harry could see her pain. It was hard to interpret before but now it was clear. She was on the motorway and he had no doubt they were there on the same day. She may have been closer to town. She sobbed. The kids looked. Harry didn't want them to see anymore distress.

'You'll survive, Harry said. 'We'll be able to get through today and find someone who can tell us what to do, we can escape this nightmare.'

She placed the notepad on the bed. Harry saw it was full of writing, probably a diary. Harry pushed himself onto the stone floor and slid across to her. His leg burned.

'Calm down. We're the adults here and we need to stay strong for the children, please,' he said. She stopped sobbing.

The kids were teasing the kitten's tail.

She reached into her bag and pulled out some tissues. Harry wanted to search the bag and find out what the tablets were, because although they looked official it seemed they had done nothing for the pain. There was a possible infection to worry about. If he had a doctor's degree the whole situation would be easier. Heck a psychologist degree would better help him understand the woman.

He was a good man and good to his son. But Molly? Was he really that emotionally unavailable as to not understand her feelings? This is deep stuff. He understood not everything could be rationale or blamed on him.

'You'd be upset if you saw what I saw. People, parents being ripped to shreds and then coming after you,' she sobbed but managed to keep it decent.

He couldn't protect James, and he supposed Sam, forever. Eventually they would know of the harsh reality of the world. James would have no choice; he would have to grow up in this horrible new world. Harry still had to tell him about his mother. Before the dead began to rise needing a solicitor applied, but not now, not at least for a while. Molly was probably dead. If London was going down then Molly's mother's house wasn't safe, they were close to the docks. Ships frequented the docks from London.

It wasn't upsetting coming to accept Molly may be dead. What was upsetting was the note about her leaving. Death could be mourned, and he could move on. But relationships couldn't without some decent whiskey. If she had become a flesh-eating ghoul, he'd have payback to exact, if not, he'd exact a mouthful of shit at her. He inhaled and his heartrate slowed.

'Did they get your parents?' Harry asked. She obviously lived at home. She was youthful wearing a sci-fi shirt. The thought he fancied her sickened him, if she was a teenager. He was twenty years older at least.

She took another tissue from the pack and wiped her cheeks before suckling on the water bottle. Harry watched it drain past two hundred millilitre's and held his hand to stop her. 'Like you said, best save it.' She laughed and put the bottle and tissues back in the backpack.

'I was reading when they came down the street. I had my bag packed after seeing the news about the city,' she said. Harry hadn't given much thought to preparing. 'I prepared and I went downstairs while my parents were asleep. I grabbed the biggest knife I could find, that thing,' she gasped, pointing to the large bloody knife on the floor. Harry turned and picked the knife up and slid it under the bunk, he didn't want the children playing with it. 'I didn't have time to wake them. They broke in the house before I could, so I ran back upstairs and climbed out of my window. They were everywhere. I jumped up onto the roof, it was soaking, and I jumped onto the neighbour's roof where I heard the crying. I saw them crazy people everywhere and waited to see what I could do. I thought they spotted me, so I laid down. It was pitch black on that roof, even the birds scared me. Then I saw you, on your roof. I waved but you couldn't see me. Then when you jumped down and ran across the road I thought you were coming to help me. I prayed that you would help me. You didn't help me. My parents were dead, and I was alone, so I decided to climb to the window and help, otherwise I would still be stuck there,' she panted and picked the notebook up and began reading it.

'I'm sorry I didn't see you, I was afraid,' Harry consoled. The moment was descending rapidly into depressing silence that went on, and on.

The kids giggled and the kitten was clawing at the oversized pants James wore. He had no clue what to say to her. Was this it for him? Dumped from a marriage and stuck to an awkward twenty something.

'How old are you?' he asked. The answer surprised him.

'Nineteen, and yes I know I still live with my parents but I'm going to move out soon', she said, emphasizing the yes. Wow what a relief. She's of adult age. Harry was blushing and pulled himself back onto his bottom bunk. The leg pain was subsiding.

He didn't care that she still lived with her parents, he had until he was twenty, in his youth living with parents at eighteen was considered loitering and for bottom feeders.

'What's your name? I need to know your name if you're going to be near me and James,' he said. Looking into her eyes. She lifted her head; her cheeks were stained from mascara.

'What's yours?' she quipped. Harry laughed.

'Harry, I practically live on the opposite side of the road, but I've never seen you.' He smiled at her and hoped it wasn't inappropriate. He wasn't sure how this would work. A teen and a stranger's child, this was more like a commercial advert that advertises coffee with the world's most perfectly unfitting family. Those adverts were blatantly all smoke and mirrors. That was television though. This was real and needed to be better than it was. It was going to be better, it had to be.

'Meghan, my friends call me Meg,' she said and returned the smile. The conversation was going well until the little kitten ran to her leg and she booted it back. The kitten ran back to James after it shrieked.

That was a nasty move but given the circumstances and her losses it wasn't unreasonable considering he wanted to kill Molly earlier.

Progress was being made with Meg. Communication was key to survival. The circle of survivors in the bunkroom were in for a hell of a journey and they needed a new plan.

No fire crew had shown up yet. They'd probably went home after the phone lines were cut. If anyone had a fire, they'd have to use extinguishers and pots of water.

Society wasn't completely ruined because there were still human beings wandering the earth. Humans had survived for millennium; survival was integrated into people.

Existence would boil down to food, water, medicine, homes, heating, cigarettes, flashlights, batteries, oil…the list goes on, a headache of worry to come.

'Meg we're going to need a new plan,' Harry said, leaning back on the stone wall. 'I think we should stay here and check the building in the morning. We'll worry about everything else at dawn.' He hoped to bounce ideas around but had no energy.

'We need to formulate a plan now, before daylight. You can't check the building. This rooms safe enough for now, the door is heavy,' she responded firmly.

'I say we hold off here until the Government do something,' Harry replied. 'It wasn't meant to be permanent when we voted to come here. It was out of desperation, having a second chance I would have said the church, there would have been people there,' he added. His calf had numbed.

The room didn't have air conditioning, it was hot and made his underarms clammy.

'And after?' Meg queried. He wasn't sure and shrugged. The town hall was an option; it had heavy doors.

'Town hall?' he said hesitantly. Meg placed the notepad back into the backpack and tilted her head at Harry. Sleep was tugging at him.

James and Sam had fallen asleep on the floor, the kitten was curled up on James's stomach. It didn't look comfortable, but Harry didn't want to wake them.

'We stay here till sunrise and then we'll escape. We're going to have to go somewhere with police. So yeah, I guess the town hall will do,' Meg said and laid down on the bunk. Harry did the same. The mattress was firm.

Meg was hesitant and Harry wasn't convinced she was on-board with the plan. It was a matter for the morning. The bright lights annoyed him, but he covered his face with his hands and sunk into the sheets.

CHAPTER 20

Others

Harry woke up unwillingly. A hand shook in front of his face. He barely slept two hours.

The lights beamed bright; his senses reoriented after scanning the room.

Meg was rubbing his shoulder frantically, she was startled.

Harry smelt the familiar copper odour; groans of the dead cloaked the silence. The dead were outside the fire station. The groans reminded Harry of football chants and drunk fans swaying, spilling beer in blissful ignorance.

Only time would tell how long the door would last. Coming here now seemed like a terrible idea. They should have fortified the neighbour's house, maybe the attic. Harry recalled his dream. The dead were slow in his dream. He had run across the beach, weaving through a horde, when he understood his lucid state he had suddenly broke to a walk and he escaped. That was their weakness, their slow pace. In numbers the dead were strong. If Harry was smart during the run then he could get James, Sam and Meg to the town hall safely.

'Harry, wake up,' Meg said prodding his shoulder. 'Did you get up last night?' Harry attempted to push her away, but he noticed knew stains of blood on the floor in the shape of feet. He sat up; his leg was no longer in agonising pain.

'Where are the kids?' he asked. She pointed to the top bunk. Thankfully they were sleeping. James and Sam needed new clothes. The kitten was meowing at the foot of the bed, rubbing its back on the metal frame. They all needed food and water.

'Was it you who did that?' she asked and pointed to the blood feet on the floor. He hadn't gotten out of bed all night. Unless he was sleep walking, which was unlikely. Harry leant his elbows on his knees. Meg reached for the flask of water on the other bunk and passed it to Harry. It had a mouthful left at most.

'Has James had any, what about Sam?' he asked. He handed the flask back to Meg and she scorned, Harry did not like it one bit.

'I tried to give them some when they woke up earlier, they sipped some and said it was horrid, so I left them,' her voice shaky. Harry took the flask back and licked a few drops from the bottle. The kids had to be first to get rations to keep their strength.

'They're always first,' Harry said pointing to the bunk above and handing the bottle back to Meg, she stored it in the backpack on her bunk. 'We're stronger, besides we have running water don't we?' Harry said. Meg walked to the sink and turned the tap, nothing came out.

The kitten had pissed on the floor and it mixed with the bloody boot stain. Then it ran and pounced at Meg's bunk and clawed at her backpack. Harry expected her to throw it off.

She walked to the kitten and picked it up and stroked it. She was becoming more tolerant. Meg trotted across the wet floor, opened the door and tossed the kitten out of the room. No, she wasn't.

The kitten scratched to get back in for a minute. It would attract the dead right to them. The kitten was another mouth to feed. There was no running water and electricity wouldn't last much long before the government shut the power grid off. Still, *cinnamon* could have been like the toy car.

'You need to calm down Meg,' Harry said. 'That cats going to attract more undead. We're fucked already, so try not to make it worse.' Harry reached for the bunkbed frame and lifted himself to his feet. The ground rocked. Harry looked down at his bare feet. He should have scavenged for a pair of shoes. His feet were filthy.

'It can't get worse than this, we're in an empty fire station with a creepy stalker watching us, what is wrong with you?' Meg yelled. It reminded Harry of Molly. Meg sat down on her bunk and pulled out the notebook again. Harry could find some shoes whilst the kids slept.

'Let's just find a radio, clothes and water. Surely there's a kitchen in here somewhere and a control room,' Harry limped across the floor avoiding the blood. He opened the door, Cinnamon had gone. The kitten could have been a food detector. At home he could go to the fridge and take out chicken slices and then make a chicken mayonnaise sandwich.

'Where are you going?' Meg asked. He scanned the corridor. It was empty.

'Radio, food, water and clothes,' he said. 'If you're coming hurry up otherwise we're fucked staying in here.' Meg was testing his patience. Fortunately, the hallway was well lit. He let go of the door, held the wall for support and began to walk back towards the receptionist room.

He walked past a white wall clock, it read eight am. Cinnamon was gone for now. Harry couldn't see any blood trail. As he walked closer to front office he spotted the bloody boot trail. The bloody footprints were close to the wall, as if who-ever-it-was had tried to sneak. They could have been evading the dead. Harry peered through the glass frame into the office, it was empty, the front doors were closed.

He turned back and headed back to the bunkroom and heard footsteps in the distance.

A shadow was cast on the wall in the distance.

'Stop, who are you,' he shouted and paced along close to the wall. Meg peered from the bunkroom door and Harry carried on down the corridor.

He should have brought the knife for protection. He reached the end of the hallway, in front a door led to the staircase and to the right another corridor. He turned right and saw the sign on the wall for canteen. He chased the elusive shadow, it appeared again at the end of the hallway. Every room he passed contained useful items, but no people.

This mysterious figure was an annoyance. He didn't have time to chase it.

He stopped and leant against the wall. The door in front had gold letters in a black border engraved in the wood. It read: Chief Fire Inspector. Below that: Ronald McCormack. The name sounded familiar, but he struggled to recall where he heard it.

The doctor's office flashed into his retina like a bad nightmare. An image of a silent hallway crumbled in his mind. The hospital flashed before him. Jamie and the others huddled around Charlie's body. He couldn't escape the visions. A mirage of trauma. A sea of dead faces was talking. A woman asked if he was okay, he jumped, Sheila's face was decaying, blood poured from her eyes. He was paralysed. A snake latched onto his leg and the fire station came into view.

'Shit,' he cried. It was the kitten, clawing at his leg, meowing repeatedly for food. He sighed and petted it, Cinnamon purred. Footsteps distracted him; a large shadow was cast on the wall further down the hallway.

He picked up Cinnamon and pushed into the fire chief's office. The room smelt of vanilla. Papers were stacked neatly on the desk. The floor was covered in boxes of paperwork and shards of glass were scattered beneath them.

He knelt on his good knee. He could hear heavy footsteps approaching. He put Cinnamon under his arm to keep it quiet, but she clawed into his bicep. The footsteps stopped outside the office door. Harry crawled over to the desk and hid behind it.

The door opened. Harry saw the blood-stained boots enter the room, then the black trousers and a well-built torso in a yellow shirt. The guy wielded a bloodied fire axe. The stranger crunched on the glass. Harry wasn't going to leave that office alone.

'Come out from there, before I splat your head on the desk and wear your eyes for medals,' the man said. His voice was coarse. Harry shuffled to his feet and stepped out from behind the desk.

The man had black hair and was rugged. He bore a frown, that looked permanent.

Harry released the kitten and she jumped to the desk and clawed at the paperwork. Hiding made Harry look like a wimp. A man with a kitten under a desk. Not cool.

'I'm alive,' Harry said. 'Who are you?' The man lowered the axe to the floor and leant on it like a cane.

'The fire chief. You though, are here without good reason, it doesn't matter what's happening outside, you shouldn't be here,' the chief said. Harry couldn't be bothered to question his title.

'Ronald,' Harry replied. 'As you know I have children and we aren't safe out there, or in our homes. We needed, and I emphasise *needed*, to come to a building secure enough to hold out in, if you have a problem with that then go fuck yourself,' Harry instantly regretted saying it, but the pain had returned.

The chief didn't own the building, it was public owned. Everyone knew it. *Ronald* didn't look too pleased and then approached Harry. Ronald was Harry's height. Ronald's muscles were larger than Harry's. Like Charlie, Ronald could defeat him.

'Can't argue with that, you need to keep you kids safe, I respect that. But you have twenty-four hours left here, then I'm kicking you out, this is my place, I'm the Chief and I run it, so what I say goes,' Chief said. He walked backward to the office door, opened it and left. Harry's spine tingled and his legs went weak. He sat on the table.

Harry was lost. Staying long enough to formulate a plan wasn't going to happen, because with Chief Ronald wielding that axe, they weren't safe. Twenty-four hours, not generous. They'd all have to leave the station by eight am. He hoped Meg could fit any scavenged food in her backpack. He was hungry and his belly rumbled. The kids were too. Twenty-four hours.

They bagged up the blankets into Megs rucksack before heading to the canteen.

They found bread, butter, milk, tea, coffee and an assortment of biscuits and cakes stuffed in little oval tins in the cupboards.

Harry drank two black coffees and ate three digestive biscuits within half hour. Meg ate toast. Sam and James ate toast at Harry's insistence, they needed real food before indulging in soft mini chocolate cakes. It would suffice for now. Meg had put a full pack of digestives and tea bags into her backpack. Harry gave Cinnamon a bowl of milk. Cinnamon quit meowing after drinking it. The Chief hadn't returned to them. Thankfully.

The canteen was large, four stainless steel tables were plotted around the room covered in a polystyrene white sheet. The countertops were covered in crumbs after their preparations. There were windows behind them looking out to a grassy yard.

Morning dew lingered on the weeds. The dead swayed past occasionally unaware of their presence. Harry was facing the windows. He could see more zombies in the distance. The glass was thick enough to block out sound. They couldn't hear the kids playing or hear the kettle boil. The kettle was already full when they arrived.

There was a bitter bottle of water in the fridge. Harry discarded it after trying to drink it. Luck and miracle were keeping him, his son, and Sam and Meghan alive. They weren't the only survivors. There would be others. Evidenced by Chief's existence. There would be many more survivors scattered through the remains of Beach Town. A once thriving populace.

The town was decimated, over the year's numbers had dwindled and businesses had struggled. Harry feared he would lose his job before the outbreak. Business was dying in the opera house. Shops had frequent sales to pull customers in. Many stores on the beach front had gone bust and were boarded up. The town was dying from a poor economy. Now it was dead.

Having Sheila's girlfriend Wendy as house planner probably contributed. Wendy used to rant on about being keen to replace parks with houses. Ugly council houses. The cheap brick. Unattractive and uneconomical. The dead rising could be the boost that Beach Town needs. It would make a funny museum. Harry laughed.

Harry had found stronger painkillers in the cupboards – ibuprofen and aspirin – they relieved his leg pain. The coffee and biscuits energised him. Watching the dead walk past as he ate biscuits was unreal.

'Did he say anything else?' Meg asked. She was munching on burnt toast crusts. Meg was unaware she had a splodge of butter on her lip.

'No not one word, but he said something about a nuclear meltdown,' Harry joked. Meg spluttered her toast out with a gasp.

'What the hell,' she yelled. She shuffled the chair across to Harry.

'Calm down I was joking,' he replied.

James named the kitten fire cat much to Harry's disappointment, Harry preferred Cinnamon. The kids desperately needed clothes and Harry needed shoes.

'Chief didn't say anything else,' Harry said. 'We've got a while though before we have to go, so don't worry.' Harry grabbed a gluten free biscuit from the plate of biscuits on the table. He preferred chocolate digestives. He was unpleasantly surprised at how disgusting it was. It was tasteless. 'Probably best to find some clothes and water, we need to stay fresh as long as we can.'

The dead walked to the window. Harry froze mid bite and placed the cream biscuit on the plate.

Meg laughed at something. The dead gazed in watching them. Their black eyes unnerving Harry. They needed to get out of there. The bloody faces swayed, not attempting to break the window.

'Kids stop now,' Harry whispered. The dead were taunting Harry. Fresh flesh dangled form their mouths as they gnawed into the air.

Meg turned around.

The corpses were covered in mildew like the grass. A few dead children wore ripped pyjamas amongst the crowd. A woman with no ear shambled into a man with no cheeks. The zombies began to hit the glass.

The canteen door bust open and they all jumped. Meg dived to the floor. Harry had a shockwave of low blood pressure. It was Chief, he was pale and stuttered his breathing.

'We have to go, now, they got in,' Chief panted.

Harry speedily stood up ignoring his stinging wound pain. He marched to Ronald glaring for an explanation. The Chief was sweating, thick beads trickled down his face onto his shirt. He looked like he had killed someone and run a thousand miles. His hair was drenched with sweat.

'Where?' Harry's asked, concerned for the safety of the kids. Chief watched the dead at the window. Chief walked to the canteen door then stopped and turned around. The axe was slipping through his fingers.

'No time, let's go,' Chief said standing at the door. Meg grabbed the backpack and slung it over her shoulders. She grabbed James and Sam's hands.

The zombies broke through the canteen window. The dead clambered over the broken glass. Harry went and grabbed

James's hand and swung him onto his back. James held the kittens fur letting her swing like a cuddly bear.

The zombies fell across the broken window. Limbs ripped on the glass and black goo dripped onto the stone floor. Chief waited patiently for Harry and Meg to get the kids.

Harry saw a dead police officer rise from the ground.

Chief Ronald escorted them right from the canteen back through to the main corridor. Chief headed directly for a fire exit in front. Chief opened the fire exit and the zombies dived forward. Harry held James tight. Meg had Sam in between her knees whilst scanning the corridor.

'Kill it', Meg yelled.

Ronald swung the axe. Harry had to jump back. The axe spun around and decapitated three corpses, their heads rolled from their shoulders and their bodies dropped to floor.

James and Sam cried. It was disgusting. Harry hurled up biscuits and coffee onto the stone wall. Chief swung his axe again. It latched onto another zombie's neck. Blood spurted onto Chief's shirt and face. The corpses head was half ripped off its shoulders and Chief raised the axe and split the zombies head into two. Chief kicked the heads outside and slammed the fire exit door shut.

Harry saw the beasts infiltrating the corridor, pouring from the canteen. Chief opened the door on the right, the stairs. Harry ran through the door, then Meg followed by Chief. They climbed the staircase one level. Harry was exhausted.

Sam was being dragged by Meg, she failed to realise when the bone in Sam's wrist snapped and he screamed. There was no time to stop. Chief darted in front and opened the door to a brown carpeted hallway. Paintings of Beach Town and landscapes were placed along the corridor. They marched forward. A painting caught Harry's eye. A stencil outline of the opera house in black and white. The walked past two doors until Chief opened a third door on the right.

'Through here, hurry,' Ron said. He held the door open.

Inside wooden benches lines the side of the room, a metallic fireman pole was going through a hole in the floor in the right corner. Hooks were covered in large yellow fire man jackets and hefty steel cap boots were under the benches. Harry could take a pair.

Harry placed James down on the right bench. James cried and Harry hugged him, James smiled but looked exhausted. Meg sat on the left bench. Chief leant his stained axe against the door. Harry looked for Sam, he wasn't here. Harry hobbled over to Meg who was routing through her backpack.

'Where's Sam?' Harry asked. Meg ignored him and continued to search the backpack. Meg had snapped Sam's wrist. Harry hoped to get him painkillers. Chief looked to Harry and then looked around the room, but he didn't say anything. 'He's out there,' Harry said. James looked to Harry and the Chief stepped to the door and opened it.

'Get out there quick,' Chief said. Harry moved to the door and into the hallway. Harry saw Sam crying on the floor near the staircase door.

Harry headed for Sam; the Chief followed. The dead burst through the staircase door. The sheer weight of the horde had bust the door handle.

'Run,' Harry cried. Sam struggled to get up, his left wrist was limp. It was too late.

Harry couldn't watch. The dead piled onto Sam. Harry rushed forward, but Chief grabbed his shoulder's. The zombies tore into Sam as he lay in his wet pyjamas, Sam cried for mummy. Harry wailed.

'We have to help him,' Harry blubbered. Chief pulled Harry by the arms back into the changing room. Harry watched the zombies knock the opera house picture to the floor where the dead trampled it. The Chief shoved Harry in the room and walked off to the crowd of undead.

Harry slumped against down the wall next to the door. His forearms ached. His face was sticky, and he needed water.

Harry watched in shock, Meg was calm, legs crossed reading the notebook on the bench. The kitten was sleeping on James's lap and he was stroking it, smiling. James would be heartbroken when he found out Sam was dead.

Chief shunted the door open. Immediately Harry spotted an inch-deep bite wound to his battle-scarred forearm.

CHAPTER 21

Times Change Quickly

It could have been anyone one of them. If it was Meg, they would fight to retrieve her from the dead.

Meg hadn't moved and continued to read her notebook. Probably unintelligible rantings of a teenager.

Harry sat on the bench next to Ronald. Harry took slow breaths to calm down. Meg was a malicious and deliberately selfish teen. Harry could see clearly now. Chief grunted occasionally as he tried to stop the wound bleeding.

'We need to cut the wound-out Meghan, get your knife out,' Harry said. Meg took one look at the bite and shook her head in disapproval.

'What do you mean?' Chief asked, gripping his wound.

'I was bitten on my leg,' Harry said. 'Meghan cut the wound clean out, a rather smart move.' Harry sharpened his words like razors. Sarcastically mocking Meg. Chief rolled his eyes in disbelief.

'Forget it, we'll use bandages,' Chief argued. Harry was edgy, his son's life was at stake if Chief wasn't taken care of.

Bringing the kitten was the best idea since portable games. James hadn't stopped playing with her. They hid under large fireproof jackets, James teasing Fire Cat's tail.

Harry wanted to take Chief out to protect James.

Harry lunged for the axe after Chief shut his eyes. Harry wielded the axe, it was heavy. He carefully stepped next to the Chief. The pole hole was to the right of Chief, he could kick him down there if need be. Chief was a good guy, but survival was survival. Chief opened his eyes. Harry held the axe against Chief's chest.

'Let's talk about this,' Chief pleaded. 'I need my arm more than you know it,' Chiefs pleads fell on empty ears. 'Meghan, please, stop this,' Chief grunted.

'Meghan,' Harry quipped. She looked at him. 'Stop reading that fucking book and cover James's eyes and ears. Do it now or you'll be next.' Meg did as he said. Harry used the flow of energy from his chakras to gather the courage to perform the act.

Meghan reluctantly walked over and covered James's face. Meg whimpered and Harry had no pity or sympathy anymore. She killed Sam through her selfishness. Chief raised his arms his arms and Harry lifted the axe above Chief.

'Sorry,' Harry said. The axe fell just as a blade on a beheading. Chief screamed as the axe sliced through the elbow cutting the forearm clean off. Chief's went white and blood pooled over him. The forearm lay on the ground, fingers were twitching. Harry jumped up, placed the axe against the door and then returned and kicked the wriggling forearm down the pole hole.

Harry watched the arm fall. The dead swarmed around it. Naked residents and a mailmen and policeman amongst the dead. A sickening sight to behold. Harry vomited onto the heads of the crowd below. Harry had lost a ton of water from vomit. He was woozy, the coffee hadn't helped.

Harry waved to Meg who removed her hands from her face. Chief was unconscious bleeding to death. Harry didn't want another situation like the hospital. There were no blood bags here. Chief could die but he wouldn't return, the disease was removed from his body.

Harry was going to ask Meg for help but had no patience for her. He grabbed a fire jacket and rolled the thick sleeves up. He knelt next to Chief and wrapped the coat around his arm, tying the sleeves around the stump. Harry looked at Chief's other arm, it had a bite wound as well. Harry was gutted.

'This is bad,' Harry murmured. Meg stepped next to Harry. Her hair brushed on his shoulder. She was stood in blood. She could have been deliberately rubbing her breasts on him to make amends. The cushion of her flesh was disarming.

Harry lifted Chief's arm up to examine the bite wound. It was a deep wound that ran from the thumb to little finger. Black pus had begun to multiply in the hand. Harry watched the goo physically changing into spirals and expanding. Meghan examined Chief's pockets and pulled something out from them.

'What is it?' Harry asked. She held up a small black box. It looked like a wedding ring box. 'Well, open it then,' Harry pressured. Meghan opened the box, inside a piece of paper. Harry remembered the sorrowful goodbye from his wife. Harry hobbled over to the bench and searched the bag for the knife.

'Stay away from that hole,' Harry said to James. James was smart but Harry wasn't taking risks. James cautiously pulled Fire Cat to his lap and dropped a jacket arm on her head before grabbing at her tail. She hissed. Harry laughed. He returned to Chief.

'Step aside,' Harry said. Meg did so.

'What are you doing, you can't leave him with no hands,' Meg exclaimed. Her opinion carried no weight with Harry anymore.

Harry wiped the blade on Chief's shirt before proceeding. He pointed the knife like a screwdriver and began to make incisions in Chief's hand. Blood spurted on Harry's shirt. black goo seeped from the wound. They needed face masks; the disease was best not ingested accidentally. Harry held his elbow across his mouth.

Harry cut the wound out and the flesh slipped out onto the floor. He dropped the knife and it clinked as it hit the floor.

The corpses who had feasted on poor Sam were thudding to get in the door. Each thud shook the walls.

Harry picked the flesh off the floor with his index and thumb. The skin was white and flesh black. He tossed it into the pole hole. He could hear the zombies feasting on it.

Chief opened his eyes. Chief shouted in Harry's face. Harry jumped up.

'What the hell have you done?' Chief gasped. Chief's eyes stigmatised.

'You had two bite wounds, another on the hand and I cut it out,' Harry said. Chief flipped Harry the bird. Blood dripped from his hand.

Chief reached for another jacket and wrapped it around his hand. His arm was still bleeding heavily. Chief's head hit the wall; he was unconscious again.

Meg had to drop her precious book as she darted for the door, nearly tripping over the jackets. The door was buckling.

The dead were opening the door. There was one option left, down the hole or die.

'James get Fire cat now,' Harry shouted and lunged at the door shunting it. Torn hands strung in red tubes reached around the doorframe. A hand grabbed Meg's hair and she cried out. Mere seconds until they had to flee. The dead groaned as they attempted to grab Harry.

A screech echoed through the corridor; the eye jelly of Harry's pupils trembled. The screech was sharp, cutting rusty slices down into his torso. It reverberates in his chest.

'I can't hold it, we need to get out of here before they get in,' Meg yelled. Harry struggled to hear here over the zombies. The dead pushed the door further open. Harry saw James holding Fire Cat waiting next to the pole hole.

'We have a few seconds at most, so we need to get down there, no stopping now.'

The hands grabbed her hair again. The bloody fingers tore her brown locks that once swayed elegantly. Harry watched the dead tear her hair off with a rip reminiscent of Velcro. Harry pushed as hard as he could, but the horde was stronger. Meg cried out.

The screech returned. It was close. Whatever it was, it was debilitatingly frightening.

The dead were bricks pushing down on butter. They had to go now or die.

Harry's brain was ablaze with lethargy. The stench of the dead was stomach curdling.

Dead arms reached around the door, they were almost in. Rotting faces munched at Harry and Meg as they pushed inwards.

'We go now, or we die,' Harry said. He let go. One wrong move and he was dead.

He stumbled backwards onto the floor next to James, his leg throbbed.

Meg finally let go. The axe was next to him, illuminated in the heap of blood.

Harry reached for the axe and Meg dived for the kitchen knife. She picked the knife up and began to stab skulls. Harry stood to his feet and began to swing.

Harry swung the axe into a zombie's jaw, slicing its head in half. He kept his mouth closed tightly, so he didn't inhale the blood. The smell made him gag.

Meg jabbed at their faces and held the knife like a sword. They were both covered in blood. Harry swung the axe round like the Chief had done, imitating a baseball swing he cut the arms of another zombie and it fell to the floor. He lifted the heavy axe and brought it down on it's neck. Their mini battle accumulated corpses and limbs next to the door.

Four zombies remained in the corridor. Harry ran and shut the door. He stared into the blackened eyes of a middle-aged woman outside the door. Meg drove the knife into a zombie that continued to wriggle on the floor. The floor was a mess of battered bodies and limbs.

Meg tossed the bent blade to the pile of zombies. She slid against the wall and wiped the blood from her face. She was hyperventilating, panicking. Her tears helped wash away the blood. Harry tossed the rough-edged axe to the pile of bodies and returned to James. James shook with fear and stood wrapped in a fire man jacket on the bench with Fire Cat.

Harry lifted the jacket, James was crying heavily and struggled to catch his breath. Harry slid the fire jacket off James hugged him. Wary not to put his bloody face near James's face.

Harry looked at the pile of bodies. Nine bodies in total. The plan to survive was disintegrating. The fire station was unsafe. Chief was bleeding to death and Harry doubted he'd survive without a transfusion or proper medical treatment.

Harry waited for the energy to do something other than hold James. His arms ached and he was fuzzy. Meg was holding her head in her hands.

'We need to move, there's no way we can stay here or go through that hole, that idiot has gotten us into a right mess,' Harry said pointing to Chief.

Meg walked to her backpack and placed the Chief's black box in it, which Harry couldn't understand. He couldn't comprehend the act he just committed. The hospital, the supermarket, the fire station. There would be other incidences. This was a brutal axe happy slaughter. The decapitations were soul wrenching. Harry couldn't concentrate through his pain.

'Stop telling me what to do, I have my own mind and I can think and decide for myself what's best for myself,' Meg moaned. Meg's words were empty and dull. Harry wanted to give her a mouthful. She pierced him with enigmatic eyes, a soul emerged in front of him. He was confused and betrayed. 'You can't blame him for this mess, you said fire station, you said come here it's safe, so you take the responsibility you moron, try learning about people before commanding them like some army general,' she yelled. Harry wanted to offer an apology. He sincerely wanted to but then that evaporated. 'And if you want to leave this room, then leave, because you seem to be under the impression that I'm *with you*.'

Harry and James watched in awe. Meg's face looked sobering and fraught. Harry believed she was with him. She climbed onto the neighbour's roof to help the children. She must have wanted to find help. It had been for her survival, nothing more.

Chief shuffled towards Meg interrupting her disenchanted rambling. Harry saw Chief's milky eyes, resembling dirty fish water. Chief stumbled to Meg. The coat fell off Chief's stump revealing green and black gunk. Harry wanted to try and save her, but it was his chance to escape. The dead Chief grabbed her, she cried as Chief started to bite into her arms and then he bit into her eye. Harry vomited down the pole hole.

Harry lifted James and grabbed the backpack, flinging it over his shoulder. Harry did a double take on the axe and decided to take it. Harry walked to the door; Chief ignored him as he munched on Meg's stomach. The dead had given him a wide berth since he was bitten.

Meg sat up groaning. Harry opened the door; the dead had shambled back towards the staircase. He walked into the hallway carrying James and the axe and shut the door, locking Meg and Chief away forever.

CHAPTER 22

The Phone

The chances of getting out of the fire station alive were now slim. Once Harry had managed to get into the hallway, he realised the staircase was the only exit to the ground floor.

He'd carried James two doors from the pole hole room into a room with a first aid sign on the door.

The room was distastefully small. It was an office with white walls and four desks in rows of two.

James sat on a foam cushioned desk chair and placed Fire Cat on the table. The only desk with a computer. Fire Cat played with the computer wires. Harry pulled her off before she electrocuted herself.

Harry couldn't believe that it had been a day since escaping from his house to the neighbours and then the fire station. It was taking a lifetime to get out.

The dead were already banging at the door. Their fingers scratching at the black lined glass.

Harry picked a sheet of plain paper up off the desk along with some cello tape and walked over to the door and stuck it over the glass so they couldn't see them.

James had a confused expression when he looked at the dead. Harry noticed on the run from the canteen. James hadn't asked about Sam yet, but should he be told? It was best to avoid telling him until he asks.

It was sad when Meg went out. There was no proof she let go of Sam deliberately. It was nonetheless heartless of her not to ask for help.

Harry walked to the far desk next to the window and slumped on the chair. A breeze blew in from the open window, it was refreshing. The loss of fluid was nauseating. Plan A was fucked. Was it worth attempting an escape or waiting?

Chief had the strength and courage Harry needed. Harry felt hopelessness. Harry wasn't the bravest man left alive. He had saved Charlie's life at the hospital because he went out of his way. It wasn't brave. It was adrenaline.

He'd been bitten and now the wound was pulsating. Harry grabbed the desk phone. He looked out of the window, staring at the dead shambling down the road. In the distant intersecting street roads, more dead people. Not enough time. He placed the phone to his ear.

The phone buzzed sonorously. It was a miracle. He put his elbows on the wooden desk. Why had they left the fire station phones working? He couldn't understand the logic. Maybe the entire town had the phone lines restored. Harry wondered if any fire crew were lurking in the station somewhere, too afraid to come out. If they were as helpful as the Chief, it could have been worth searching, but the time had passed for that.

James was pulling strips of ripped paper along the floor for Fire cat. She was stalking, waiting to pounce.

The plastic phone stuck to his sweaty cheek. Harry used his index to carefully dial Sheila's number. He changed his mind and thumbed the disconnect button. The dial pad had a button covered in red tape that read: emergency. Harry thumbed it. It rang.

'I'm hungry,' James said. James was used to having a filling breakfast, not toast and cheap butter. They were both used to having a large bowl of oats with raspberries or blueberries. Then Molly would serve up delicious syrup covered pancakes. Harry's stomach rumbled. Molly did the best pancakes. His father once said, "those are better than the entire towns, I know, because I've tasted them all". Harry couldn't argue at the time, they were first class.

His father had gained weight after developing severe depression. He would wander the streets like a lost dog, and scout through every café in town. He had been prescribed pills, according to the doctor he would feel better in a few weeks. Harry suffered from depression but not to the extent of his father.

Harry reminisced; it wasn't going to help now. He found solace in those memories.

The phone clicked. 'Hello, anybody there?' Harry said, freezing with anticipation.

It was a soul crushing pre-recorded message.

'This is a pre-recorded message from the Beach Town Police Department, we are sorry we cannot answer the phone right now, please leave a message for us after the tone.' Harry prepared to speak but the message continued. 'If you are calling about general enquiries, then please contact your local neighbourhood safety team, if you are calling with an emergency and cannot get through…' Harry was in an emergency and couldn't contact the police. 'Then please phone for the fire department, and press two, thank you and have a good day.' The voicemail beeped. Harry investigated the little holes in the speaker end of the phone, the holes were clotted with grease and grime.

'We are at the fire station, we are all fucked,' he was sombrous. He placed the phone back on the dial pad and spun the office chair towards the window so James wouldn't see the tears streak down his cheeks.

The sky was decimated with scattered clouds interweaved with tangerine and pink streaks. A lovely sight. The birds whistled and chirped. The moans of the dead carried in the wind.

James walked over to Harry and grabbed his hand, startling him. James passed Fire Cat to Harry. He wanted to speed throw it out the window. The kitten's glistening eyes disarmed him. He held her up like a baby. She meowed, blinking tirelessly.

'Cute isn't he, he needs a proper name though, Fire Cat is a bit pretend isn't it?' Harry said and cuddled the kitten in his lap, stroking the fluffy fur over its spine, it raised its back end in agreeability.

'Yes,' James said, holding his thinking finger to his lips. The paper on the door fell off, and Harry was unpleasantly greeted by a gawping bloody face. 'Sam,' James said and began to stroke the kitten harshly.

It was a saddening name to choose, but honourable. James must have known Sam was dead. Harry was relieved he didn't have to explain it to James. It was a gruesome death Sam had died. He wouldn't be coming back; he was shredded to pieces.

Another lesson learnt. A small victory. Everything mattered. These dead mattered despite his best intention not to care. First he learnt they were slow and dangerous in crowds. Harry now knew that not everybody returned. Was it a lesson or was a connection not worth making? Some people were so badly eaten that coming back was impossible. It wasn't immunity. It could have been god calling us to hell. Harry scratched his head. More god questions popping up.

He was an intruder in his own mind when he pondered the big questions. They were too big for him to ever understand. That was the key to human nature, he could not fight it. Humans were built to acquire knowledge. They were also built annoyingly with the desire, the obsession to find the answer to everything.

'Sam, that is a delightful name,' Harry said. 'Should Sam be our scout leader?'

'Yes,' James said, no hesitation. Harry grinned.

The phone that Harry believed held no salvation, rang. Harry, James, and Sam the cat, froze. They looked at the phone. Sam jumped to the desk purring. James ran over to another desk and began to mess around with a stack of printing paper.

The phone rang again. He hesitated and then picked the phone up.

CHAPTER 23

A Saviour

The church goers had gathered in the church basement. The survivors sat on beds that lined the stone floor in rows with walkways between the beds. Bedsheets were thin.

Candles were propped up on warping wooden tables. The ceiling lights didn't work.

Dean had brought the group to the basement after sitting on a bed in regret and despair for a while.

Dean had walked back to the main hall and told them all how he secured the area for their safety. Dean's creaking mattress annoyed him; he wanted a refreshing drink.

The room was cold, dim and had a musky aroma. The room was poorly ventilated. There was one window at the rear of the cellar, about two feet wide and rotting from the damp. Fallen branches littered the lawn outside the window. The ventilation was adequate for now, Dean had opened the window and gave orders not to close it.

The chaos from last night had rattled everyone, especially the priest's wife. Dean had awoken this morning and given a speech about rationing and how it could save lives, and how cooperation could rebuild them. The crates of tinned food, and twenty-five litre water bottles, could not sustain them.

He'd rounded up a few do-gooders and told them to hand out the daily portion. The survivors had a positive attitude most of the time. Kids had calmed after digesting breakfast.

Dean could envision his temporary police force forming out of the group. Now though, they would follow Dean's orders, otherwise Dean might have to get deadly serious with his pistol. Even an empty pistol could coerce people, nobody would question him when looking down the barrel.

It was live or die. The hard choices had already been made.

Dean sat on the bed scanning the basement bunks. People rustled on their blankets, rolling uncomfortably, trying to sleep the day away. Metal food can keys, gulps and slurps of bottled water pierced the silence.

The people were pale, ghoulish. The survivors nearest the window were lit up from the sunlight beaming through the window. They crammed next to the rotting frame trying to inhale air.

Dean stood off the bed. He forewent the water ration, the kids needed it more. He didn't want old water that had sat in the dark for months, that could be contaminated. Nobody had turned ravenous or crazy yet. That was a relief. His palms had accumulated a glue like sweat.

Dean scanned the room hoping to see a familiar face. Hoping to see one of his few friends, Jamie. His deceased friend. He would struggle to forget what he witnessed at the supermarket. Was it preventable? His forehead stung as beads of sweat trickled down his brow. They needed air conditioning. The officers had opened fire, government orders, save the food and ration. Jamie was trampled as an innocent man looking to survive, not to loot. The image burned into Dean's head; his eyes pulsed. If he could go back in time, he'd keep Jamie in that station as an on-call emergency doctor. Jamie had been forced to cooperate with the processing of people. That wasn't his fault, neither was being trapped in the hospital.

Then, another totally irrelevant thought crossed his mind. Dean saw the image of a lady holding her little boys' hand, speaking softly to him. Their eyes met, she smiled at him and the little boy smiled back. Dean's mind was in a dark place. He had tried to forget many years ago, his dearest friend of twenty-seven years, Marcy. She had been his rock, a partner, that was a long time ago. The candles flickered as a gush of breath blew over them by passers-by and a mystical daze overcast his flickering consciousness.

Marcy had wanted to move to the city to find a better home, to live the city life dream. "It's more money", she told Dean. "Better career", and "more stimulating." They discussed it regularly when they frequented the pub together. She had returned after a dreary goodbye some months later. Her news hit Dean first, he was first to know, even before family.

Dean felt a pin prick scrape his spine; the memory flooded over him. She had returned to tell him she was moving back to Beach Town. Her house hadn't sold and that was the good news. Dean crustily remembered the sad news. She had little to no time left to live, maybe months. The city doctors told her. That day his emotions had plummeted beyond the core of the earth. The whole church shook with a malevolent howling wind that penetrated the cracks in the walls. The cool breeze snaked past Dean's feet. Tears falling uncontrollably down his cheeks. Dean watched the room of survivors, teary eyed, smiling. Dean remembered the final days he spent with his former friend. The image of the mother and son faded away.

He could not stop the disease that had killed her, but he could help prevent the deaths of the people in the church. They were lost and scared. Only one person could give them guidance – Dean – and he revelled at his position.

He would help them. The dead were trying to break into the temple, and they needed to fortify the doors.

CHAPTER 24

Church Breach

Dean was out of breath standing on the stone staircase leading back up the main hall.

He had to get things locked down before taking official charge, he'd have to barricade the church and then find a way to communicate with the station. That was the goal. Dean hoped the station was holding out. The town hall and police station were the only buildings capable of receiving the government orders. Dean stepped through the door into the main hall.

He scanned the empty hall and recalled a hostage situation two years ago. A gang had taken the church goers hostage and wanted a ridiculous sum in return for their release. Swat had a tough time breaching the building, but they succeeded in the end. Now all that mattered was getting the benches flipped upside down and pushed against the door. If he was lucky (he considered it unlikely), he could go back to the police station and leave someone in charge of the church, a deputy sheriff.

He was mayor, albeit battle trained and dangerous when desired.

He needed a shower and more ammunition. The outbreak was more of a pain in the ass than he expected.

The hall reeked of foul flesh. The air had thickened. Wind blew through the gaps in the stone, and morning dew was settled on the stain glass windows.

Dean crept forward, the floorboards let out a shrilling creak and clank. Dean glanced to the bell, the priest's legs in a pool of coagulated blood.

He stepped down the stone path in the middle of the benches. The front doors were very dangerous, the banging hadn't subsided.

He glanced at the man impaled by the scaffolding pole. He had reanimated, clawing in the air, unable to get up. Its eyes were black, and green goo seeped down the metallic pole. Its ribs clanked on the metal sending a razor down Dean's neck.

Dean stood next to the church doors.

He placed his palm on the wooden door, and then his ear. Moans and scratching radiated through the wood; Dean pulled away. The chants of groans were like a gust of wind. It was no wind. The sun beat through the stain glassed windows. It was them and him.

The wooden doors shook as the dead pushed against it. Dean stumbled back, the church doors were rocking back and forth. The wood creaked and cracked. Pushing and chanting corpses.

Dean wanted to call for help. The shaking doors reverberated along the stone walls. Adrenaline surged through his chest.

A beast screamed as sharp as barb wire wrapping around Dean's face. It channelled through the building. The floors seemingly rumbled.

Dean frozen like a mannequin. His legs were facing the opposite way to his body. A creature screeched again. The window's rattled. Dean's breath was shallow, his nose dripping. The screech was a rancid sting, an electric airwave speared into every crevice of his being. Dean had never experienced anything like it, it was haunting, petrifying.

Dean quickly headed – avoiding the poles and planks from the scaffold, to the cellar door. The refugee camp door.

A stain glass window above him smashed, a rainbow of glass shards fell onto him.

Dean had seconds to escape. He shook the shards of glass of. A piece had cut through his neck. A million pieces had left a thousand cuts over his forearms. His forearms stung and he ran tripping and crunching on the glass as he hit the floor.

Dean gazed around the hall. It was empty. He lifted his head to see what had smashed the window. The creature he saw made his eyes bubble dry and his lungs incinerate.

Blood dripped from his forearms and neck. He pulled himself to the bench, staying low. Dean crouched to the wooden platform past the bell. Whatever creature was in the window, it did not see him moving.

Dean kept looking over his shoulder as he hurriedly lunged for the basement door.

Dean watched from the door. The beast leapt into the air, screeching as it did so. The noise was brain sizzling. It came crashing to the stone floor and a crack rippled through the stone floor to Dean's feet. Stone and dust spat into the air sporadically. The dust settled; the creature had formed a hole in the floor. The creature was at least eight feet tall. Thick fangs protruded from the mouth and it had an overcoat of thick black sludge.

Dean slammed the basement door shut and bolted it. He hurried down the steps. His heart pumped steel ants around his body.

He had to stop, he had to admit, he was fucking petrified beyond belief.

He had to shake the fear off, he realised he was the saviour of the people in the basement. He needed to look strong for them, especially the children. A scared officer didn't look good any day of the week. He should have taken backup to fortify the door.

They needed to get to the North of the island. It had a small community. Hope was better than fear.

CHAPTER 25

Disagreements

Dean entered the basement and was met with a sea of desperate eyes. Unique souls watching him pant and fall onto the nearest bed. It was occupied by a woman. Dean recalled her face; he'd seen her in the main street café. The times when he had no choice but to go there after the station coffee machine conked out and all officers were stupefied by it. She got off the mattress and scoffed at him and sat on another bed.

Dean wiped his forehead with his hand and dried them on the bedsheet. He tried to rub his palms dry. His hands were clammy, like the cheeks of survivors who couldn't come to terms with the situation. The people sat in silence laying and glaring to the darkened ceiling.

Some children mocked one another whilst others nagged their parent's with grumpy moans, they wanted more food. It was tough, they couldn't have it yet. Dean's gut churned.

He thought it was a case of the heebie-jeebies, however it had a new and bitter meaning now. It didn't dissipate, like death had transcended upon his neurons, destining him to the grave.

Screeches couldn't be heard between the stone walls.

Dean stood off the bed and faced the people. 'Plans screwed,' Dean said. Everyone looked to him. 'We need get everyone out of the church and to a safe, secure location. Bef…'

Dean was cut off by a man wearing an American flag t-shirt and black joggers. The man's eyes were red from lack of sleep. The man shot Dean a stern scowl, he appeared fed up.

'This is safe, this is secure, we can't move now we have to make do, you should know that by now,' the man shouted, more people began to stand up and approach them. Kids stopped bickering; the vicar's wife sat holding her rosemary beads.

The crowd had encircled Dean and the man, like a school yard fight. An unbearably ideocratic action. It would only go Dean's way or no way. He was the official leader for now. Throwing them a few big words should help.

A petite woman with thick lips and moisturised skin stepped into the circle wearing a purple night gown. She was quick to speak.

'I agree, we need to go, there's hardly any food here at all,' she said, pointing to her son, who lay curled on a bed, pale. Dean concurred; the food situation was dreadful. The vicar was mistaken, supplies hadn't been stocked in a long time. There was enough food for another two days at a stretch.

Everyone had already eaten their daily protein bars and drank the instant-coffee. That was over half of the rations. This place wasn't viable.

The tired man turned to the gowned woman and gobbed off into her face, right in front of everyone. Dean watched, amazed at the audacity of the man.

'What are you siding with him for? Are you the useless police too? We stay and we wait for help, this is safe and this is secure, we do not need to go out there with those things, whatever they are, we need to stay and fortify, the only logical thing that buffoon has suggested,' he shouted, teeth gritted. Dean grabbed the man's shoulder with a firm grip, some of the crowd huffed non-agreeably and others nodded in agreement. Idiots.

'Calm down, keep calm and nobody has to spend their time chained to a bed, okay?' Dean smiled, trying to diffuse the situation. Perpetrators were hard and intimidating. Today this man was as frightening as a kitten.

The man swung his left fist at Dean. Dean stumbled back, gripping the man's shoulders. The crowd stepped back, nobody intervened.

Dean swung his right fist and the man dodged and returned an uppercut to Dean's stomach.

A lump propelled with unimaginable nausea into his chest. He hadn't been hit like that for a long time. He was unaccustomed and fell back onto a bed spluttering.

Dean held one palm up to the disgruntled man. He didn't take kindly to the hand and Dean was unprepared as the man grabbed his shoulders and kneed him in the chest. An atomic bomb of stomach acid galloped to his tongue. Dean was overwhelmed by the nausea, but he wasn't ready to give up.

Dean grabbed the man's arms and threw him across the bed. The man rolled across the mattress to the floor on the other side. He quickly jumped to his feet, agile and unaffected.

Dean stood up; his ribs ached. Dean held his fists up. The man copied Dean.

People lined the walls; the makeshift boxing ring was the size of the room. Some people had gone to lay down near the window. Parent's pulled their kids close to them.

'Stay back,' Dean shouted. 'Someone help me take this psycho down.' The survivors watched, too afraid to help. Dean waited for someone to step forward and was caught off guard.

A steel boned fist impacted his right cheek. The bones cracked and blood shot from his mouth. His tongue cut on a broken tooth. This guy was strong, Dean was dizzy and wanted to use the gun, but he didn't have the gun anymore. It might be excessive force anyway.

Dean lunged forward and rugby tackled the man's waist. Dean had tackled him onto the bed and onto the floor. Dean managed to pin the man under his legs. Dean punched left-right on the man's face, uncontrollably.

The man was weakened and tried to push Dean off. It was hard to tell if he had lost consciousness, his face was mashed in, bleeding. Dean stopped punching him.

The man was unrecognisable, purple veins bulged from his eyes. Black bruises formed over his face. A red river flowed and seeped at the embankments of his ears down onto his cheeks. Five teeth had fallen out onto the floor. His forehead lacerated with deep cuts. Dean thumbed his carotid artery for a pulse. He was breathing, he was alive, and he knew who was in charge.

Dean stood up, muscles aching. A pitiful snake bit into his oesophagus, the stinging nettles of a thorn bush wrapped around his body. Dean's belly a lead pie. He had won, no doubt about it. There was no sign of a struggle. Dean laughed.

People began to approach, and a few assisted the man on the floor. The crowd was white, shocked, speechless with gaping mouths.

'You needed to take care of that, and you did, thank you,' a woman said, standing behind Dean, placing a meaty hand on his tingling shoulder.

Dean waddled back and sat on the bed. He turned his bloodied face to her, his ribs cricked as he turned.

'Yes, I did, and you know what?' Dean said, grinning but his lips stung. 'There was no sign of a struggle, ma'am.' He wiped blood from his tongue onto his sleeve.

They needed to evacuate now and use anything in sight for a weapon, they could go through the rear window onto the lawn. It would be a slow crawl through back gardens.

Dean was horrified when thumping began on the cellar door. A screech pierced the cellar. It was like a demon choir, screaming to get into heaven, pissed at god. Everyone felt it, it rattled the candle holders. A candle fell to the floor and was extinguished by a man.

Dean stood up, his hips were rusting and unoiled. He needed some tasty food and fresh water.

It was now aware of their location. The window was the only escape option.

CHAPTER 26

The Run

Harry gripped the plastic, desperate for an answer. It was nerves wracking. His heart and breath silhouetted.

A crackled and distorted remnant of words was transmitted. Nothing human, nothing that could help. If he had put the phone down he would have missed the vital information. It was only spoken once, quaintly.

The office room had a glow, a migraineurs aura shimmered around the window ledges. Fizzy static lines danced around the corners of the desk. Harry would have a throbbing headache soon. Dehydration didn't help.

The anticipation made his hairs stand on an electric edge, hungry for information, he persevered.

'Hello, please, who is this?' He spoke with a loose tongue, each word fed with trepidation, frustration. His elbows were sore from the desk. His nether was soaked from the trickling sweat. A singular presence rose in his spine to his neck. A reply.

'Code…emergency…transmit to…. niner,' a man said. The cackling subsided. Harry clasped the phone, James watched, smiling. Harry saw the dead outside the door becoming more erratic. He turned to face the lawn. 'Niner, echo, niner, echo, foxtrot.' The dead horde shambled across the lawn to the station.

Harry quickly grabbed Meg's backpack, unzipped it and searched for the pad and pulled it out along with the pen. He jotted the message in the notepad..

He had a lot of questions. Why are they phoning the fire station? Is this being transmitted to all emergency services? Why by phone? Why hadn't they transmitted via the radio or television before it went out? Harry tore the page out and stashed it into his trouser pocket, and then put the pen and notebook back into the backpack. The information was safe. It sounded important.

Hopefully it was the national army, or international corps, deployed at full force. He had to take control of his breathing. The lack of water and light from the sky outside – cumulous clouds, blue sky– rattled his brain.

James was occupied with Sam, hiding under the desks as the cat tried to claw his hands.

A scream shattered the glass in the door.

The scream radiated through Harry. James froze and cried, Sam pounced onto his lap, hiding.

Harry's heart pounded. His palms sticky. The room was like a sauna.

The glass shattered into a million pieces onto the office floor.

The room shook, a thundering vibration emanated from corridor. The screech was so loud that Harry's ear cooled. He felt his ear, blood trickled down his cheek.

He stood up and staggered to the door. He daren't look away from the door. A ghastly creature came into sight.

The flesh was inhuman, it was oiled in a thick coating of black tar. The arms thin. The fingers, twigs.

The scream had disabled – that was the only word he could think of – the other zombies. The corpses had fallen face first onto the floor, squirming as they tried to stand up. Harry was sympathetic. They had been people at one point. Now they couldn't even walk straight.

Harry ducked behind a desk. James and Sam were cuddled together under the phone desk near the window. Time warped, Harry was anxious. It was if his neurons gave up halfway to their destination. His hands and legs were shaking with lactic acid. He clambered across the floor to James. James's body took on a thick black outline. What was happening?

It wasn't migraine, which had sought to destroy him since he entered the damn room. A sharp sting snaked through his chest around his neck. A pop echoed in Harry's skull; he was disorientated. James began to cry.

Nothing was right, forwards felt like backwards and arms heaved as rocks. A disturbingly strong sensation of thirst and hunger washed over him. He wanted to feast upon the flesh before him, and the cat too. They were appealing, very much ready for consumption. Their fear odourised his buzzing brain, he scrambled like a tiger towards James.

'No!' James cried, pushing himself backwards with his legs, hugging Sam tight.

The dead resumed their moaning, the room took on a strong stench – a freshly cut grass aroma. Harry wretched from the pain in his calf. Was it time for him to find shelter for his son, and go to die somewhere alone? He didn't want to give up yet.

Harry pushed himself to his feet. The office door creaked and cracked, as if it were about to break open. He approached James. James retreated under the desk, afraid. Harry looked to James's teary eyes. His son was afraid of him. It couldn't end like this. Harry could turn into one of them or worse, die.

'Sorry,' Harry said. 'I can't stay strong forever, but I will fight it until you are safe, whether it takes weeks or months, I will not rest.' Harry gulped his words; it could be months before salvation arrived, if it were coming. It could be months before they find safety. Harry reached his tired arms out to James who grabbed them.

The window shone with hope. The drop was worth the risk. It was better than becoming torn spaghetti guts that would satisfy some sick diseased bastard. Harry reached for the backpack and slung it over his shoulder. James held his fathers' hand, and Sam was nestled under his right arm.

The window was open, and a desk slid against the wall below it. Harry assisted James onto the desk before climbing on himself. They peered out at the lawn. It was eerily quiet. The office door cracked, the wood splintered, and the door smashed open, the hinges were bust. The screaming black tar beast stumbled in, followed by a bloody mouthed mob of the dead. Each zombie with a blank stare limping towards them.

White clouds cumulated overhead; a rung-out sun now heated the earth. The heat could be a killer. Sweltering heat was not uncommon on the island, and with a lack of water it wouldn't be long before he experienced seizures or heatstroke.

There was absolutely no time to ponder. The dead fast approached the desk, the jump looked higher now, and Harry had butterflies. The worry James or him would be injured conjured up images of becoming crippled after the jump and becoming grass and meat pies if the zombies jumped after them. Harry grabbed James's shoulder and they both jumped out.

They landed hard on the grass. James whimpered and Harry grunted as his throbbing legs gave way. The bag had banged against his spine and the bruised ribs. Harry flicked his neck round to look at the window, his spine cracked. Groans whistled with the breeze. A wild-eyed zombie leant out of the window - a woman, wearing only white pyjama bottoms with purple blotched skin – fell forward.

Harry pushed James out the way and got to his feet. He grabbed James's hand and began a fast limp back towards the front of the building.

Harry looked back, the dead fell one after another out of the window, on top of each other. Bones snapped and the dead struggled to get up. They were not free yet.

Harry pulled James along and he dropped Sam.

'Wait,' James cried tiredly. Harry halted to let the extremely lucky cat be retrieved. There was no way the cat would survive this; Sam was a big hindrance.

Harry watched the zombies begin to pursue, their broken arms swinging like dolls. They continued towards the front of the building.

Harry couldn't hear or see the screaming beast anymore. His ear stung from an aching eardrum, it was burst, he couldn't hear anything out of it.

As they reached the front of the building, more dead shambled from the right. Harry slowed.

The church stood out, a hundred or so zombies lined the streets. The dead turned, they began to walk towards them, some fell over in the excitement. Another wall was coming to block Harry. Harry could feel the sharp dread creeping up his arms and snaking around his pelvis and spine.

'To the church James,' Harry gasped, before leading his son over the muddying terrain towards safety. The muddy grass clogged his stride and then he stepped onto the concrete. They were close, they could do this.

More zombies trailed after them, undead neighbours poured from the houses. Harry couldn't tell who was alive anymore, if anyone. The road was covered in blood and Harry heard distant screams. Harry turned around; the dead had gained on him.

Harry couldn't react, the pursuing dead with their excitable hunger latched onto his shoulder. Harry pushed James forward out the way. The dead swarmed him. James sprinted off towards the church with Sam. Harry could see a figure, possibly cannibalistic, waiting.

Harry had a feeling they were both about to die. Time slowed, and the sky lit up bright pink and orange, his vision began to sink into darkness and scratching began to surround his head. He shoved and kicked. The dead were strong. He understood this was it, this was the only chance he had, this life was the only life he had and dying was not an option.

He swung his left arm and walloped a zombie in the face, its cheek cracked, and black pus squirted onto Harry's filthy clothes. Harry saw James had reached the distant figure, safe.

Harry felt his arms go limp and he collapsed onto the road. An oblivion of fuzzy warmth encompassed his skull. The clattering of devilish teeth and a dozen hungry mouths were chattering around him, the stank of guts was vomit-inducing.

Harry was conscious, and even though his eyes were closed, he could see. His vision was cloudy, he was looking through his eyelids. Dean appeared, holding Sam's hand. Two other men and a woman accompanied him.

Harry was silent, unable to move, but able to see the dead dropped to their knees. Their heads bobbed around his body, they were smelling his flesh, they might claw at his stomach.

Dean was keeping an eye on the situation while simultaneously gripping James's hand. The zombies had a good smell and examination of Harry's unconscious body. Then they rose and filtered away from him. They were disinterested, their sights now set on Dean and his companions. James's face teared and little Sam meowed. Harry was hopeless to do anything.

The zombies were stumbling around him, their ghastly bloodied faces pursued Dean instead. Dean seemed reluctant to run, instead looking to Harry. Whatever Harry had Dean clearly wanted. Harry listened, and he could hear the Sedan doors open.

'Get in and keep him inside,' Dean shouted. Harry hoped Dean would come back, help him.

A scream echoed from the church. The dead stopped and then continued as if they were being called forth. The cries of men and women and children came from the church, probably being ripped to shreds. Whoever was in the church, it was too late to save them now. Only a Deus ex Machina could save them now.

Harry watched through closed eyes as Dean limply jogged towards Harry's body. He was weaving round the dead, ducking and diving as the dead tried to grab him.

Harry watched; a gunshot rung out. Dean stopped and searched his person, probably for a gun. It wasn't surprising that people would take up arms, however limited. Two more shots went off, closer. The birds overhead scattered with a squawk. A few zombies fell to the ground. Harry watched Dean get closer.

Dean crouched; he was being grabbed at like items in a black Friday sale. One of the zombie bastards had ripped through his shirt.

A gunshot deafened Harry. A corpse fell beside Dean. Whoever was behind Dean held a gun and was approaching fast. Harry heard the group in the car shouting for Dean to turn around. Dean did so.

A gunshot fired point blank into Dean's skull. His body limply fell and rolled over onto the patch of grass next to Harry.

A bulky man wearing leather stood over Dean, shotgun in one hand, knife in the other. His eyes were red, and he growled as he stood over the body.

Dean's blood stained the wet green grass brown. The killer laughed before driving the tainted steel bowie knife sideways into an incoming corpses head. The killer's hands bulged.

The shotgun smoked from the barrel. He shot more zombies, but they continued to come, oblivious to their fate.

He chuckled as he blasted the crowd of undead. The shotgun clicked empty. The man approached Harry and knelt next to him. The man's face was clear. Charlie had found him again.

CHAPTER 27

Hostage

The main street of Beach Town had once thrived with shoppers, parents and toddlers alike. They would swing bags merrily and weave around the vine laden cracks in the sidewalk before basking under the sun.

Main street was now laden with bodies of dead families. Previous neighbours who had fought each other to get into the supermarket, only to be shot.

The police stood guard at the doors of the police station, picking off the dead who would stumble by now and again. Many of them had washed further into the urbanised area, main street was a post-war zone.

The armed police officers waited for orders, orders that would not come. Medical personnel had been placed inside the station due to unexpected problems with the temporary tent out in the rear car park.

Very few survivors remained, none of which were particularly talkative. Who would be? The docs had to continue to collect blood samples and the officers had to scour the corridors, their boots grimy. The officers were determined to detain the man still broadcasting from the radio station. Beach Town was being fed a bogus broadcast, a seriously uncontrolled version of events. It had to be stopped.

Pink cumulous clouds were scattered through the sky, the rain droplets spitting like ice stones as they hit the pavement with a clink.

The scene outside the supermarket was uncleared, a half-eaten mess. The dead had had a buffet on their way into town.

The motorway was now going darker under the pink evening sky. The highway was the only viable way out. Not one officer or doctor or survivor could have known the true extent of the situation. The bridge was blown to bits, the concrete destroyed, flung to the shoreline below. An oil tanker had rested underneath the bridge, and now it had sunk into the sea as waves crashed against the blackened rocks of the shoreline, black with oil which leeched to the sands.

Three military tanks were stagnant, the olive-green camo was barely visible in the dusk light. Soldiers surrounded the tanks, there was a commandeering chief giving orders, and a man with a radio on top of one tank, his broadcast short and repetitive, his shallow nod not reassuring the other soldiers.

Harry and James were caught by Charlie. Sheila was boarded up in her flat, arrogant to any help. Many residents were at home unaffected, unaware of the shear reach of the dead.

* * *

Charlie had driven as quietly as he could through the dead from the fire station lawn, but not before leaving the two men whom Dean had brought along and duck taping the woman's mouth shut. He had no need to tie her hands, the shotgun deterred her.

Blood trickled down Harry's forehead. His son was next to him, trying to wake him by prodding his ribs.

The car had rolled through the built-up area and approached the beginning of main street. Charlie investigated the rear-view mirror, the houses in the distance were alight. Houses were on fire, not from the zombies emotionally attacking the décor or wooden porches, but because many houses had been out of gas for a few days without realising it. The boilers had run dry and then sparked. Charlie knew the fires would die down in a few hours, then chuckled, to which James and Sam watched in awe.

Charlie turned right down main street. He could see police officers outside the station and wished he had gone the other way. There was a dirt road that led from the back of the estates to the motel. That would have been better. He had gotten what he needed.

A couple of cars blocked the road. Abandoned-doors-open style, the radio station drowned the silence with a monotone voice, a pre-recorded message. Charlie couldn't believe the radio hadn't attracted the zombies. But right on cue, he saw a few corpses pop up from the bar, the officers tiptoed down the station steps, equipped their guns and knelt. They fired their guns, three or four bullets pierced through the crowd of dead drunks. The stragglers were down before the officers retreated up to the door where they holstered their guns.

'Smart', Charlie remarked, noting the silencers attached to their guns. He eyed his shotgun; the brown barrel was cracked, and the grip worn down. He needed something bigger and silent.

The car rolled forward, the fuel light was lit. The stench of possible sewerage engulfed their noses. The cat meowed loudly and jumped down under the seat.

Charlie unintentionally ran over a few zombies who hadn't seen the car coming. After it ran over a second body, it conked out and stopped, no fuel.

'Shit,' Charlie groaned, scanning the street trying to determine a safe route around the police station. Or a safe route into the station. It was too risky going back to the motel, once was enough.

The women wriggled, muffling and whimpering for help. Charlie had forgotten about her and dug his elbow into her ribs. Her tears began to loosen the tape. Charlie knew he'd be able to use her as bait if needed. The kid was a problem. Charlie was sick of children; he should have left the kid back at the fire station.

'I'll deal with you very soon,' he told her.

Charlie grabbed his bloody blade from the dashboard. He twisted the blade in his hand and brought the steel close to his face. Charlie inhaled and let out a sigh before dropping the blade, it clanked down onto his shotgun in his lap.

Harry was still unconscious; Charlie couldn't hear him, that was good. Harry had gotten on his nerves at the hospital. But this kid, he continued to prod and to entertain the kitten.

'Name?' Charlie asked the woman, using his index and thumb to peel back the tape from her mouth.

'None of your business.' Charlie roughly dug his thumb into her cheek and the tape stuck again.

It was a literal nightmare of a decision. Police would not sit idly, and watch Charlie carry Harry's body around and with a noisy cat and gagged woman. The only other option as Charlie saw, was to get into the radio station and call for help.

The car conked out two shops from the radio station building on the left, another building or two to the police station on the right.

Thick coagulated fog and mist whipped and snaked over the dead bodies lying in the street and around the building, a sackcloth of ashlar. A mysterious silence drumming the air, piercing Charlie's brain.

The car seat was uncomfortable, and Charlie shuffled his sore glutes to a better position. His ass scratches itchy. It would not be safe for long, sitting vulnerable in the car in a haze. The creatures would surely wobble back to main street at the first smell of flesh.

'Your time is here, so be useful,' Charlie leant over the woman and ripped the tape from the lady's face, she whelped and curled into a ball. Her body small, her clothes skimpy tight. Charlie crumbled the tape in his hand and pushed opened her door.

The creaking passenger door attracted the attention of the police officers. They were looking, Charlie froze and then shoved the woman to the damp road surface. The woman would allow enough time to get the kid and Harry out and to the radio station. Charlie could then radio for help, possibly going back to the motel, he wasn't keen on the idea the kid was his, he probably wasn't.

She groaned and clawed at the floor before dragging herself into the sheet of fog and out of sight. Charlie had only glimpsed a wound in her leg, perhaps a bite.

Charlie carefully opened his door and swung his legs onto the concrete before stepping out.

Everything sounded crystal. The wind slipping around his ears. The smell of the salty sea air invigorated him. Charlie was tiresome trying to move, his stitched throat giving him sharp needles from the icy breeze. The sedative lingered, Charlie had a moment of clarity, but it faded, and moans of the beasts started to echo down the street. Adrenaline buzzed through him; his sense of survival heightened. He turned and opened the rear car door.

Inside the rear passenger seats, nothing. The boy and the cat were gone. Charlie quickly scanned the area; the kid and kitten were escaping from the front passenger door.

'God damn it!' Charlie shouted, about to pursue, when a wave of fear trickled over him. The beasts appeared through the thick smog, surrounding him, five or six of the bastards. Charlie went for the gun and knife he had left on the driver's seat.

The corpses were translucent, their face ghostly in the condensation. Half torn hands, spaghettis of ligaments, boned fingers began to claw at his jacket. Bastards were tearing into the leather.

Charlie's adrenaline gushed into his heart, he darted into the driver's door, reaching in, grabbing the knife and turning and jabbing it rapidly into the dead's afflicted skulls. The beast's oncoming in numbers unseen. More and more, a sea of unchartered proportions.

Charlie was primal, a beastly presence took over him, he would not go down without a fight to the death, not now, not ever. Fucking kids. Harry was still unconscious in the backseat.

Charlie battled throwing fists and knife jabs in an ever-thickening smog. The darkness of night settling over the town and where the mist met the night sky a thin blue line of hope faded.

The woman had crawled through to the police officers and before she could speak, they had shot her dead. Their silencers leaving the dead and Charlie unaware of their actions. The police officers now sneaked side by side, crouched, into the street where the light of the open car door revealed dancing shadows that were falling fast. It was Charlie, the police had locked on and kept their eyes down the sights and fired.

Charlie was caught on the leg by a weight, a heavy clay of dead bodies fell as they were shot by the police. Charlie fell to his stomach, his ribs cracked, and his spine stiffened. It was increasingly painful on the tarmac ground as the beasts piled upon Charlie and within thirty seconds the recognisable faint whips of air of the silent pistols went dead themselves.

Charlie struggling to move or breathe, bodies were crushing his spine, some of the bodies barely clothed, some of the creatures' guts were spilling onto his jacket and pants. The stench was foul even by Charlie's standards.

Charlie heard the officer's approach, their boots clip clopping on the road. They were unaware of him; god help him if they saw him move and decided to drop a slug or two into his skull. One of the officers knelt next to the bodies and rooted through the corpse's pockets. Charlie had one eye on him, dirty copper, killing and stealing. The officer retrieved a pack of cigarettes from a dressing gown of a man and a pack of tic tacs from a woman's jeans. The other officer was peered into the car door, his gun clanked against the metal door. Charlie knew they might be tempted to take the shotgun. More groans echoed through the foggy mains street. The officer had found Harry, as he stepped next to Charlie's face to look in the rear passenger door.

'Looks like this one might be alright, slightly bruised but nonetheless looks human,' the officer said, reaching in and grabbing Harry's body.

'Hurry,' the other officer said, 'they are coming.' Both the officers went in to grab Harry. They both stowed their pistols and cradled Harry's arms over their shoulders. Charlie watched in anger, desperately trying to retrieve some grip. They slung Harry into a supported position over their shoulders and walked off into the fog. Charlie's eyes burned from trying to watch everything. The blood pooled into the forehead; rage coursed his arms, but he was taken back. Charlie could see footsteps emerge from under the bonnet and there he was trailing after the police and Harry, the kid carrying that kitten.

Charlie sensed fresh beasts closing in, the stragglers - unaware of his presence – coldly encircling the car.

CHAPTER 28

Negotiations

Sheila had resorted herself to the only act she was comfortable with, the only foreseeable way to spend the end of days, drinking jasmine tea and hanging on to the hope that rescue might be coming.

She had pushed her furniture, the cracking coffee table and her smaller two-seat sofa against her bolted flat door.

The entire floor must be vacant, Sheila had not heard a whisper from the neighbouring flats. People she never knew personally, they were distant memories of a life now stolen from her. The dead has fucked her plans.

She had watched as residents had evacuated from the lower levels en-mass. It was depressing to see them leave, but Sheila was certain others had stayed, noises and bangs had echoed from below. A sure sign that someone was still in there.

Sheila gazed out of the flat window, dreaming of that interview, of the city. Creatures that had tormented and destroyed people's lives at the hospital were now invading the entire town. The corpses mere shadows spread across the grass.

The corpses were clumsy, they fell over inanimate objects like the bins and benches and tripped over each other's feet.

Last night was one of the worst she had come through. Cold and lonely. This night was darker in every sense of the word. The streetlamps had dimmed and gone out about three hours ago. She kept the clock next to her on the window ledge. 2am, but she doubted it was correct, it never was. It had caused many late awakenings with its faulty hour arm.

Drinking tea was becoming repetitive, a naïve attempt to escape boredom.

Outside her flat door, someone must have been wandering the corridors because someone began to bang and dig their nails into the wood. Not friendly.

Sheila jolted and her tea spilt over her lap. It was cold and she frowned. Spilling tea didn't matter anymore, so she tossed the cup at the door and it shattered, the ceramic pieces spearing onto the sofa she had pushed against the door. She scowled with a savagely shaking upper lip. Whoever it was stopped immediately.

Her desire to escape had risen, and the rage was more than she could handle. Her choices for escape, and where to escape to, were slim. Attempt to go down the stairs and hope last night hadn't given rise to a break in. Gangs rendering the hallways free of corpses with shivs and 3inch blades, or stay and die of starvation, thirst, or hypothermia, because this apartment was freezing without heating.

Sheila leant on the window frame. Her books propped up on the ledge, a selection of old and new interests. Through her haze of uncertainty, fear, she spotted a text on languages, specifically Spanish, to which she had become accustomed to some years ago. It had been useful on holiday and family holidays, but those days are gone, like the heartbeat from most of the towns people. The thought made her chuckle. A memory, albeit temporarily retrieved in time to save her from jumping. She also spotted a small, rough-edged box of matches wedged in the middle of another two books, and a bent cigarette beside the matchbox.

She plucked the matchbox from between the books and examined the damp corners. Sheila held the matches and gazed into the night sky, a sea of stars shone brighter than she ever recalled, she had no memories of this, or a time when she had pondered the universe or life's big questions. She picked the cigarette up and straightened it out. She opened the matchbox, and there was at least five or six left. She stuck the match and lit the cigarette.

The first inhalation was foul, and the taste made her gag. She tossed it to the floor and stomped it out.

She examined the matchbox again. It was dampened from the condensation, but the italic black lettering was visible. It read 'Harry's matchbox', at first sight it seemed mundane, but Sheila was overcome with tears and she wished she had stuck with Harry. To think she declined to go with him after he specifically came back for her was a terrible mistake, an utter fuck up.

The plastic window frame was chipped along the bottom and the corners were damp. Sheila lifted herself higher, she had to stand up, her legs were beginning to lose circulation. She lit a match, and then another before lighting the matchbox on fire and throwing it onto the sofa that was pushed against the door. The sofa was the most flammable thing she could see in the flat. It was rapidly alight, and a blazing flame tore through the fabric. Her mind was whirling, the flame was hot and that relieved her.

A few days ago, she was on her way to an interview, on her way out of Beach Town. Now she was staring into fighting blue and red flames and cackling as the plastic buttons of the sofa melted. She did wonder in that moment, whether she might have got the interview.

*

The main reception hall of the police station was housing a half dozen officers, equipped with assault rifles and pistols. The receptionist was miraculously still alive, but she was not an officer in the modern-day sense, her role consisted of strictly paperwork.

Dean had given her a day worth of firing training on a field range. Dean was no longer alive, and he would not be coming back, not even as one of the undead. The officers awaited obliviously for Dean to return. In the centre of the entrance hall, now candle lit as the station didn't have generators, sat a metallic table from one of the interview rooms. On top of the table a matte-black portable wireless two-way radio.

Harry had been placed in the corner on a makeshift bed – consisting of nothing more than emergency blankets and a spare pillow from the cells – he was showing signs of life which was promising. James and Sam slept soundly next to him.

When the officers had realised James was in pursuit as they had carried Harry into the station, they could not shoot him down, physically they couldn't grab their guns to do so.

Emerging from the darkness of the staircase were the only two doctors on hand to help with anything. Since the dead were in no way treatable, they became mere assistance to the officers rather than the objective givers. They carried first aid bags and one of them also held a briefcase with the red cross symbol.

The officers gave them a wide birth, as one doctor headed straight to the officer with the radio and began talking to him about awaiting a response. The other heavy footed it to Harry and James, kneeling on the emergency blanket and feeling Harry's wrist.

'Weak pulse,' he muttered, leaning his ear to Harry's mouth. The doctor shook his head and opened his briefcase - a leather brown, number lock case – retrieving a needle and bottle. The doctor examined Harry's arms, the veins were evident, not for the right reasons. Harry had a black streak running along his right arm and the doctor rubbed the vein and inserted the needle. The blood did not flow smoothly, it spurted into the sample bottle, the blood was cherry red.

'Bridge evacuation…to disease…control, police station… emergency services, anyone,' a man's voice shoddily echoed through the radio, interrupted by heavy hissing. Everyone in the room went silent as they listened to the radio, and an officer darted to the centre room table, to the radio. The doctor attending to Harry paused, noting the chaos, and quickly finished withdrawing blood before sneakily tucking the blood sample into his right trouser pocket. After which he returned to the centre table, and the strange man's voice came through again.

'Evacuation to emergency services, please reply, contact mandatory, over.' It was crystal clear now, like magic. Everyone stood up, some of the officers were sweating heavily and loosened their shirts and one officer dropped his gun on the floor and sobbed as he fell to his knees. They all looked exhausted gazing in stupor at each other. The eldest officer,

Paul it said on his nametag, took the radio and clicked the talk button.

'Police services to evacuation, we're here and waiting for orders. I say again, we are here and we all here you loud and clear,' he coughed. 'We are so happy you're out there, evac, over.' Officer Paul trembled towards the end and cheered. All the officer began patting each other's backs whilst awaiting the response. The doctors gave a yawping hooray to the ceiling.

'Okay officers, we read you loud and clear too, but I'm afraid there is some sad news.' The radio went silent again and officer Paul went white, sweating heavily from his brow.

'Come on what sad news?' officer Paul yelled. Everyone else looked melancholy.

The doctor who had taken Harry's blood, peered towards Harry, James and Sam, they were all asleep still. He scanned the room, and nobody was paying attention to him. The doctor calmly placed his stethoscope onto the table and began to pace backwards before turning around and walking to the front door. The sample was still in his trouser pocket.

The radio crackled static and beeped, 'Officers, evacuation is off the table for now, we have blown the only way out of Town for your own safety and to try and prevent the threat from growing,' the man said. 'Western planet earth is a thing of the past, welcome to the apocalypse brothers. I think you may need some time to digest this, so please stay calm and maintain law and order, and rescue as many civilians as you can. Avoid the North of the island, its swamped. We can arrange a pickup further down the line when we have a safe outpost to evac to, that might be your best bet, alpha evac out.' It was a long, uninterrupted broadcast that left a shadow of fear overhanging the officers. The radio hissed before transitioning into a constant monotone beep. Officer Paul turned the radio off and put it onto the table..

'I'll be fucking damned, civilisation gone,' officer Paul paused and rubbed the sweat from his cheeks, his face whiter than his shirt. 'I expected it to be controllable,' officer Paul laughed hysterically, his wrinkled neck tightened, and he swiftly reached for his holstered pistol, pointing it at his forehead before anyone could react and squeezing the trigger.

The gunshot rang out and blood spurted from the officer's head as he fell motionless to the freshly bloodied stone floor. Everyone panicked, the officers jumped backwards, sinking their heads into their hands whilst some slid down walls wailing and moaning.

At the front door of the police station was the doctor who hadn't even made it two steps, he was screwed. An angry Charlie met him with a red eyed grin and stature that stood over the doc. The doctor gasped to plead.

The doctor received the full force of Charlie's vengeful punch. Charlie's knuckle cracked as he broke doctor's nose and blood trickled down the doc's face.

Charlie was savage, his veins bulged, and his teeth snarled. The moonlight shone on them both and Charlie grabbed the doctor and decided to snap his neck. He dragged the body to the side of the staircase and propped him up against the sidewall.

The shotgun was hidden down Charlies pants and his knife firmly in his trouser pocket, a knife that could stab a hole big enough for a gold ball.

He would have gone straight in. But it was better to lure them out then raid the station.

Charlie knelt and routed through the doctor's trousers. He pulled out the vial of blood, the blood now black and Charlie puked to the side.

Main street was silent and empty for now. The fog had cleared, and the street was a clear wreck. Dead bodies outside the supermarket, bullet holes in the pub windows and a few crashed cars ditched in the middle of the road.

'Interesting, what were you trying to do with this?' Charlie murmured and put the blood sample into his trouser pocket. He began to climb the police station steps.

CHAPTER 29

Remnants

The motel was desolated, four or five zombies wandered the car park. The only occupants of the motel – Charlies newborn child and prostitute fling – sat in the candle lit room. Luckily for Delila, Samuel was calm and had slept non-stop since Charlie left.

The zombies outside were unaware of their presence. Delila was sat on the bed looking out of the dirty motel window when a figure emerged from the darkness rapidly heading towards the room. Delila carefully placed Samuel into the pram, the cushions rustled as he lay down.

The thumps on the motel room door rattled the chain lock. Delila stood next to the window to see through the glass, the curtain wrapped around her body. Another thump on the wood, Samuel slept through it, for now. Moans rippled through the motel. Delila turned her head to see where it was coming from, the dead were shambling from the neighbouring rooms. Delila hesitated and reluctantly went to the door peephole. She could see the young man outside, cherry faced. She gripped the handle and unlocked the door chain and opened the door.

Douglas, the petrol station attendant who had made his escape over the bouldering side bank. Douglas had snuck himself into a ditch and hid until he could move, that was hours ago when it was daylight. Charlie had climbed over the boulders unaware of Douglas hiding in the ditch on the other side. Douglas had a purple bruise along his right forearm and a cut on his left hand.

'Stand in the corner over there, away from the pram,' Delila pushed the door shut, careful not to slam it and wake Samuel. She pointed to the corner, her eyes piercing Douglas who was panting, he wiped his brow. The carpet had become wet from Douglas's shoes and muddy footprints now stained the carpet. He stood in the furthest corner next to the bathroom door. The wallpaper was peeling as he leant against the wall.

Both eyed each other cautiously moving with precision. Douglas looked at the pram and the sleeping baby, Delila quickly stood in front of the pram, blocking his view.

'I'm Douglas,' he said. Delila was inattentive and Douglas twitched uneasily as the silence expanded.

'Delila,' she smiled and instantly both their shoulders relaxed, and they were more flexible. Douglas sunk to the floor, accidently peeling the wallpaper off with his shirt. He was younger than Delila, her face was bearing undereye bags and his eyes were still fresh. 'Meet Samuel, he's not too talkative right now,' Delila quipped and rested her forearms on the pram, baby Samuel no longer suckling on the milk bottle he had been sleeping with. Douglas laughed. It seemed to be going well. Douglas had a strip of wallpaper over his shoulder, and his legs quivered. The room was dimly lit. It was too dark for him to fully realise Delila's bruises.

'Where's the man that was here?' Douglas enquired; his crescent smile turned to a frown of empathy. Delila cried and a few tears dripped onto her forearm. Douglas tried to stand but had to crawl over to the bed and pull himself up. Douglas was better able to see the baby boy from the bed. Douglas couldn't help but let out a big grin. Delila didn't look impressed and pointed back to the corner.

'Stay there,' she shrieked, and Douglas went pale. The atmosphere was tense again. The air conditioning buzzing went silent, the absence of fresh air gave the room a musky appearance. All that remained in the petty motel room was the uncomfortable bed, covered in a cream pink throw over and a bathroom which housed used razors and shaving cream. Douglas had a stern look of anger in his grimace and sat on the floor next to the bathroom door once again, knees to his chest.

'I'll tell you where he is, he's gone because he doesn't care,' she quivered, her mouth agape, her eyes sunken.

'I want to help you and your baby get out of here and go somewhere safe, the town hall or the police station.' Douglas tried to sound optimistic. Delila wiped her eyes and the tears kept rolling from her cheeks onto arm. Douglas rolled his eyes, realising how difficult that sounded, exhaustion coarsely soared through the air. Delila seemed unmotivated to move. Vehicles were out of the question and the hospital was surely no safe zone. 'We could try and make our way to the motorway,' Douglas continued. 'But that means having to put up with being in a car for a few hours, that's if we find a car with keys. I know of a car, parked at the back of the petrol station, the keys are usually always stashed in the exhaust. Belonged to the owner,' Douglas spoke empathetically and twiddled his thumbs, gazing into the carpet, almost self-pitying himself.

'I don't want Samuel to be in danger,' Delila blurted. 'As for the man earlier, he's beyond redemption, I wouldn't want to find him again,' she cried and sat down on the bed, the quilt rustled.

'We don't have to find him,' Douglas said. 'You can wait here while I fetch the car, I just want to make sure you and your baby…Samuel, get to safety. It seemed unfair to leave you here that's why I came back, I could hear a baby crying,' Douglas explained, his eyes met Delila's glassy eyes, they were breaking barriers, of age and of expectations, building trust, although Delila appeared hesitant to trust still.

'I couldn't exonerate him from his ignorance, please don't abandon us like he did,' Delila sobbed, drying her eyes and reaching a hand to Samuel. Samuel slept peacefully, but for how long was anyone's guess. Douglas pushed himself to his feet and this time approached Delila with determination. He sat opposite Delila on the bed.

The dirty window was drowning in moonlight, the candle lit room surreal with compassion. He put his hand to hers, and she took it. Douglas looked into her eyes and blushed. They could now trust each other, it was hard to trust in this new reality, they were the remnants of humanity. The order they had found, amongst the moment of peace, was disturbed by the scratching on the wall. The neighbours mustn't have left. The occupants had to be dead, or at least halfway.

'We can sleep tonight,' Douglas spoke. 'There's a few hours of darkness left; I'll keep watch.' Douglas retreating to the wall next to the bathroom door, where the paper had peeled off. A content smile on his face. Delila shuffled up the bed and lay down, pulling the blanket over herself and closing her eyes.

Rain began pattering on the window frame, the inside covered in streaks of dust. The moonlight now obscured by clouds and the only source of light in the room, the candle on the bedside table, was melting fast.

***

Morning broke over the rooftops, remnants of humanity shimmered across Beach Town, scattered fires lit up parts of the neighbourhoods, corpses shambled in every corner alley and down every street. Electricity was out, water was out, phonelines were fried and emergency service numbers failed to dial. Nothing of the busy town remained, it was akin to a deserted town. The only survivors left had taken shelter in homes, some families were lucky to survive, and others fortified their front doors. The police on patrol were now rogue militants. The police station was home to a chaotic and uncoordinated team of undertrained officers. The only way out of town, blocked.

The screaming black tar creatures had gathered a following of various corpses, each dressed uniquely, some in their birthday suits – or death day suits – some were half eaten, guts trailing along the concrete slabs of the pavements. The creatures were aptly named screamers by the remaining serving officers, roaming Beach Town with a gang of the undead in tow. The officers had one way to contact each other, their radios, and that was not efficient enough, considering the radios were constantly cutting out due to interference.

It was Sheila who had witnessed the screamers inflict death. They possessed great agile capabilities and tended to crouch in bushes. They would use their hands as razors and cut the throats of the victims. The victims would fall and then corpses would pile on them.

It was as if – as Sheila had murmured as her flat burnt - *they were feeding the dead*. Sheila was watching over the town from a high, safe window. The new day shone into her apartment where blue flames whipped and flicked viciously, it was a short matter of time before she had no choice but to jump.

A few stragglers roamed the motel, clueless braindead freaks were waddling in the mesmerising crisp red dawn. People once considered smart were now walking into walls and gazing moronically at the crows and seagulls that swooned overhead.

Their slowness had given Douglas an idea, especially since he had managed to reach the Jeep behind the petrol station. The keys had been in the exhaust. He had to get it running and to the motel room quietly without attracting them. He was locked inside the Jeep. The doors secured. The distant hills behind the petrol station shimmered with a heat, the island was like that, unpredictable weather. Up and down, rain and sunshine.

Today the weather didn't matter, surviving did. Humanity now had to endure a battle of redemption, of security and trust. Douglas smirked, empowered by the sunrise, keying the ignition, a look of determination across his face and fire from the sunlight in his eyes, unmoved, powerful.

The vehicle revved to life and the brown four door Jeep shot a clump of black smoke out the rear smouldering the bricks of the petrol station as Douglas shifted to first. The bins were overloaded. The building riddled with cracks sprouting olive vines and spouting weeds from every crevice.

Around the corner an open road, he toed the accelerator and the Jeep rolled forward. Creeping the Jeep around the building Douglas saw a clear route approximately thirty yards to the motel. The ticking over of the small engine was drawing the attention of birds that feasted on dropped foods and crisp packets. Some crows rested inside the abandoned cars that had been dumped at the pumps. Fuel was spilt over the floor, Douglas spotted it and as the Jeep drove over the spillage, he tightened the grip on the steering wheel. The entire place could explode, go nuclear, if something sparked it. All it would take is a shot of fumes from the exhaust and the petrol station and motel and all birds would be obliterated.

Douglas pulled the Jeep alongside the motel room. Douglas put the handbrake on and honked the horn, a few monsters stumbled out of the other motel rooms. Naked women came from the room furthest away, Douglas admired their naked splendour with a grin. They still looked alive if it wasn't for that crooked stall paced limp. The morning dew on the windshield gave everything a fuzzy appearance. One of the motel rooms seemed to be coveted in a white smoke. Douglas could not move at the realisation that the smoke flickering from one of the motel rooms could be a raging fire inside. He shivered and his stomach rumbled which attracted the undead from the petrol station.

'Come on, where are you,' Douglas complained, his arms shaking and the car vibrations rippling through his spine with every revolution. He honked the horn again, longer.

Delila appeared from the motel room carrying Samuel. Douglas gritted his teeth hoping there was time for her to get in the Jeep without getting eaten or blowing up. Douglas spotted the electrocuted officer in the puddle, the officers burnt face and torn flesh made Douglas quiver. Delila approached the Jeep, but her timing didn't ease Douglas's grimace.

Flames began to spit from the doorway further down. The dead were fast approaching the bonnet, clawing at the metal. The sound was like marbles rolling across a stainless-steel sheet.

Delila struggled to open the door and get in, but she managed to place Samuel - who was awake and wide eyed and calm - on the seat. Douglas could not take his sight from the flickering flames in the doorway or the beasts in the rear-view mirror.

'Come on for god's sake,' Douglas cried out. 'Come on!' The creatures started clawing the doors. Delila was in and holding Samuel in her arms again.

Douglas floored the acceleration pedal. They all sunk into the leather seats as the Jeep screeched off, as Douglas turned sharp left and onto the main road. One of the corpses arms had torn off in the tire as the body was flung sideways into the motel wall. The Jeep was speedily beginning its journey to main street. The boulders side bank was lined with blood streaks and remains of bodies. There was shirts and random items of clothing scattered over the side bank.

Douglas looked in the rear-view mirror, his face dripping in sweat. The motel and station grew smaller. The flames erupted into the air, a small grey mushroom cloud appeared, then a bang rumbled through the road, followed by a pop, the shockwave rippled through the steering wheel and the glass in the rear-view mirror smashed and Delila screamed and Samuel began to cry. The journey to salvation had begun.

CHAPTER 30

The Revelation

The remaining police officers stood quietly around the radio table, watching the radio eagerly whilst sipping the last of the water from the fountain in Styrofoam cups. Charlie was making his way around the station without being noticed after slipping in the back door. Keenly spying the police and eager for Harry to wake up. Charlie had found the bandages on Harry's wounds awe inspiring. The pain from his neck scar pulsed for the remainder of his pacing. He finally settling on a darkened oak bench near the reception desk.

After removing officer Pauls body – another officer managed to find the janitors mop and clean the mess using a bottle of surface disinfectant – the officers stood twiddling thumbs and asking each other open ended questions such as *what could we do next* and *how did this start*. One of them had brought down the steel chairs from interrogation rooms.

James and Sam had woken and were merrily playing but James constantly looked at his father. Sam jumped on Harry a couple of times. The remaining doctor had to shout at him so he wouldn't claw at Harry's already wounded body.

Charlie watched with a grin. Charlie had no need to move. The two officer's stationed at the front door had re-entered. Seemingly unaware of the body that Charlie had dumped over the sidewall. Because of their obliviousness he could sit quietly, protected from the elements until rescue arrived, or however long until the officers spotted him.

Every officer had been rattled by the horrendous events that had unfolded. When the morning dew settled and the clear blue sky broke over town, the officers felt the remnants of the thundering clash of the motel explosion. The petrol station was blown to oblivion along with any survivors. It was pointless to call for any emergency services. The officers had grunted in agreement that they would stick together until rescue arrived.

Charlie appeared to find the officers amusing, bearing a jeering smirk across his stubbly face. The officers had been locking him up earlier. But after breaking one officers neck – amongst other victims – he sat joyfully watching the pigs sip the last of their supplies.

A young Caribbean male officer, unbuttoned white shirt, shaking hands and a nervous expression, walked over to the reception desk and was taken by surprise. Charlie smirked at the officer.

'I'm taking charge, get back to the radio and see if you can help,' the young officer said to Charlie. 'There obviously isn't any point waiting for the Lieutenant to arrive,' he continued. The officers slanted tag read Ken. Charlie burst out laughing, his coarse laugh breaking to a choke. Ken looked with distaste. Ken was a well-built man, and Charlie only had stature on his side, Ken could surely out manoeuvre Charlie.

The other officers glared to Charlie and Ken but didn't advance, unaware of the threat. Ken adjusted his belt. His trousers were torn along the shin.

'I'm sure you could,' Charlie replied, leaning against the reception desk and clasping his hands together in anticipation. Ken sternly gazed at Charlie.

'We should move all officers up to the roof,' officer Ken said. 'The top floor of the station. We need to get the word out to the men on the front line. God bless them I hope they are alive. To the rooftop. We'll set off the emergency flares from storage, the military isn't the only rescue,' Ken gasped with sweat sticking to his shirt. Ken rubbed his thin jawbone and it clicked. Charlie scorned.

'No chance,' one officer holding water said. The officers were beat, all of them appeared exhausted and bored.

'We should stay in the warm,' a middle-aged officer chipped in. 'We can't take our chances living on the roof.' All six officers mumbled followed by random agreements.

The doctor attended to Harry and James trying to keep his head low to avoid disagreement. Officer Ken went pale seeing the disagreement.

'You are a genius,' Charlie said sarcastically. 'We can wait on the roof until rescue arrives.' Charlie smiled deceptively. 'I think you are onto something,' Charlie continued whilst grimacing at the other officers.

'At least you are with me,' Ken sounded optimistic. The officers resumed their redundant quavering and talking, and Ken approached Charlie on the bench. Ken's shirt drenched and his face sunken.

Ken carried a pistol on his belt; the holster was unclipped. Charlie glimpsed the pistol and slowly reached into his jacket.

Before Ken could speak Charlie equipped his knife from his jacket and forcefully drove the dagger through Ken's stomach. Blood pooled from Ken's mouth and stomach down his trousers before collecting around his feet. Charlie wrapped his arm around Ken pulling him close. The officers were oblivious, but the doctor noticed.

'Stop!' the doctor yelled as his Poirot style moustache flicked.

The officer equipped their pistols. Sippy cups were dropped, and they had all pistol sights on Charlie. James coveted Sam and snuggled into his father's unconscious arms. One wrong move and Charlie was dead.

Ken was still breathing and whimpering, crying tears of blood. Charlie stood up using the dagger to lift Ken.

'Drop it,' the only female officer shouted. Her pistol was a silver colt with fire sight. She aimed straight at Charlie's head. He held Ken the Caribbean closer, ignoring the blood that spooled from Ken's brown lips onto his leather jacket.

To the right of the reception desk, the staircase. Where Harry lay unconscious on a makeshift bed whilst James and Sam hid in his arms.

She fired her colt, the bullet ricocheted off the rear stone wall.

'Whoa lady, not cool,' Charlie yelled. 'Fire again and I'll burn you all.' The female officer lowered her gun as another officer placed one hand on her shoulder.

The officers lowered their pistols. Charlie began to move towards the staircase. He reached the first step, froze and then tossed Ken forward snapping Ken's ankle. The station became an auditorium of high-pitched shouting before going silent. Charlie ducked his head and darted up the stairs.

Two officers ran for the stairs, but the doctor commanded them to stay and the officers stood down stowing their pistols. The officers turned to look at Ken's bleeding corpse, another lost warrior in the new world. Ken's eyes flickered as he exhaled his last breath.

'Another officer dead,' the doctor said. 'I think we should prioritise now. By the way, this patient is waking up and we need to secure him.' The doctor pointed to Harry who squirmed and groaned. James watched in awe, holding Sam tightly in his arms. Harry opened his eyes for the first time in hours and the doctor took a sharp intake of breath. The officers gossiped. James looked into the eyes of his father. Harry's eyes were milk white.

'Take your time,' the doctor said softly to Harry. 'You've sustained some damage, a few cuts and bruises. Heck you've been through a war. It Looks like you could do with some water too.' Harry propped himself up on his elbows. James let Sam loose and he didn't skitter off, but instead seemed intrigued by Harry, purring at him, rubbing his face on his arms. Harry gently stroked Sam. 'He can see, thank god,' the doctor added.

Some officers had been ignorant of anything the doctor had said but now they had looks of awe and respect. The female officer had moved to the bottom of the stairs, trying to see if Charlie was still in sight.

'He's gone,' she said. 'We can't let him run loose in the building.' Nobody was paying attention to her.

Harry looked pale and worn but had an expression of discerning judgement. Two officers returned to the front doors and left to guard the front. The door officers were briefed not to respond to the internal threats.

Harry was goggle eyed and his left arm shook. He felt his leg wound, it was now cleansed and bandaged, the tape neatly cut by the doctor. He felt his new clothes, someone changed him. Sam rubbed against his hands, tail up and weaving his head around. Harry smiled and then hugged James tightly. James pushed him away with a profound smile.

The doctor had walked to the table for the water cups. He took one and then pulled a strip of paracetamol from his pocket. Harry felt a pulse of relief. His head hadn't ached so much since having a hangover, but he struggled to remember when that was. Time had dilated, Harry forgot where he was and what was happening. The confusion made him tremble. The doctor now placed the cup in his hands, and Harry took the pills the doc had popped out for him. Two gulps and the water were as ice, refreshing. Immediately the officers jumped back, each startled and commenting. Words buzzed in Harry's head. The room became a glowing orb of light, and then faded to normalcy again.

'If you can't deal with it then try and do something useful,' the doctor choked kneeling next to Harry. Shakily he placed his hand on Harry's shoulder and Harry felt more confusion. 'Can you talk? Take it easy, you'll have time to recollect the situation later,' the doctor added, scratching his white stubble. Harry pushed himself up, with the help of the doctor, into a sitting position against the staircase. He felt the blanket and it was smoother than ever, it was unreally beautiful, the glow of each object intensified, and even James's skin looked vibrant and new. Harry made a thumbs up gesture with his hands. The doctor and James watched on in amusement. Sam skittered off towards the officer's. The police stood at ease, because Harry was awake and not a creepy walking dead.

Something flashed in Harry's right eye and he felt like talking but couldn't. His mouth moving jaggedly. Harry touched his cheeks with his detailed index, its wrinkles like canyons of warping black matter. The world of his hands was all-encompassing of his imagination. He thought momentarily that he was on drugs, but he wasn't, because he felt absent minded. Harry looked around at the figures appeared with a small orange simmering light around them which faded to purple and white. His throat popped air and the words croaked out as if his oesophagus were dry.

'Where…Where…Where,' Harry couldn't fathom the words, something to do with where he was. Trying to talk was a heavy pressing in his stomach. He pointed steadily to his forehead then gave a thumbs up. He knew his brain worked, but his voice didn't. God knows what other things didn't work, like his ability to walk straight. The doctor acknowledged with a smile and thumbs up.

'Good,' the doctor said. 'I'll be here if you need me but feel free to explore the main hall. Please refrain from going upstairs, some guy wearing a leather jacket has killed an officer and made for the upper levels.' The doctor stood and walked over to the radio table. The female officer returned from the staircase with an angered sour grimace wiped on her face.

Harry gulped and then realised with dread that it may be Charlie from the hospital. Charlie had been acting suspiciously after leaving the station, but had he returned, and for what reason. Memories flooded back. his lower back tingled, and his left leg ached. He rubbed the thigh, the clean joggers breathable and comforting. James hadn't moved from his fathers' side since he woke, and Harry was glad. But there was a feeling of emptiness in Harry's heart, as if he were unhappy to be alive. But he reassured himself, hugging James, that this was a brilliant thing. What he couldn't remember was the last words Sheila spoke, or his wife.

'Oh, call me John by the way, or doctor, it's up to you,' John the doctor called across to Harry, who managed a smile. His face was particularly tender. Some of the officers laughed and John shook it off with a middle finger. Harry could feel the sense of instant connection, everyone was literally surviving now so it didn't matter who was present, it only mattered that they weren't psycho's intent on hurting anyone. Harry chuckled to himself, his laugh fraught sharply with air.

'Why are your eyes black?' James asked, looking caringly to Harry. His stomach rumbled; he could use a sarnie sandwich. Then he noticed his bag and the other belongings from the fire station were gone. He did recall the phone call. The memory was brought back by hissing of the radio on the officers table. The officers were trying to contact someone, there monotone voices repeating the same message. They took turns. The female sounded more enthusiastic then the others. John was looking at a clipboard whilst taking notes and checking his briefcase. He appeared as if he had lost something.

The question James asked had shocked Harry. But he was withdrawn, and it didn't disturb him, nothing did anymore. Not after seeing a child torn to shred and a bunch of dead people shambling through a once thriving hospital. The stains from the attack were still present near the staircase, someone had done a bad job of wiping the blood up. The body had been laid beside the entrance. It was coincidental when an officer walked through the front doors, the sun and blue skies shone in the distance. The officer grabbed the bodies legs and dragged it out the door held open by his assisting officer. The body of the youngster left a trail of oily blood, it was dreamlike. Everything Harry had known was overturned. Then with a huge huff and a big inhale, Harry whispered fragilely.

'We'll be okay, James, we'll be okay.'

CHAPTER 31

Crowded

The station was at stalemate. The occupants stuck in a limbo, waiting for the so-called rescue to make contact. Evacuation could be months, if it even happens.

Doctor John had scrawled a message to be relayed over the radio and one younger officer took to reading it sharply. 'We may have an immune survivor,' the officer read the message aloud. Harry perked up to a sea of officers admiring him with a slight look of resentment.

The increasing number of zombies shambling through main street was evident by the wails echoing through the walls. Their predicament was escalating to dangerous levels. No matter how sunny it was, it felt miserable.

The officers outside the station front door were now firing their pistols, pop after pop of unsilenced takedowns.

Harry listened closely; the shouting was muffled as if muted by foam. The other officers stood around gazing at the front doors. The gunshots continued until the front doors slammed open and one officer stumbled into the station heaving and short of breath. The other officer was crouching at the entrance, popping round after round into the beasts.

'Assistance,' he cried. 'There has to be more than a dozen and they're not stopping!'

The remaining four officers scrambled to equip their pistols and darted towards the front doors.

Harry saw the variety of ripped clothes and gnawing faces the endless clawing to devour the officers before being shot point blank in the chest and skull. The moaning crescendo like waves of the sea. A thick salty breeze wafted into the hall. It smelt half sea, half dead. The dead were being slowed, but the relentless need to feed was not being subdued.

'God dammit keep them out!' another officer yelled. The officers managed to push them back and slowly but surely shut the front doors. Doctor John remained stagnant and fraught. James became overly anxious and fidgeted which irritated Sam who began to scratch at him.

The police would again be overwhelmed, and the station overrun, Harry had seen that before. The dead were unstoppable. Rescue had to come, there was no way any of them could survive otherwise.

'We have to call for rescue now,' Harry coughed. John shot him a look of scouring anger and empathy. As if Harry had questioned their authority. 'We have to leave now.' Harry pushed himself to his knees and wobbled. Dizzy and his vision sparkled. John rushes over to his aid and assists Harry by supporting his underarm.

'Take it easy,' John said. 'We have our orders. I think the police can handle it.'

A screaming officer shook them all. The officer's outside were firing again. Harry grabbed the doctor and pulled him close.

'You hear that?' Harry said. 'That's not salvation and we won't last here, we must try.' Harry's demanding felt futile. His balance was skewed as he shuffled the doctor by the scruff of his neck and gritted his teeth. Adrenaline pumped through him, a sensation of spiders crawling over his chest and then calm. John was startled as he tried to wipe his face, but Harry stopped him.

'We can try...' John replied but was cut off before he could finish, visible shook, his hands shaking. Harry released him. Another door slammed shut, both John and Harry stumbled to the side of the staircase. James and Sam patiently on the blanket.

Harry could hear footsteps pacing across the stone floors. The killer from earlier? 'What's that?' John whispered to Harry, who had regained his strength in his arms. His back ached and his half-knifed calf pulsated with each heartbeat.

'I see a shadow behind the reception desk,' Harry replied. The station windows weren't great at illuminating the station entrance hall. Harry watched the shadows eagerly, fearing the dead had breached the building. He wondered what it may be like to kill one of the zombies again. John crawled on his belly to the other side of the staircase and Harry could see his head popping up from behind the stone. John dropped out of sight and then jumped up with a squelch.

'It's okay come on in,' John said. 'We're here for your benefit.' John vanished from Harry's sight. Harry could hear a woman and then a baby coughing. Harry's thoughts were not friendly at first. Risking his child's life by sneaking in the back door. Everyone mattered now though, even if Harry was annoyed and they endangered the entire building. He put two and two together. Obviously they had attracted the zombies. James left Sam and went to greet the strangers.

Harry saw a man and a woman carrying a thickly wrapped baby. Harry pushed himself to his feet again, ignoring the pain and missing the painkillers, even though they made his head feel soft. As the survivors approached the staircase, Harry imagined the woman was Sheila. Sheila may have changed her mind and tried to find him. But it wasn't her.

He officers left outside were shouting. The officer stood around the radio table looking concerned but helpless to act. The shouting officers mixed with the bangs of metal sent shudders down Harry's spine. The mother and baby had somehow got into a death-trap.

'Douglas, Delila and Samuel meet our survivors,' John introduced them. Douglas exchanged a handshake with Harry, and he instantly regretted it, it was pointless. They could be dead soon, getting acquainted was useless.

'My name is James,' James shook Douglas's hand with a smile that made Harry become glass eyed with emotion. Soon the smiles turned shyness and James wrapped his arms around Harry.

'There's no more time, John,' Harry implored before demanding, 'we call now, do it.' Harry pointed at the radio. Douglas and Delila watched in confusion. John shook his head and walked over to the radio.

All the remaining officers gathered around the table; the radio hissed. Gunshots continued to ring out. Harry prepared himself.

'Calling Alpha evacuation, Alpha evac. This is Beach Town police station to evacuation, over,' John said. Harry's pulse quickened.

'Give it here,' Harry said as he tried to snatch the radio from John who quickly pulled it away. The plastic scraped Harry's hand.

Harry wanted to punch the doctor but being in the presence of a baby and James changed his mind. John was not as big as Charlie; John was the annoyance that Harry could deal with. Harry pondered being able to control Charlie if he turned up causing trouble. Whatever mysterious disease was coursing through his veins, it made him feel ten time stronger than usual.

'I have my orders too,' John said. 'Evacuation, Beach Town police department to evacuation, I… we are requesting emergency evacuation from the Police station, the situation has changed,' John turned to look at Harry before continuing. 'I have the package.'

It was obvious Harry was the package, but why he was he wasn't sure. The bite wound on his calf had been cut out in a brutal manner, but there was more to this disease. Maybe he was immune. But he doubted the odds and grunted it off.

The radio crackled, then two officers bolted through the front doors loud enough to startle the baby awake, he instantly began crying.

'Barricade the door', the officers gasped in unison. Harry spotted another bench next to the door.

'John give me a hand,' Harry shouted as he limped to the wooden bench. The officers managed to lock the bolts above the door. Outside dark figures emerged, their bodies covering the station window, the smell of brains and guts seeped through the glass. Harry pushed the bench and John pulled the bench to cover the door. After pushing the bench against the door Harry felt embarrassed, it was a pathetic attempt at barricading. Harry was sick of nobody taking charge, the same happened at the hospital.

'You two, stay guard,' Harry commanded the officers. 'Make sure they can't get in.' After hesitating they began scouring the hall for some other benches. 'John get back on the radio.' Doctor John did as he was told. There was no reply yet. 'James stay with Sam and make sure he doesn't go wandering off.' James had made a den from the blankets and appeared content to hide there with Sam.

The empowering feeling of taking charge gave him butterflies. Harry's palms sweaty with blissful hope. Being in charge made rescue seem possible. The smell of the dead was overpowering. Seeing so few faces in the hall made it feel strangely crowded. Harry imagined it was the dead outside that gave that effect. It was affecting his concentration.

'Alpha evacuation, I have the package, we have a survivor without symptoms, over!' John shouted. Delila sat on the staircase trying to shush Samuel, his crying quietened but continued. Douglas remained very wide eyed and vacant leaning against the reception desk. If Harry had the time he might have enquired, but he assumed it was shock. The radio cackled in John's hand. Harry placed his hands on the table and gasped. John held the radio against his ear.

'Alpha evacuations to survivors,' a male voice spoke, Harry let out a sigh of relief. 'We have new orders following your information, we can evacuate the package and three other survivors who haven't been exposed, if there are any, over.' John went pale. Harry felt humiliated and guilty. Harry and three other lucky people were going to make it out of town alive. But they still had the lunatic upstairs to worry about.

'I'll stay,' John said with a sad gauntness gaze. 'You need to get your son out.' Harry began tearing up but wiped it away and looked at James hiding under the blanket.

'What about you?' Harry asked. 'I thought you had orders?' The front doors were being frantically scratched at.

'Screw orders,' John continued. 'I've lived and I think it's fair that your son has a chance to live a life, don't you? That baby and its mother need to go as well.' Tears trickled down John's face. Harry could see John's wrinkles clearly now, it was the right decision, John was used up. Even if John hadn't given James that chance, James would be leaving with evacuation no matter what. Harry had come too far and through too much destruction to let James die now. He realised he might have to contend with Douglas and the officers.

'Good,' Harry said and patted John on the shoulder. 'It means a lot that you would do that.' John cleared his tears with his sleeve and placed the radio against his mouth again.

'Alpha evacuation send rescue to the police station. To the rooftop, we've been trapped in the main hall,' John said. The officers removed another bench from a side room and placed it against the front doors. The doors were close to breaking. Baby Samuel had stopped crying. Douglas had his arm around Delila as they sat on the steps. Harry kept a watch on James.

The radio clicked in a Morse code fashion.

'Survivors, evacuation has checked the map and rescue from there is not possible,' the man explained. 'There is no landing pad, the nearest is on the roof of Beach Town Hospital, can you make it?' Harry rolled his eyes in disbelief; the rescue team really had no idea of the situation. John even laughed at the comment.

'Are you serious evac? We can't even get there, that's the fucking source of the outbreak as well!' John yelled, his screech as chalk on blackboard.

'What are they playing at?' Harry commented to John.

Then, the front doors smashed open and the officers rapidly equipped their guns and opened fire. The officers that had stood on guard shambled in before being popped in the skull and dropping to the floor. Corpses were obliterated backwards as bullets penetrated their bodies. Blood spurted onto the officers clothing.

'Hold tight,' evac said. 'Head to the roof, we'll try to get there as quickly, eta ten minutes, Alpha evacuation out.'

CHAPTER 32

Evacuation

The events of the last few days had been gut wrenching, the last few hours, even more so. Once the hungry choppers of the zombies gnawed their way into the police station, vacant expressions and gargling and oozing blood, the fear cranked up a notch.

'Go,' John cried as the zombies swarmed in, the officers firing the remaining bullets to no avail. 'Get to the roof, we'll hold them off.' John equipped a concealed pistol hidden in his back-pant pocket. Harry was shocked at the number of zombies stumbling into the hall and he rushed to grab James and Sam from the blankets. John opened fire, the shots hollowing through the coppery fuelled air.

'Come on let's go', Harry called to Delila a she cradled Samuel on the staircase. Harry shook, emerging from behind the staircase, the dead. Stragglers must have gotten through the back door. Harry recognised one of them was a doctor from the medical tent's outback, his undead torso ripped. Arms outstretched and limping, the corpses came in wonky pursuit.

Douglas jolted towards Harry. Delila began to climb the staircase. The dead closing in fast. Baby Samuel was screaming and gunshots beckoning made Harry woozy.

'Back door,' Harry shouted. One of the officers turned to fire, a bullet pierced the skull of a beast about to devour Harry's face and the zombie dropped motionless to the stone floor. Delila was ahead, expressing confusion. The other officers diverted their attention to the back door, and the three remaining walkers became shredded brains among the stained floor. The officers had no choice but to now boot the dead back. The police had slowed the zombies advance. But Harry could see the officers struggling to breathe and he could hear their guns clicking empty. John was sweating profusely, dousing the dead with lead.

'Move,' Harry called out, Douglas was assisting Delila onto the first floor now, but he left her at the top of the staircase and darted back down into the main hall. James's weight was bearing down, and Harry's scratched arms stung.

'Go Delila,' Douglas cried. 'I'll hold them off.' The hall was riddled with corpses that Harry could not stop watching. It was captivating and surreal. Then Harry grabbed Delila's arm and with an almighty fathom of strength began to forcefully assist her through the first-floor corridor. Douglas, John and the other officers faded from sight. All that remained of those heroic people, Harry thought, was being eaten or suicide. Their legacy, their honour would live on through Harry and James, their stories would not go untold.

The struggling police cried out, their gunshots ringing out through the stone buildings, a nerve wrenching cry channelled the station. The dead had taken down another victim.

The first floor was empty, and the vacant offices were ghostly, an eerie sense of a supernatural presence lingered, the sensation of death.

They continued to climb. 'Keep going,' Harry said. His legs pulsing, his heart was racing, and he felt like he was going to pass out. The second-floor corridor also empty, this time papers were scattered across the floor and paintings and pictures had fallen off the walls. Harry spotted the sign for the staircase. Each floor they had to travel the length of the hallway until reaching another staircase at the end. Four more floors to go, but how long until rescue arrived. Ten minutes was nothing and Harry suspected there may be two to three minutes at the most. Evacuation had better wait for them, he thought. James sobbed as they reached the rooftop staircase, metallic, Delila had handled the climb sportingly and was well ahead. Harry was seized by a gripping stitch of exhaustion pinching his lungs. His torso burned. As Delila pushed through the door to the rooftop Harry was met with a refreshing breeze of salty air. It invigorated him, and he pushed through to the roof. He could hear the zombie's ferocious growling. They were well past the first floor at this point. Rest in peace, John. The groans were monstrous chants. The door to the roof had been left ajar, but Harry thought nothing of it.

On the rooftop, the salty wind snaked around Harry's cold nose, it was a huge relief. A sense of purpose and rejuvenation was beginning to overpower him. They had made it. Seagulls swooned overhead. It wasn't salvation, but it felt as if it were redemption.

The air conditioning vents were silent, and the stone roof cracked and sprouted weeds. The sky was clearer than Harry could ever remember. Delila took a seat on a vent, comforting

Samuel. Harry put James down – James held Sam tightly, his meowing continued – he looked exhausted.

Harry walked back to the rooftop door and closed it, the creaking hinges enough to scare the crows away, there was a rusty bolt at the top and he locked it.

His limp was causing him to wobble and he couldn't imagine climbing into a helicopter. Harry walked to the edge of the roof, he stared thoughtfully at the dead who had amassed to greater numbers than he thought possible. The zombies shambled around every shop, building corner, crevice and car, lamppost, post box and window. There must have been hundreds, the Beach Town residents shambled aimlessly. Each biting into the salty air, their arms swayed, as they attempted to grab at nothing. Harry gulped; this was the end. Thank god rescue was – hopefully coming – if it wasn't, he might have contemplated jumping. But he had James and Sam to look after. Then he remembered Sheila, he missed her greatly, even more than Molly. Harry looked to the distant hills, to the hospital in the distance. An epiphany struck him, he realised that Sheila was much better company and he preferred her companionship, he revelled in it. Tears trickled down his face and he smiled. He wanted to be with Sheila, it took the end of the world to realise it.

Harry's reminiscent mind went black, he was pounded in the face and fell on the stone floor. A large figure stood over him. Charlie, looking bulkier than ever. Charlie grinned and clenched his fists.

'Long time no see,' Charlie remarked. 'So, you're waiting for an evacuation, huh?' Charlie equipped his knife from his jacket and swung it at his side, as he had done with the wrench. Harry was confused how Charlie could possibly know that.

'How do you know about that?' Harry snarled. Charlie booted him in the ribs. The kick had cracked a rib and the pain was unbearable. Charlie paced around Harry. He struggled to catch his breath. Charlie huffed as he looked over the edge of the building.

'Fancy going in with them instead?' Charlie said. Harry looked over to Delila and James, both were sitting on the vent, James was smiling. Charlie watched them as well and Harry was red with anger. 'What are the chances of that,' Charlie chuckled. 'Are you trying to steal them from me?' Charlie knelt next to Harry. His breath meaty. As Charlie bowed next to him Harry spotted the walkie talkie under his belt. He must have listened to everything.

'I don't know who they are,' Harry said, contemplating whether he should mention the limited spaces available on the evacuation chopper. Charlie probably knew anyway. Harry's chest was cold. Charlie stood up and leant Harry a hand. Harry was both surprised and relieved. One of them couldn't board the helicopter, and it had to be Charlie.

This was Harry's worst day, beaten and bitten, torn and thrown around and now, as he recovers from his wounds, discovering he may have to fight Charlie, possibly to the death. Charlie held his knife in a threatening manner, the silver blade glistened in the sunlight.

Harry had a chance to grab the knife and protect his son, and Delila and her baby. He suspected Douglas was too young to be romantically involved with her, but this was no time for procrastinating.

'Me and my son are getting out of here,' Harry said, 'Delila and her baby are too.' Harry pushed himself to his feet and Charlie brought the knife slowly to Harry's neck and he froze. Intimidating and unnerving, one wrong move would see his throat slashed. How many people was Charlie prepared to kill to survive?

'I'll be on that chopper, Harry,' Charlie said, 'you can stay here, and I'll take care of your son.' The winds picked up, the amalgamation of salt and brains wafted across the rooftop, the whooshing of something drowned out the zombie's moans.

The whooshing was louder, something was approaching. Harry and Charlie looked around. Sure enough, Harry spotted the helicopter in the distance coming from the hospital. The chopper was still a distance away and Harry knew it was maybe two minutes out.

'I'll be taking care of him,' Harry scorned. 'You can rot here with everyone else.' Harry instantly regretted it. Charlie was gushing with saliva as he gritted his teeth. But Charlie tossed the knife to the floor with a clank and he pulled out his shotgun and tossed it to the floor as well. Harry had a few funny heartbeats, and as adrenaline poured into his brain, his surrounding became crystal.

'No don't!' Delila yelled. Harry turned to see James hiding beneath the air duct shaft. Good boy, Harry thought as he turned to face Charlie, but Charlie punched him in the jaw as he turned around.

Harry stumbled backwards, regaining his balance and holding his fists up in defence. Charlie towered over him and lugged his right fist at Harry, beating Harry's arm as he blocked the attack. Harry manoeuvred sideways. Harry tried to jab Charlie in the kidneys, but he missed, and Charlie thumped his cracked ribs. The rotor of the helicopter was drowning out the dead and the seagulls departed. It was over main street. The fight ceased whilst Charlie watched the black helicopter. The crew were pointing to the rooftop.

'Perhaps you aren't going to make it after all,' Charlie snuffed. Harry was angry and lunged at Charlie, shunting him backwards into the wall as he began digging his cut fists into Charlie's ribs. Charlie was taken by surprise, but not defeated. Harry looked to the knife, laying in waiting for him. 'No chance,' Charlie said. 'We do this the old-fashioned way.' Charlie kicked the knife across the roof, and it landed next to a hiding James. Delila was weeping.

The helicopter hovered over the roof, the gushes of wind propelling debris around the rooftop. The crew slid the side door open and a man in a black helmet began to guide the helicopter down. There was no room for it to land, they would have to climb on. Rescue was here at last; civilisation had not forgotten its humanity just yet.

Charlie kicked Harry in the thigh, and Harry whimpered. He returned a hard-upper cut to Charlie's face and he stumbled back again. It gave Harry hope that he could reach the chopper alive. He smacked Charlie in the gob, Charlie was visibly disorientated, his eyes rolling as he clasped at his nose. Harry kicked him in the balls and Charlie grabbed them, swearing out loud. He managed to smack Harry's face, but Harry continued through the pain. Charlie was closer to the edge with each blowback. Harry continued his left right jab attack. Charlie unable and struggling to get a punch in. Harry glanced to the chopper.

One of the crew had deployed a rope down to Delila and Samuel and was assisting them as they were being lifted to the helicopter. He could not see James and assumed he was onboard.

Harry's distraction meant Charlie got few punches to his face. Harry's nose was bleeding. Charlie grabbed him by the scruff of his neck and swung him round, holding him over the edge of the police station roof. Charlie began to punch him in the face. Harry was losing consciousness, each hit like bricks being thrown at him. Harry managed to twist around Charlie's arm, and he kneed him in the stomach and shoved him towards the edge.

The crew of the helicopter watched on, helpless to assist. Harry had one chance now to end this, so he took it, booting Charlie in the stomach causing him to fall onto the edge of the rooftop, trying to hold onto the brickwork as he lay facing Harry. He was losing grip. Charlie's face bloodied just as Harry's was. Harry was empathetic. Stupidly turning to leave. Before Harry could turn, a tremendously loud gunshot rang out beside him. The shotgun.

Harry prepared to fall and die as his heart dropped to his shoes. He felt his stomach and it was intact. He turned, gobsmacked to see James wielding the shotgun.

Charlie had a gaping chest wound, blood pooled onto his jackets, filling the cracks in the stone and dying the weeds red. James dropped the shotgun. Harry was shocked.

Charlie was red, then he fell backwards, and his body rag dolled from the rooftop. The sound of his body splattering on the pavement attracted the dead and Harry watched on. Looking down as Charlie's broken boned body was devoured.

The chopper had waited, patiently. Harry kicked the shotgun to the side and picked James up, wondering where Sam was. But Sam was not far behind and he pounced up onto James who caught him. Harry brough them to the hovering helicopter. The crew took James and Sam first.

Harry took a moment digesting the week's events. The disaster that had unfolded and carnage that may come. The splendid beach and the deliciously cold ice cream of Beach Town was no more. Harry wrapped the safety jacket around himself and was lifted painfully aboard the evacuation crew's chopper.

As its ascended birds squawked overhead. Harry could see buildings burning in different directions across the town, the corpses scattered far and wide throughout the streets.

There were two pilots in black uniform with no identifiable badges. The man in the back has his face covered with a black helmet and remained quiet. It was the beginning of a new life. Harry wanted there to be time for Sheila.

The matte black Bell military helicopter laden with olive camouflage and a UK tail number continued its ascent as it flew towards the sea. Harry had an unobstructed view of the town. Up in the air was a bumpy ride, the pilots were struggling with the gusts of wind. The hordes of the undead unrecognisable from this altitude.

'Take us to that tower block,' Harry said. The crew member in the back who hadn't taken his gaze from the window, looked to Harry. He pushed a button on the side of his helmet. The chopper was weaving faster through turbulence.

'Sorry, no more detours,' the man's voice sharply cut through the helicopters communication system, 'unless there's something there that might save the world then we can't divert. Don't worry ETA is twenty minutes.' The helicopters radio buzzed, increasing in intensity.

Sam curled up on James's lap to take nap. Delila cradled a snoozing Samuel. The tower was still close enough. But it was burning, right from Sheila's floor. Harry became fraught with anxiety; it must have been Sheila's flat. Below in the school lawn and park, men were firing into oncoming hordes of undead. Surviving police officers clustered in a small group, the dead encircling them. Harry wasn't hopeful for them. He needed an excuse to get Sheila onboard.

'I thought you needed three other survivors. Children don't count,' Harry said. The man with the black visor helmet leant to the cockpit. His black uniform was coveted in patches, one of them was the flag of the United Kingdom on his upper right arm. He was holding the microphone away from his face and whispering something, he glanced back at Harry.

'Who is it?' he asked with a deep voice. Harry was attentive, the man's neck was black. The chopper was now leaving central Beach Town and heading approaching the sea front. Distant echoes of metallic bangs continued to ring out. The humming and beeping of the rotor blade were irritating Harry.

'She's female and she witnessed the outbreak,' Harry asserted, 'we both did.' The burning tower block was growing smaller in the distance. 'Please, go back,' Harry pleaded, his face sinking with despair.

If there was someone whom he could survive the apocalypse with-it would-be James. Sheila was the friend, the love and the comfort where James could not provide it.

The man's spoke deeply, his impactful words strong and cutting through the noise. The rescue chopper flew over the beach reaching the sea.

The air was thick with clouds and salt, the tepid whirling breeze that caressed the sides of the paintwork showed no sign of slowing.

'We can't go back; we have our orders.'

Printed in Great Britain
by Amazon

82169514R00161